TERRA-INFINITA
THE TRILOGY

CLAUDIO NOCELLI

CLAUDIO ÁNGEL NOCELLI

ISBN: 978-631-00-0925-4

Printed in the United States of America

CONTENTS

Course of Humanity

WEBSITE:

https://nosconfunden.com.ar/

YOUTUBE:

*https://www.youtube.com/
@nosconfunden*

YOUTUBE 2nd Channel:

*https://www.youtube.com/
@nosconfundieron*

INSTAGRAM:

*https://www.instagram.com/
nosconfunden/*

INSTAGRAM - Personal (Author):

*https://www.instagram.com/
eddienosconfunden/*

(In the case of not being able to enter any of the social networks due to any error, they will always be updated in the main website, you can visit it to be informed about possible updates, thank you very much for your understanding)

Nocelli, Claudio Ángel
    Terra-Infinita : the trilogy / Claudio Ángel Nocelli. - 1a ed. - Ciudad Autónoma de
Buenos Aires : Claudio Ángel Nocelli, 2023.
    410 p. ; 16 x 23 cm.

    ISBN 978-631-00-0925-4

    1. Ciencia Ficción. 2. Ovnis. 3. Novelas de Misterio. I. Título.
    CDD A863

- THE NAVIGATOR WHO CROSSED THE ICE WALLS

WORLDS BEYOND THE ANTARCTICA

TO ANTARCTICA

My name is William Morris, and the story that you are about to read, It is probably going to modify the current way of seeing the world, I know most of people will find it incredible and believe me, even having experienced this adventure, having seen it with my own eyes and with all my senses, it was also incredible to myself, but the evidence is irrefutable for those who want to see it and the memories indelible, such evidence will be presented and science will also change its perspective, another path will be opened in the human mind forever.

 As for my personal life, I was a member of the Continental Navy, as the American naval force was called in the Revolutionary War, I was married to Lucy and we were thinking of enlarging the family, but the war postponed every plan, as it usually does, with that pain that probably feel cutting the root of that shining tree that gives life to the garden, that immense pain that produces to move away from your loved ones and go to hell itself.

One peaceful night after the surrender of Saratoga, we were sailing through the northern Atlantic Ocean, rounding the islands on our way to Charleston Harbor, the full moon was the only light that illuminated our way and during that night, thousands of stories and anecdotes arose among the boys over a little whiskey to calm the anxieties of a raw war.

Even then, there was talk of James Cook's voyages and his obsession with crossing the "Antarctic Circle", although it was not clear who was behind his funding or why the obsession, as

I was not well steeped in the subject the talk had not captivated me enough, I did not pay much attention and the boys went on with the stories.

Captain Butler, well respected in the group, joined in the sailing stories by commenting that it was possible that there was a passage somewhere in the Polar Circle, and that this passage could be the connector to other worlds, he said it seriously without a moment's hesitation.

My attention turned to him, and the five or six of us in that cabin were speechless listening to his story, we expected him to say that it was a joke but that never happened, we could not believe that a captain was seriously telling that there could be lands behind the Antarctic Circle.

Butler commented that he knew from good sources at the highest levels that they were researching and funding voyages to penetrate the harsh climate and barriers in the southern latitudes to find possible land and perhaps civilization beyond the Antarctic continent, and that they were in a hurry to carry out these missions as many civilian navigators were circling the area and did not look favorably on anyone else coming along.

This story was even longer and in great detail, he also commented that he observed with his own eyes a map that indicated the coordinates that could be the opening of such a passage, and although he was stupefied by this story and I think the others too, the fatigue and stress generated by a war conflict could not be wasted, it was the perfect moment of happiness that generates a breach of peace to be able to sleep a few hours.

Time went by and after the famous war, many of the ships used by the Continental Navy were rented, destroyed, captured or sold, as at that time I was a person of good economic standing, especially after a war that we could say "triumphant" (if after a war can be called so) I made an offer for one of them and managed to keep it, although my colleagues always scoffed at me because of that, as they say it was ridiculously high for such an old ship.

The idea of the exploration trip to the south, after Butler's story, generated even more interest for me to bid and keep the ship, although it needed repairs (therefore some extra money) I felt no guilt as I felt it as an investment, although I did not know the real danger of such a trip, I needed to provide myself with a great navigation equipment.

Although Lucy was not happy about this plan, I was planning to leave Charleston by the end of November and head, with a few stops along the way, straight to the Antarctic continent.

During the idea of forming the team, I talked to former colleagues, some of them made the most ridiculous excuses, and I don't blame them either, the idea of such a trip was really not encouraging, two of them, who were there that same night that Butler told his story, wanted to join as soon as I told them about the plan, But the most difficult part was to convince Butler, who had knowledge in navigation based on his experience and leadership, and also knew the coordinates where we should go, after gathering courage for a few weeks, I contacted the captain to tell him about my project and add him to the group.

It was difficult to convince the captain of such a plan, and although in his voice I noticed some enthusiasm, he declined my offer, and it was like that for a while.

Unexpectedly on the morning of October 11th he showed up at my home with another companion named "Fint", he had maps that I had never seen and was full of documents that very few eyes had read, he told me that he accepted the deal but that he was willing to understand that it could only be a one way trip, then I understood that we had to take this trip professionally, the adventure was about to begin.

THE CUSTODIANS

After such a phrase from the captain, we finalized details and agreed on a departure date, it would be November 14th, his mysterious partner Fint, as he introduced himself, would also join the team, my boat would be ready even a month before.

Those were days of much anxiety and little sleep, a lot of reading and meetings with the team about the trip we were planning, we fantasized about the most incredible adventures but reality was about to surpass any possible fiction or imagination.

On November 12th, just two days before leaving, Fint (Butler's partner) showed up at my door with another man who looked even more mysterious than him, all dressed in black and with a strange accent, he told me it was urgent and I made them enter my home.

Fint had a briefcase which he opened as soon as he entered on top of a table, inside there were many documents and among them he took out a kind of ancient manuscript, and began to recite a part of it:

"Then by demand, I subscribe in major importance, here by desire of our lords that the doors of knowledge be closed to those who refused to be part of our glorious path and liberties granted", the text went on for several more lines and then at the end the so called "Poem Regius" was recited.

As soon as he finished his reading, I commented that it seemed that he was in some kind of initiation rite, it was then when

Fint commented:

- Exactly comrade, precisely those who did not pass this initiation, are the marginalized, better said, we are the marginalized.

Fint, I demanded, please explain a little, I am not understanding anything, what does this text mean and what does it have to do with our trip?

- Look, Fint commented, I am going to explain a little of the situation, this manuscript belongs to "The Custodians" as we call them, or as they call themselves "The Sun-Gods" and they found out about your trip through Butler, the high spheres are aware of it and it does not make them happy, this manuscript raises that they will not let anyone leave these lands by demand of the Lords.
The situation could not get any worse, an adventure that was already risky enough due to the harsh weather and everything that could happen to us due to natural events, now we were adding these unknown enemies.

Who are these "Custodians"? I asked.

Fint went around in circles, and his strange friend opened his mouth for the first time, interrupting, he commented that these Custodians were not happy about our trip and that was the only thing they could tell me.

Fint then suggested that We should cancel it, that it wasn't worth risking our lives, he said it with a threatening tone, that's when I then invited them to leave my house immediately.

His strange friend looked at me defiantly and they left, after a few minutes I tried to communicate with Butler to ask him what was happening and comment on the situation of this strange visit, Butler never answered, neither that day nor the following ones, I gathered the emergency team to analyze how to continue, this travel plan was becoming dark and sinister, but an inner force pushed me to continue, the passage to other lands was becoming even more real but also more dangerous.

We met with the whole team, Butler was not there, nobody knew about him for weeks, he was missing, I told them the whole sequence about the visit of Fint and his partner, also about the Manuscript, Walter said he had heard something about "The Custodians" but he was not sure who they really were or if it was a secret organization.

The situation was not at all encouraging, Butler did not show up and the plan without him seemed impossible to carry out, besides the risk it seemed to entail against an unknown organization that was chasing us without even having left port.

We made the decision to postpone the trip again until we could find Butler, we would try again to find him at his home the next day.

As expected, we were unable to find Butler, and the chances of the trip were being destroyed by the minute along with the concern of the captain's whereabouts, the team also communicated with other known people and members of the naval force, nobody knew anything about him, it seemed as if he had been swallowed by the earth.

November 14th arrived, with the plan already cancelled, someone knocked on my door and to my total surprise, it was Captain Butler with provisions, maps and everything necessary to leave, he commented to me as if it was nothing, "It is time to leave, comrade".

I asked him as many times as possible where he had gone, and I also had to explain to him the strange last two days that the whole team had spent, he looked at me very coldly and commented "it was to be expected, I had to hide for security and priority to protect the documents needed for the plan", especially this "map" while I was unfolding it on the table in my living room, it was huge.

There was land I had never seen before, Butler ordered me to assemble the team and that we had to leave today.

I asked him if he knew "The Custodians" and he told me that there was a lot he had to tell, "the story is not the one we were told, William" "the creators of the Pyramids and another race, as they also call them "Custodians", have no interest in us crossing the South Pole", he told me that they found out about our travel plan via Fint, who had betrayed him, and that the trip had to be made today or we would never be able to make it, he also commented that we would have plenty of time later on to give me more details about all this once we are sailing.

I hurried to gather the whole team, once we were all together, we left the port of Charleston, we had a few stops before reaching the frozen areas of the South.

WE HAVE CROSSED THE WALLS

We set sail at last from Charleston harbor, Captain Butler was leading this adventure that we calculated between a few stops to arrive with enough provisions, we would be reaching the cold Antarctic waters in about 140 to 150 days at the most.

As we left we all had a mixture of excitement and panic from everything we had experienced in the previous days, we were also not quite sure why Butler had hidden himself in this way, had we become the enemies of a force we were going to be able to actually face? Butler also mentioned "another race" what had we really gotten ourselves into.

The days went by and everything was going very well, we had plenty of provisions and the companions were encouraging each other, beyond some sporadic storms the ship withstood the winds very well, when crossing the Equator we made some stops and stocked up again on the advice of the captain, who told us that the trip was going to be longer than we expected in the case of being able to cross the South Pole, We were also able to bring some cases of bottles of alcohol, although the heat of the tropic at that time did not let us think clearly, it was known that times of darkness and cold in the black waters of the south were approaching.

The second night of leaving the last port straight to Antarctica,

I was on deck looking at the horizon and thinking about this adventure, the memories came all together to my mind, everything I left behind and if this turning against someone powerful was really worth it, I had an inner fire of curiosity, to know about this passage, if it was really possible to cross it, I wondered what would be behind, while all this was going through my mind Butler approached.

- Already cold, comrade? You can't imagine what awaits you then, he asked me.

- So you've been there? - I asked again

- Where do you mean, in the southern waters?, yes of course, Butler affirmed.

- That story you were telling that night, was it about you?

- I was there William, I saw that passage with my own eyes, that's why I'm wanted;

All doubt left my mind, the captain then gave a clear version about his past voyage, the lights went on in me and illuminated all curiosity, I couldn't wait to fill him with questions, but he stopped me right there almost as if reading my mind.

Then he told me, don't worry William, you will see it too, you will see what I saw with my eyes and you won't believe it either, and I'm not just talking about the passage, but I won't talk about it until we can get there.

The captain closed the conversation at the best moment, I had as many questions as the reader will have at this moment and I assure you that they will be answered in due time, the intrigue ate me inside and my face was the same tone as the reddish sun that began to appear on the horizon.

At one hundred and thirty eight days we were in the icy waters and the sudden difference was abysmal, the water was dark and as dark as the waves that swung us from one side to the other, the storm that had been chasing us for eight days was getting worse, the captain was calm and that gave us some security, but every time a wave crashed against our boat in our minds we could not not remember the warm home we were leaving behind, but I was confident in this mission, I knew somehow that it was going to give us its fruit.

We crossed a huge mountain that we had as a reference, where warm and cold winds intermingled even under the snow, as strange as the waters we were sailing, it is very difficult to describe this place, it is simply unique, it has a beauty that enamors even being aware that a second is enough to end your life against the huge masses of ice floating around.

We were now sailing parallel to a giant wall of ice that loomed, we calculated that it would be between 80 and 90 meters high, and in some places there were peaks of even more height but it was impossible to see it, the sleet could be seen up to a certain height, what we noticed and called our attention (except the captain who had already experienced it) is that reddish and yellow color that sometimes appears on the horizon, as if a ravenous fire of some forest was raging behind.

Near this giant mountain, blocks of ice fell like absorbent cotton on a mattress of snow forming a steep slope where the snow water melted and cascaded into the sea, an imposing image with this kind of reflection of fire behind, if this were portrayed in a painting, they would pay millions to have it, this view overwhelmed with a unique beauty and a sepulchral silence accompanying the lonely boat that the team decided to name "The Secret".

The weather was inhospitable, it did not give us any respite, the fight was daily against the waves and the wind, the danger of collision against the great masses of ice and the water that fell on us like an eternal cry from the sky, we decided then to approach again to the enormous Mount, The strange heat emanating from the melting ice all around gave the strange appearance that it did not fit, that it should not be there, but it even seemed to generate a different climate, we decided with the captain to skirt it as much as possible and investigate thoroughly this strange portion in front of the giant ice barriers.

Butler shouted my name and called me on deck, a passage opened up behind between the giant frozen walls, the happiness that enveloped us was unexplainable, but we knew that we would not be there for a long time.

Butler did not hesitate for a second and we were all stunned, the ship was heading that way, the captain seemed to know what he was doing and left the boat parallel to the promontory, and then a kind of current took us inside without even thinking twice, we were dragged by an enormous force, fear paralyzed us, we brushed the edges of that wall several times, all this panic lasted three or four minutes but inside us it seemed to be eternal.

Suddenly and once we were sailing on this current that was dragging us, calm seemed to invade our surroundings, the storm ceased and although the cold was still lashing it was no longer overwhelming, we were in an inexplicable ecstasy, this narrow passage was opening more and more and gave way to an open sea, my eyes did not lie although I doubted them several times.

The captain shouted, "We made it! We made it! And we all celebrated with surprise and amazement, we were in waters that only very few reached, or so we thought at that moment at least.

The dark waters began to clear, the ice walls were still visible but were being lost in the distance, the sun that contemplated our feat was falling on the horizon, it was time to boast.

I gathered the team by decision of the captain, who called us all with some seriousness, he was going to make an important announcement, he began by saying that what he was going to comment was not about him, nor about the team, nor about the known Earth we were leaving behind, it was about the whole of humanity and its past.

THE WAR BEHIND
THE ICE WALLS

When we were all in silence waiting for the words of the captain, who was going to tell us something that seemed to be unique, a colossal sized craft loomed and seemed to be coming straight at us, one of the boys went up to see what he could spot and shouted as he descended in a violent manner, "They are coming towards us", "it is something gigantic".

We all panicked but Butler ordered to remain calm, although he remained calm, he seemed a bit nervous compared to what we had been experiencing before, this made me more uneasy, who would be coming towards us in this giant craft?

As it got closer, we did not change the north course, it had a reddish color and as it got closer we could see that it was more and more immense, I will not deny that I feared for my life and that of the team, I could not believe that we had just left the walls of ice behind, something was going to prevent us from continuing to investigate this unknown ocean, I also thought that we were the only ones who had come so far in these areas, we did not know exactly the depth but the ocean still looked dark.

A deafening sound enveloped us we could hardly stand it, it was a screeching sound like some kind of horn, then a voice with a perfect English accent came before us, saying the following;

"Dear visitors from the walled lands, some of our men will come down and approach your boat, we will do you no harm, please remain calm."

This message sounded even more frightening, inside me I thought they might attack us but it's not like we could escape from there either, this ship was gigantic and looked like something out of a fictional tale from a far future, Butler reassured us by acknowledging that he was aware that something like this could happen, to stay calm and welcome this new visitor in a kind way.

Three men were making their way to our ship, this was the first time we had ever had a visitor and we were not even sailing in familiar waters nor were any familiar people coming aboard, the men had white suits and some emblems stood out on them, there was a flag flying on top of their ship, if we could call it that, said flag was completely blue with a white circle in the center.

We helped the men up and they greeted us kindly by shaking our hands.

One of them introduced himself as the captain and asked us what we were doing sailing in this area across the wall.

Butler spoke for us and informed him that we were sailing around the Antarctic Arctic Circle and that a current had brought us to "the other side", and that we had decided to sail through these areas to investigate it, it would be my impression at the time but I had noticed a certain camaraderie between Butler and the officers.

The same man turned to look at his other two companions and they were amazed at such a feat, they commented among themselves that it had been a long time since they had seen something like this, he apologized for the way they should have approached us and also the way they had to approach, saying the following words he explained to us the reason for this concern;

"We are very sorry that your visit does not seem to be welcome, it really is, but it has been a long time since we have seen people crossing the walls, in fact we do not know how they left them either... but it does not matter now, I will give you this map with directions on how to get to safe lands."

This last sentence was not well taken by any of the group, we looked at each other with some fear, I encouraged myself to ask then "safe lands did you say? are there then unsafe lands?".

"Well, the lands where you come from are quite unsafe" replied the man standing behind, "don't worry, you will get there fine sailing in this direction".

It was a unique moment to be able to understand the situation a little, I spoke again as the owner of the boat, "Excuse me, where do you come from?", I had millions of questions in my head.

From "The Ancestral Lands", sir, - the man answered me in a bounded way, adding later "don't worry, I understand that you have many questions at this

I promise you that they will give you all the necessary information when they arrive to these lands that we indicated to you, we will inform you that they will arrive so you can receive them immediately".

The men withdrew quickly, looking in all directions as if searching for something, the strange visit left us with more questions than answers, Butler did not hesitate for a moment and as a great leader, he woke up the group that was still fearful and somewhat hesitant, the destination was clear now, we were heading to new lands called "The Ancestral Lands".

We sailed for quite a while following the course indicated by these men, Butler indicated that it was important to follow this direction rigorously, when several of us from the team asked the captain about what he was going to tell us before the visit, he preferred not to continue with the subject, as if he had changed his mind outright, although he told us the following,

"After what happened I think we all have to open our eyes, fortunately we ran into these people and we can

We ran into these people and we can head to safe lands, I think we would not have had the same luck if it was another boat that visited us, let's remember that there are people we left behind, very powerful people who do not want us to be sailing these waters, or knowing all this, let's wait to arrive as soon as possible to The Republic and then they will understand more about the situation, it is something complex, but I am glad we have crossed the walls, the journey has just begun comrades, it is time to understand that we are in a war zone, doing something unique".

The last sentence left us speechless, we all asked in unison, "What do you mean, in a war zone?

War zone, what kind of war, what kind of war, what kind of war?" all the questions were directed to the captain, who answered them all by saying, "comrades, pay attention and let's get to these lands indicated, everything will become clear as soon as we anchor".

The temperature had changed quite a bit as we moved away from the walls, in about 30 days the area enveloped us with a temperate climate, as indicated we would be close to these lands, birds of various types began to be spotted, and vegetation on the waters that were now clearer, I had an inner feeling that we were making history forgetting a little the captain's phrase that we were in War zone without knowing it, in that case I would like to know, who was the enemy.

THE HUMAN REBOOT (RESET)

On a clear night we could see in the distance, different lights that went from east to west illuminating the way and our hopes in a mild but very dark night, Butler observed the group that was stupefied by such beauty, it was a giant and silent city, it seemed an electric world out of a book by Thomas Browne.

We decided not to wait any longer in unknown waters because of the possibility of being attacked by an enemy that we still did not know because of the warning of the ship that had intercepted us when we crossed the walls and alerted us about the danger and about this supposed war that was being fought, although we were supposed to have arrived to safe lands, nothing seemed safe at that time.

We arrived at the port of what looked like a large and modern City, we were on deck waiting to be received, in less than two minutes several agents dressed in similar Uniform that those on that ship were wearing approached us, and in a very respectful way they welcomed us;

- "Welcome to the Ancestral Republic", one of them pronounced while shaking hands with Butler.

- "We are happy of your visit to our Lands, it was something unthinkable, we were informed that you would come but anyway we could not believe it until we saw it with our eyes, your visit is so rare not to say impossible, but here is our joy to receive you" - he pronounced.

Butler thanked on behalf of the whole boat, and introduced me as the owner of the boat, I was going through all the emotions together that can be imagined and immediately wanted my questions to be answered, although the fear of being in unknown lands in many occasions overcame the strong emotion of having discovered something immense, I was carried away by the latter, I think the whole team started with the idea that this trip had every chance of going wrong, but here we were in the land behind Antarctica and being welcomed by citizens of a modern city, it was time to ask everything.

It is an honor to visit these lands that until today were unknown to us, I proclaimed.

Before I mentioned anything else, this agent interrupted me saying that he had to take me to the Office of the President of the Republic himself, since our visit was almost unprecedented, that furthermore the President was aware of it and had notified that we take him immediately with him. He asked me to accompany him and looking at Butler who nodded his head, I went after him among some people who observed the situation, we were strangers who came from inhospitable lands, I think this generated such confusion in people as in ourselves.

A vehicle that I had never seen in all my life was waiting for us, there was not even a corner, at least in this part of the City, that was not reached by the illumination by the great lanterns that adorned and generated the sensation of being in a tale of the best writers.

The silence of the City was now more understandable knowing that there were no carriages, horses, or any type of vehicle that I knew from my experience in big cities like New York, the difference was abysmal in everything, their clothes were also colorful, the agent that accompanied me had in his hands a luminous device that transmitted different images and voices, the language that was spoken was different and I did not understand a single word.

A huge stone building stood out among the rest, with large and clear letters it said "Presidential Office Rebirth" and the flag of his country was highlighted by a perfect illumination, the blue circle in the center seemed to stand out.

When we arrived I followed the agent until we entered this immense building, there were connections for the passage between each room, there were seats of different types, the lighting was dim, when passing to one of those rooms I touched one of the walls, which were as cold as marble, I had again some fear about everything I was living, I understood the protocol that our visit was not common but I was already dizzy between so many stairs we climbed.

The agent asked me to wait for him in one of the comforting seats, the truth is that I could have waited there for hours, the comfort of those were indescribable, a tall man with a mustache came out to greet me:

- "So you are William Morris from the United States of America?" - he asked. That's right, I answered

This gentleman shook me tightly by the hand, commenting that he was sorry to receive me in one of the worst situations experienced in that Republic, in fact he commented as follows:

- "My name is Fhael, I am sorry that you have arrived in these times we are going through, it would have been totally different your visit and our reception in normal situations, you will know how to understand now when I put it in context."

I had so much confusion and questions that I could not say a single word.

- You see Mr. Morris, the situation is extreme and there are moments of tension, this war was usually seen from afar and now we are part of it, I should explain many points for you to understand, but I will have to be limited because I have many men sailing at this time and they need valuable information.

I nodded my head as if pretending to understand everything, only to give way to the story, hence some answers that could place me in situation.

- "Maybe you don't fully understand it yet, but we are part of what we could call "the old humanity", I mean, we were not part of the last reboot process, do you understand me?"

I would have every desire to be able to say that I understand but the truth is that I am lost in all this, what do you refer to as ancient humanity? How many humanities exist or existed?

- "There were many humanities in different times, as well as there were many resets or reboots, this happens every certain time already stipulated or it is done before that date for external reasons, I mean in a way intentionally created before reaching that time, as far as we know here in reality it always happens this way since the "natural" way is also carried out by the same by manipulating the environment where you come from."

What is this "human reset"?

- "The reboot is a process they carry out in their lands to annihilate every human being leaving only their newborn babies to repopulate those lands and carry out the same process over and over again, the reasons for the reboot according to our information is carried out when something gets out of the control of those who rule on the other side of the Ice Walls, the factors can be several and they do not doubt it, believe me, the knowledge of other lands can lead to a reset, it could be by pests, floods, fires, plagues, wars, missiles or war bombs they call asteroids, or it could be all that together, it doesn't matter how, the fact that we have escaped before is reason enough of a threat for them not to want us breathing, do you understand me now William? "

My head was spinning, I felt dizzy and thought I would fall there in front of this Mr. Fhael, while I understood the situation I could not believe that all that was happening in the lands where I was born, I sat up in a hurry and started to sweat cold.

- I understand your feelings, William, I wanted to go straight to the raw history so you can understand the situation, there is much more to know but you will learn it with the days in your stay here, although these lands are considered out of the conflict, nothing and no one is out of this conflict in these days, now if you allow me I am sorry that the conversation has been so short but I must leave urgently.

He shook my hand again and rushed back into a room, the agent next to me looked me in the eyes as if he understood my pain for the lands I was leaving behind, it was a before and after, I could not believe that all this was happening.

We returned to my boat where I had many things to tell the group, Butler was not there, I gathered everyone and told them the situation and how little I understood of everything I had experienced in President Fhael's office, the group was more stunned than me, they began to question me that I should have asked this or that, but with a confused mind immersed in the darkness of the story told it becomes difficult to even breathe, we were all in a crisis of not having anything clear, I began to ask where Butler had gone, they told me that he had left the boat as soon as I left with the agent, we do not know where he was going, again we lost Butler but now in unknown lands.

We were silent, pensive, all this was going around in my head, the old humanity, the death of all of us intentionally, who could carry out all these macabre plans and with what intention? When all this came to my mind a deafening sound suddenly invaded from the skies, and an explosion made us lie on the ground, the earth shook and the water shook our ship as if it were made of paper, everything exploded around us, our eyes were wide open and we did not understand what was happening, we ran to the deck and saw the worst war landscape that anyone could observe, not even in our times of war we lived something similar, everything was destroyed, people screamed in the streets, an alarm sound was activated who knows where, but it was heard throughout the city, a voice tried to calm people down, but it was too late, they had reached the Ancestral Lands.

ANAKIM, THE GIANTS OF THE SOUTH

Stunned by what had happened and still not fully understanding the dramatic situation that was taking place in these lands, many images crossed my mind, surely derived from the fear and helplessness of seeing the suffering of my new brothers before my eyes, there were people on the ground under the dust and rubble, like the tragically famous Sodom and Gomorrah, "enemy crossfire" could be heard in the distance, I saw innocent people die that day, everything was getting out of control in just a few moments, we watched the sky full of small silver spheres with red lights that followed the whole scene, I was not sure if they were from the Republic or enemies, but there they were without missing anything of the gloomy scene.

We ran trying to help those we were crossing on the way, but the reality is that we had to leave the boat as soon as possible, we were all going in different directions, the voice that before tried to calm us down, now gave orders that were almost pleas to go urgently to the building of the "Presidential Office Renacer", that's what we did those who were left standing in the middle of a rain of debris and some detonations.

Anguish and anger fell on me like lightning in the ocean, I raised my eyes to the sky begging for some kind of mercy, the sky was in a furious red tone, I could observe that the sun's glow did not burn my sight, it had a dark tone and what I thought was the Moon, stood out in the distance in a totally black color, as in the middle of an Eclipse. I thought then that it was the strangest sky that anyone from the "Known Lands" had ever witnessed, added the strange spheres that danced in the air in all directions, they were like silver eyes observing everything, the next question resounded inside me immediately after:

Who was controlling these small objects, and what was their function? As far as I could see in the midst of it all, none of them were performing any attack maneuvers.

The situation at the time was really heartbreaking, the building was intact and I could enter without major problems, although for obvious reasons there had been some turmoil at the entrance, anyway and despite the existing fear, people respected each other in an extraordinary way, I can not even imagine the chaos that could mean a similar situation in my homeland.

I had lost the whole group in desperation under enemy fire, I felt concerned for the others and with the responsibility by experience in the Continental Navy to put myself at their disposal to help in some way to the city that had just received us in the best way and now suffered the onslaught of an enemy still invisible.

The wounded numbered in the thousands, there were so many equipped rooms that in the face of such an attack of dimensions never seen in my humble wartime past, I was shocked.

I tried to find the team but it was impossible, I could not

even recognize one of them, the people who were there in the different corners of this huge building looked at me with some suspicion, I was a "newcomer" from other lands and with me had also come a fierce and fatal attack that would leave at least a quarter of the city destroyed.

I tried to go through the different floors without getting lost and to find the Office of President Fhael, I needed to talk urgently with a high command, I wanted to satisfy my many questions about the enemy, I wanted to put myself at his orders, this attack was not going to be one like any other, it had touched my heart so much that I felt equally part of these lands, as much as the others who suffered at my side, as if my blood had been born here long ago.

To my surprise I found Fhael with a face of extreme concern with Captain Butler, I called his name without being able to wait to arrive among so many people around, Butler performed a kind of typical military salute from afar, without losing customs, I was glad to see a familiar face and it generated me confidence among so much atypical War madness.

I saluted Fhael as best I could, with a faltering voice, who said everything with his melancholic look, he showed to be depressed by the situation, which was not for less.

I put myself under his orders to help in what he needed and required such a situation, Fhael thanked the gesture but commented that nothing we could do but wait for the moment, although in a failed way I tried again to deposit my many questions, the moment deserved it in my mind but Fhael was in a heated conversation in a kind of tiny communicator, where the other voice repeated constantly and the following was clearly heard:

"We are requesting support from the Anakim, we have no choice Fhael, this was a planned attack to destroy a civilian and secure area, there is no turning back."

Butler turned back to me with the typical look of leadership reinforcing my idea that what I had heard, are they talking about what I imagine? I asked Butler lowly, he nodded his head, they are the "Giant Warriors of the South", William.

Fhael heard him and blurted out a sentence that left me even more intrigued:

"Not only that, they are the saviors of our people, the ones who led us to these lands before the reset of our time" he then commented to Butler that he should leave but to do what was needed, and quickly returned to his office with three agents following him.

Butler asked me to follow him and so I did as best I could among thousands of agents coming and going, another attack was feared, war was brewing on the very land we had only set foot on a few hours before.

The captain told me that it was time to rest before embarking on a new journey and another destination, I stared at him as if expressing my fear again, besides I was not sure if our ship was still standing, I could hear explosions outside, it was then when I thought to ask: Where would this destination be and the reason for it, was it something that Fhael had requested?

He explained to me that it was not exactly Fhael's plan but that the moment required it, he would go to look for the team first to gather them here, and once they were all here, we would undertake a unique trip to the Anakim Lands, but first we would pass by their home, I was stunned trying to digest these words, I wanted to have said so many things but my voice barely made a sound that made no sense in any language, Butler then clarified in case it was necessary before my desperate way of expressing myself:

"I'm sorry I couldn't tell you sooner, William, I am as much a part of these lands as anyone else you see suffering here, I was born with the ancestral blood and I am watching my brothers die, apparently they want to repeat history even in these Lands, it is time to save again the only humanity that has survived a Custodial reset, and who can save us all, who better than the very ones who helped cross the Ice Walls back then?", Butler then marched off and got lost among the agents waiting outside.

I lay down on the most comfortable bed my body had ever been in, intending to sleep but who was going to sleep after all I had been through? How would my reason process so much information from a human story never told, How could I not see the eyes of my new brothers falling in pain and not feel that we were on the right side, and that we had escaped from a sinister place that I used to call home, these feelings hit my chest with a resentment and deep venom, I would want at that moment to open the doors to the innocents we were leaving behind, to the loved ones of the Known Lands.

THE DISEASE
OF THE HUMAN
BEING

I had been able to fall asleep after several failed attempts, among so many thoughts and explosions heard in the distance, thinking that maybe none of this was real, it couldn't be happening, it was too much information to process in my confused mind.

I was abruptly awakened by the captain's voice, "William up, it's time to march!" he said in a firm voice, almost like an order, I could barely grasp the situation and again be aware that we were under enemy attack, an enemy I was still almost completely unaware of.

Butler had gathered the whole team together, everyone was safe and it brought my soul back to my body, we embraced each other as the great team we were and for all the situations we had been through, an almost brotherly reunion in an unknown continent where only negative things were happening all around.

We went out to the central corridor that crossed with President Fhael's door, the captain was worried and ordered us to hurry as much as we could, the thousands of people that were crowded in the building were gone, what had happened to them?

I didn't even have time to ask before the boys commented as they passed by, that the "evacuation plan had been activated" one of them with astonishment told me "we saw big trains and thousands of ships overhead carrying many people at incredible speeds, William".

The captain came back to us saying, that is exactly what we are going to do, we will get on one of those ships that has to leave in twelve minutes, hurry up the pace then we will have time to talk about everything that is happening, I know you have so many questions that will be answered as soon as we arrive to safe lands.

We had barely arrived to the supposed safe lands and now again we were looking for other lands, it seemed that we were turning the lands into unsafe, we were arriving and hell was falling around us, I feared that people would think that we were cursed and we were bringing calamity with us.

Practically running through the desolate streets destroyed by the bombs that had fallen, I managed to look at the sky again and those little spheres were gone, but in their place were passing at incredible speeds some big bluish triangles from one side to the other, I could not help stopping for a minute, when the captain noticed my fault, he returned to his pace shouting at me "William, leave the skies for a second, now is not the time, those flying birds are friends, "the Iron Blues" are making the enemy retreat, now please let's get to our destination urgently".

I had no choice and gave in to such a plea, although it was quite hard for me to let pass such a majestic flight of those blue birds, they were flying from one side to the other, they were flying in a magnificent and singular way, I could not believe that they were being directed by someone or something else, they seemed as if they had a mind of their own.

When we arrived at the supposed destination, there were many agents apparently waiting for Butler and therefore for all of us, although they seemed to be relieved to know that the captain was alive then they reproached us for our delay, and that they only had to wait a minute longer, they practically "put us" quickly on a silver platform and it took us to the top, while we were contemplating a contradictory view, between fire, death and desolation to the other side of a modern city with structures never seen before that represented absolute prosperity. In the sky "the Iron Blues" were still battling against these spheres that were already far from the coast, the captain asked if this view did not remind us of the portraits of Nuremberg and Basel, but we all looked at each other without understanding what he was referring to.

As soon as we arrived at the top floor, some agents greeted us with a warm welcome, commenting that we were about to have a unique experience touching the clouds, these ships were not at all like the ones we had in our minds, if we could ever imagine such a thing.

The structure was huge, and they seemed to be made of one piece. There seemed to be routes in the skies, leading two different ones separately there and back.

These supposedly large iron structures were lost in the horizon, from what I was told by the same agent who received us, they connected every point of the big cities, he told me to prepare myself because the first experience of traveling in these great ships was something that would never be forgotten.

A dark blue ship was waiting for us, once inside the opening closed automatically, I sat next to Butler in seats of 4 people, the interior seemed even bigger than it was on the outside, soon to sit down it started up but we could barely hear a faint whistling sound.

Butler and the agents asked us to try to relax, that getting used to these iron giants was going to take some getting used to at first but then we wouldn't notice. As soon as the trip began, one of the boys was the first to collapse with a fainting spell, but he came to quickly.

I felt dizzy and missed Butler's conversations with the agents, I tried to relax and join this frantic trip that seemed to be ejected like a ball from the most powerful English cannon.

At times we would enter long tunnels, and everything would go dark, at those moments I thought I would pass out too but I got around this feeling of temporary nausea and dizziness as best I could and after fifteen or twenty minutes we were all traveling smoothly.

It was time to pay attention to the beautiful landscape of the Ancestral Republic, "Renacer" in the distance was the most modern and prosperous city that not even the great literary minds could have imagined, the surroundings were tinged with various colors due to the large plantations of vegetables, flowers and fruit trees.

The green was predominant, it was a really emotional view that invited to live in this small Eden, in fact according to what I heard there were some nearby islands called "The Islands of Eden" that even provided a greater spectacle, and its name described them perfectly, although I could not afford to miss listening to the interesting conversation of Butler with the others about the war strategies that were developing.

At a moment when his big talk of plans and strategies ended, I knew it was my chance to again satiate my questions, I had as many as the reader will surely have at this point, I didn't know where to start.

Butler beat me to the punch and outlined the next question:

How much did the last air measurement yield, how much damage do we have in the area? One of the agents replied that they were sure they had acted in time, and for this reason the attack was made in the same area where the numbers showed possible poisoning of the air and nearby plantations.

I could no longer bear this conversation that seemed like undecipherable codes to me and to the whole group, so I got up my courage and asked: "Can you explain to us, which poisoning are you talking about?

Butler looked at the group somewhat with compunction, and explained succinctly:

"They poison the air, let's see, how do I explain? The human that is born in their lands, gets sick quickly due to the work that the Custodians do, this disease is usually implanted in the first humans or better said, the babies left from the last reset, or maybe the second generation as well to make sure, but then this is passed from generation to generation automatically, it is also not uncommon for them to poison the air they breathe, which is the most common way, sometimes to continue to ensure future sick generations or simply docility, it is a very cruel race William, I am sorry that you have to find out all this in such an abrupt way, but sooner or later you have to know.

We were all stunned again by such a statement, what do you mean by poisoning our air? And what is this disease? Or what harm does it cause us? - I asked astonished.

"This disease is practically new, it was used in the last reset," clarified the agent who was listening to our conversation, "we are still studying it closely but what we know is that it makes their bodies age rapidly, and that only a small part of their lives are useful and profitable for them to then give way to the next generation quickly, They prefer it this way because the past longevity brought other conflicts, people had more time to analyze the situation in which they found themselves, they modify the human and mold it to their usefulness avoiding any conflict, the idea is always to fulfill the cycle called "natural" of the next reset".

- Does this mean that they shorten our life span?

"That's exactly what I'm saying, we in the Ancestral Republic live three times longer than you because there is no such modification in our bodies, but they tried recently, they want first to shorten our lives to achieve their control."

Butler interrupted with a blueprint he had in his hand and started to ask again about War strategy issues, I could not fully understand the situation, it was all so confusing and it generated such anger in me that it was hard to handle, I think we all thought the same at that moment, the guys were asking each other and analyzing this trying to understand it. The Custodians were shortening our lives and making them miserable, I understood then that there was no freedom of any form in the Known Lands, how could we free our people from this perverse power?

How could we declare war on an enemy of which we were unaware? And what was the human like without this foul control?

The answer was right in front of my eyes, absolute prosperity was below us, in every boy and girl who ran through the fields freely, where their life seemed to be happy and carefree until their old age perhaps at 240 or 250 years old, how wise could an elder of the Republic be then? How free was a child born there? How much evil existed within each one without the cursed Custodial control?

We arrived at the Capital called "The Ark (El Arca)" in the stipulated time, there were no delays there, except for our delay of one or two minutes, the doors opened and we stopped on a platform where everything was covered by a kind of crystal, if the scenery was already inexplicable by then, the reader will understand that I could not add any words for such a description, these are the moments that I regret not having been born or trained as a literary great, but I assure you that that day we lived the best sunset that someone can have in his life.

There were structures never seen before that touched the skies, besides hundreds of flying wheels, they were like two wheels that joined together forming with other material a sphere that could carry one or two passengers on it, something magnificent to see, another incredible detail was that in spite of seeing the biggest, most illuminated and fullest city of all, there was no noise, everything happened in absolute silence.

HUMAN GREATNESS

The Capital "El Arca" received us, but as things were going so far, it was clearly not going to be a pleasure trip, at least not at the beginning, Butler ordered us to follow him and after saying goodbye to the other officers, we immersed ourselves in this immense luminous and modern city that my mind so lacking in imagination would never have imagined.

We tried not to lose sight of the captain who never looked back but as is his custom as a leader, he expected his faithful companions to follow him without losing track, it was complex to do so because we were enraptured by the environment at every step we took, the whole group was really surprised, people filled the public spaces, restaurants, and vehicles seemed to always collide but never did, their maneuvers were almost perfect.

In the sky big transparent spheres were walking from one side to the other, most of them were occupied by one person, but in some occasions even two were seen driving those strange balloons that floated and crossed the skies.

Even when the news was fast spreading in every part of the Republic, the citizens of "El Arca" were happily strolling around, as if no war had broken out just a few miles away.

Separating from the captain would have left us in big trouble as the language they used in the capital was not English nor any language I could decipher, another question was already adding to my mind, would this be a native language? Perhaps the oldest one anyone could have heard, from an earlier humanity, and if so, where did it come from?

I sank into my thoughts as I automatically followed the captain, the land of the Anakim, imagining what such a place might be like? A part of me even doubted its existence, it was unbelievable to even imagine the possibility of seeing giants, giants? I asked myself an inner voice. It was even strange to repeat it in my own mind, I think the whole group was in the same situation.

We approached a place that appeared to be a large harbor, many boats were resting, Butler asked us to wait for him while he went over to talk to the officers there.

We took the opportunity to talk to each other, we were all living in a dream that at times turned into a nightmare, from the Eden that could be seen from the heights of the great forests full of colorful flowers to the deadly and bloody roars of these, apparently famous "Custodians" of which we had barely heard until now, and that perhaps I would have liked to never know.

With the experience of a past war and battles at sea that I had under my belt, I could notice that the group was very united and with a lot of strength, I guess that the uncertainty and this knowledge with which we had collided unintentionally, transmitted an immense desire that arose from within us to want to know more and more, we wanted as much information as possible, to unravel this unknown human history in the lands where we were born.

We also began to doubt about the recent attack, was it our fault for escaping from the Known Lands, was this our punishment, were those great walls of ice perhaps artificial, were the Custodians perhaps other humans or were they a race we did not know? Giants, new races, new lands and artificial walls, we began to dig so deep that our theories already bordered on the ridiculous, but everything was already beginning to be unknown then nothing became logical either, our world was changing every second and it had done it forever, like a divine sentence.

Butler approached us and told us that we would take that boat over there (pointing with his hand), it was the boat that stood out the most, similar to the one that approached us as soon as we crossed the Walls, everything was ready to leave for the Anakim Lands, but first, according to Butler, we would have an obligatory stopover in the Captain's lands.

We were able to visit every corner of the luxurious and modern ship, everything was from a different and distant era to the one known to us, difficult to understand, in case it was not already enough to have noticed, that technology was advanced in light years.

They explained to me that we could practically say that these ships handled themselves, besides that we could hardly hear the outside, they were very silent, fast and we could hardly notice the movement in the water, anyway the sea was calm and suddenly this made me realize that the waves were always in this state, their calmest and most neutral form in these lands, at least in all our experience in our trip here. Then that led to another question that added to the immense list that I already had to my credit, did these waters have a totally different way of behaving compared to ours? I was sure of one thing, and that was that the Moon shone at least three times brighter, the color of the Sun was totally different from the known, and there was also another sphere of a bluish-black color, which I noticed when the iron blues battled overhead, at first I imagined that it was part of some technology I did not know, but it was still there, static, in a part of the firmament.

After a few minutes of sailing at truly extraordinary speeds for the whole group, the captain ordered us to prepare to descend, although the situation was tense and certain precautions were taken during the short trip, we breathed a different air as we arrived at this island that had a small and humble port, not so different from those we knew in America, and in the distance many low houses of shiny white color that peeked out from among the green hills.

Butler left his few belongings on the floor and suddenly a little girl who seemed to be no more than six years old ran into his arms, behind him a woman with a pale face smiled as she saw the captain arrive to port, after a deep embrace she introduced us, it was his wife and daughter who welcomed us.

Butler with a cheerful tone confirmed what we all thought, welcome to my land comrades, this is my family and I hope you are comfortable here as long as we can stay.

We settled in some houses adjoining the captain's house, who also invited us to enter and gave us all the comforts, we did not think we would be there long because of the urgency required by the situation in which we were, but Butler said later, it was just over a year since he was at home, and he was not going to waste the time to stay as long as he could with his family.

We stayed two nights on that simple but beautiful island, and during this period I was able to talk to the captain about several points that kept nagging at the back of my mind, that I needed to externalize, I was looking for answers over and over again, my mind would not slow down for a second, Butler knew this and anticipated it as he always did, he was a man who walked several steps ahead of us in every decision and thought.

- "Their minds are somehow modified, to put it in a way you can understand me."

I tried to follow him with my eyes, in an act of inner emptiness, only waiting for him to develop that interesting and disturbing point.

- Butler then went on to say "The ultimate humanity is dependent on your mind, in a totally noxious extreme, you do not detach yourself almost at any time with exceptions, you imagine what exists and what is based on your thoughts, your image created by experiences and through others who also feedback on others thoughts, creating an immense network where each one identifies himself according to where he was born, his status quo or physical condition, but this only does nothing but move away from the true human essence."

"We, those who have blood of ancestral humanity, do not have that permanent attack of the mind with infinite thoughts mostly degrading, and that also mostly are inventions of situations that no longer exist or that will never happen, Humanity in each reset was approaching what the Custodians want from us, because they were modifying both their bodies and minds as the environment, the Lands you left behind is an isolated world, unreal, where evil stands out, wars abound and degradation becomes almost unbearable, but those humans, your brothers and mine too, although from another era, they are not what their minds think every day, that is why history is hidden, because if human greatness were known then nothing could stop us in our growth, because no one would live kneeling if they knew who is tying them with the invisible leash there in that world inside the ice walls.

- I had nothing to say, I remained silent and I kept my words to myself so as not to cry with impotence, I had never heard the captain be so clear, his gaze was lost in the horizon, I kept that night as one of the many unforgettable nights I would have in these glorious and revealing lands.

I asked some other important questions that you will soon understand from the story of what will happen, the next morning when that strange sun would shine again, it would find us sailing towards the lands of the "Anakim".

THE ORIGIN OF THE HUMAN BEING AND THE REVEALING BOOK OF SHE- KI ABOUT THE OTHER WORLDS

The journey to the islands of Giants went without major inconvenience, the only strange and remarkable thing was that there was no night, the day faded barely on the horizon, but the first night a full and clear Moon appeared in the firmament, and we barely noticed the transition, like an eternal sunset of fire in the distance.

I saw two iron blues pass across the sky at different parts of the last day's journey to the islands of the giants.

It was hard to fall asleep because of everything that had been going on in our lives and around us, we were all waiting for the big moment of contacting giants, it was something we could not even imagine.

We finally arrived at a fairly modern port, perhaps with fewer structures of the majestic in the Capital of the Ancestral Republic, but their ships differed quite a lot from those I had seen before, a certain decline towards military ships stood out, some even seemed to have weapons that I had never seen on top.

As soon as we descended, a man with a very long reddish beard and a woman with a beautiful face and long blond hair welcomed us, first they spoke with the captain and then introduced us to everyone.

Although they were tall, they were no more than 2 and a half meters tall, it was enough to pass us by several long feet.

Stupefied to step on the ground of giants we shook their hands and followed them, the city was not so silent, and that was more like a rural area.

The language they spoke there was also unintelligible to our ears, the captain could not speak it either, but the woman who introduced herself as "She-ki" spoke our language, albeit in a very strange way, but she was fluent and could make herself understood.

We entered the part that seemed to be the center of this village on a remote island in an ocean also hitherto unknown to us. She-Ki invited us in, their houses were domes of different heights, and there were also huge white towers finished with domes on top, in some there were even figures of giants watching everything, I think I would not want to leave this island without going up there at the top to see that majestic view to who knows where.

I noticed that we were already beginning to naturalize situations that until weeks ago were unthinkable and that we would surely faint if we found ourselves in the situation we are in now, in front of the "Giants Anakim" without having gone through all of the above.

I had in my mind the imagination of barbarian giants, with only some basic clothing that covered them, but the reality is that this advanced race seemed to come out of some story of parallel worlds, their attire was colorful and adjusted to their large bodies, we could see later approaching the central area, that there were thousands of giants of all sizes, but never descended from two meters twenty or two meters thirty, and we have come to see giants as high as four meters.

Butler told us that this race of giants was so important to know our past, since there was in them ancestral human blood and pure Giant blood of the Ancient Lands of Anak. He told us that later they would tell us a little of the history of our race link, how the ancient and pure giants joined with the ancestral humans to bring forth one of the most powerful forces that ever existed in "The Known Lands" to confront the Custodians.

Known as the Great Tartary, which could have changed the course of our history forever, and that in any case marked a before and after generating radical changes in the "Known Lands" as well as in the surrounding worlds.

She-Ki approached where we were with Butler talking about this topic that I was trying to follow closely without missing any detail and making a mental note of the thousands of questions that arose in my mind at each advance. I noticed that the giant had in her hands a huge book that she offered me saying that this would help me to understand much more about the past of our races.

As soon as I opened it I noticed several maps, she marked a special page where our home, "the Known Lands", and its surroundings were specified, below and on the following pages she also detailed what was known about the Lands, their races and history.

Again, when I thought I had seen it all I felt again a fire burning inside me with each page, stupefied my face was hard in expression trying to imagine this new personal discovery.

She-Ki noticed in my expression that I was sinking in information, she told me not to try to digest it all at once, "with time you will understand and assimilate it", she tried to reassure me.

How many lands are there? I went so far as to ask at his expression with a smile understanding my frustration.

"178 known worlds, at least, according to the information we've been able to gather," he commented.

"But that doesn't count all the lands and islands that exist outside of them," Butler then added.

The kind and beautiful Giant-human as she went on to summarize a bit of some key topics as she showed me some of the pages of this wonderful and unique book.

We stopped at the "Anunnaki" lands, there her face changed, the "Anunnaki" race has always behaved in a hostile manner towards humans since the beginning, and he also commented that they were bound by an old treaty with the Custodians.

Would it be the most awaited moment for me? Would it be the culminating moment where I would know the true beginning of human life? The true origin?

I will not get ahead of myself for the moment, I will only say that this conversation, in case the trip itself had not already done so, changed my life completely, I will go on to detail and transcribe this conversation in the next chapter.

THE DOMES, THE LEARNING OF THE WORLDS BEYOND THE ICE WALLS

The past of the giants or Giant-Humans was hidden forever, their technology and bones were as sadly hidden and forgotten as the greatness of their history, and new discoveries of giants will be today and, in the future, simply ridiculed, some even intermingled with beasts that never inhabited these lands. The eternal "Known Lands" where their oceans are stained with ancestral blood, which could have changed everything.

The Custodians made a pact, never the human of the new reset could know, that a force was possible to defeat his invisible colonizer, he would not even know this time that there was a force above that controlled his lands and his environment that made him live an empty life, where the messages would be based on his exploitation of all kinds, his degraded spirit, in this chapter we will see the origin of the human being, an essential being with infinite spiritual potential, as well as why the other races are interested in him. Those who want to keep them in an almost unbearable oppression and those who want to make them escape towards their immense spiritual freedom, is this possible?

The previous day had been so important that I had not even fallen into the world of dreams until my body tried to reconcile in a strange night of sky illuminated by that mysterious and huge full moon.

It was so hard to sleep that the whole group stayed up until what we imagined was very late even though we didn't see the Sun peek out before finally getting a wink of sleep.

Conversations obviously revolved around everything that had been happening to us, but especially the little we had been informed had already fallen like a fierce storm overseas, our minds by then were mere vessels in search of survival, the storm was the truth that not only fell on our face and plunged into our interior, but also generated the most gigantic waves that made each of us reel abruptly.

Have they conditioned our minds so much? We repeated to ourselves over and over again.

Is this story real? But how can we doubt this story when we are in the lands behind the ice walls, and living with the same ancient Giant-Humans? I think that from so much analysis we passed out until a few hours later.

Butler woke us up, we came out of these Domes that maintained a strange temperature that seemed to be regulated, it was always cool in there and outside, the heat was sometimes unbearable.

There were fruits of all kinds, we had never even seen or tasted most of them, some vegetation peeping out of the distance also had strange colors that were hard for me to decipher.

She-ki was wearing a very colorful and summery dress, her face was more beautiful in the sunlight, I think several of the group had been enraptured by her mere presence.

After breakfast we were able to have a private chat together with Butler, and She-ki began to tell me other details of the Book and the history of the races.
Yesterday I told you about the so-called Old Treaty, which was made between parts of the Custodians and the Anunnaki.

- What were they looking for with that treaty? I dared to ask, I think that this question even came from within me driven by the same anxiety to know everything, but it also generated the way to what was going to be without a doubt a unique conversation. She-ki continued her narrative by saying:

"William, first you have to know that the Custodians and Anunnaki have something in common, and that which unites them is that their technology is primarily based on armaments and military development because they are colonizers from birth, when they arrive in a certain "circle" they look for ways to penetrate it to see how they can benefit, study the life found there and if it serves them they could own it or create different agreements for their benefit in its development."

"In fact it is the seed that they implanted in the ancient humans. The Custodians are also known for their advanced ships and for being among the few to know the 178 worlds or circles around the known."

- What's that about the great dome, what does it mean? I asked innocently.

"William, each circle is divided by one or several different Domes depending on what encompasses that circle, this dome is a kind of membrane that divides a system, this information is very advanced for the time where you come from, but I imagine you have heard of the cellular theory, these circles we could roughly compare them to what we call a cell and its plasma membrane."

"This Dome-Membrane, is a wall invisible to our eyes (although some races can make it out) that divides two systems that are similar or may differ in their totality, but have connections in different parts, what we know from the information taken from the Custodians, is that all the circles or worlds that are known have some connection between the inner and outer system, except one, which is considered the most important and which led just to this Old Treaty between Custodians and Anunnaki."

"These races are adept at manipulating environments as they have sufficient technology to do so within the dome of any known world.

These connections between inner and outer worlds are not simple to find, but the races that have managed to get out and those that base their technological advances both in conquest or in their mission to explore, make long journeys with the reason to gather information from other worlds also developed different types of systems to find the way to find these entrances and exits more easily.

There are also portals that connect different lands but that is another subject that you will discover throughout your stay outside your homelands and how much of the technology works here."

"Now, that circle that I was telling you about the 178 known ones was impossible for them to access even using the most advanced Custodial technology and then this became their obsession. These lands where no one could enter, or at least no one could enter and get out of there alive, are the 'Celestial Lands', and as each Custodial attempt was thwarted an agreement was made with the Anunnaki to jointly develop technology that could open the way inside and unveil the mystery of what was there."

"The reason for their obsession was the rumor that in the Celestial Lands would be found the secret that would lead to being able to penetrate "The Great Dome" that divides the known worlds from the outside."

- What do you mean by the "Great Dome"? - the question came from inside me almost without wanting to interrupt but with the anxiety that all this generated in me.

"Of this Great Dome we have very little information that we were able to gather from the Custodians, what we know so far is that it would be a great Dome that envelops the 178 worlds inside, where the theory goes that no way out or in has ever been found and there is no information regarding what lies beyond."

"The Custodians and Anunnaki worked together with their great scientists to carry out a never-before-seen development basing their technology entirely on discovering the impenetrable Celestial Earths, what would be found there? On that question they based their development of their long years to come.

They reached the point where their technology had advanced exponentially, so much so that they were able to pass through the first Dome, but another problem arose, the beings that passed through the first Dome died pulverized almost instantly, they found no answer to this and tried in various ways and with the use of various races, but they all died in the same way."

"Later in their extensive study of such lands they came to the conclusion that within did not exist physical bodies but a conscious energy which they called "The Source" or "The Source of Life". The theory goes that this energy began to perceive the danger of Custodial and Anunnaki technology and acted accordingly to safeguard its environment."

"Then this conscious energy split taking the body of the "Five Masters" who gave life to the Human Being, occupying lands around your home or homelands.

They first started with "Asgard", to the north, a remote place bounded by mountainous areas very difficult to discover, then as they developed, they took lands in Lemuria, Atlantis, and the center of their lands which they called Hyperborea, which in turn had a direct connection to the outside world with Asgard, their land of origin, by means of a connecting portal".

THE GIANT-HUMANS AND THE GREAT TARTARIANS

Nothing mattered around here more than all this information I was receiving from "She-ki", it was incredible just to imagine where I was and that a surviving gladiator, who had also helped our ancestral humanity to survive, was telling me in great detail about the true human history.

She-ki then continued: "These men animated with the vital energy of "The Source" began to increase in numbers as well as in technology, first they based their technology on race development and welfare, although later they came to develop defense weapons, but they never reached the same Custodial level.

One fateful and dark night the Custodians penetrated the Known Lands and found abundant gold and other minerals, in their eagerness they traveled through every point of these lands arriving to discover outside the first Dome between a zone of high mountains, the famous lands of Asgard, and with them they also collided with the humans living there.

This group of Custodians were surprised by light defense weapons that attacked and automatically pulverized the enemy, igniting an alarm to the other lands inhabited by humans, what was feared was really happening and by then the energy of the Celestial Lands that animated bodies of human beings was not prepared to face them.

Moreover, the Custodians outnumbered the humans by 1000 to 1. Then, a few days later, the inevitable happened, humans surrendered to them.

This was the beginning of a great nightmare that would last until the present day, but why didn't they behave as on other worlds where looting as many minerals as they needed was enough to march on?

Simple, they tried to send humans to the Celestial Lands as a test (it was not strange to think so since they had tried it also with other races) and although the human bodies burned as soon as they entered these lands, they noticed how this energy that lived inside them, always went directly to the Celestial Lands, no matter where this body met death.

In this way the Custodians and Anunnaki have been studying the human being since ancient times, all that effort and development to enter these lands now turned to the possibility that through the human as the fundamental vehicle it could be achieved.

But there was a missing connector that was not simple at all, and this was the power to manipulate these souls or energy that left the human bodies, but that was never possible.

At first they performed the ancient and cruel colonization of lands carried out by these beings in a general way, most of the population is annihilated leaving only their newborn babies, then comes the education necessary to give the new colonized the purpose or function that the Custodians desire.

This attempt to use humans to enter such lands led to countless numbers of beings dying senselessly, in fact in past "resets" led to the sacrifice of many humans together to see if they could manipulate this great energy at will, the great and well known blood rituals by past civilizations.

As I was saying. rituals, diseases, catastrophes, they tried everything, but nothing worked, they even tried to resurrect bodies and a lot of different things.

What happened next is not clear, some historians say that they simply continued with the control of humanity to continue trying to enter, and others say that they only continue to do so for fear that humans can defeat them because they see in them a unique and immense potential among the many existing worlds. For this reason they control them with "resets", and then the famous lies in their education, shorten their life, create plagues, diseases and miseries.

But you are so important that they are not going to let you go just like that. Because inside each one of you is "The Source" which is the most important thing and which keeps alive all the other beings in these circles.

The giants saw all this from the outside, they never got involved in these wars, but then in time they decided to help humanity as they realized that if "The Source" fell, probably the 178 circle-environments would fall as well.

(Here again it is not clear whether the Custodians tried to use any race of giants for the same mission of accessing the Celestial Lands, since it is said that they tried all the races they could find among the 178 Worlds).

After a while the Custodians lost interest in the human as they began to believe that this energy or soul that came out of the human bodies and returned to the Celestial Lands were not the same energy or that failing that, if it was the same, they had no way to manipulate it, also the Anunnaki began in a crisis in their environment due to the lack of gold and minerals essential for their development.

What to use then? They began to use the newly reset human to be able to extract the gold from the harsh and deep intraterrestrial darkness. What better way than to make them believe that they were their Gods and that they would have to worship in obedience to what they required.

The period of creation of many of the known Pyramids was carried out at this time, by the humans themselves with the help of Custodial technology, these Pyramids were nothing more than energy generating centers, which served to control the human and

generate catastrophes if they wanted to, they also tried by this means to control souls again in a failed way.

The Anunnaki Pyramids were deliberately spread over the Known Lands and the other lands, it was also another ancient way of colonizing lands, they leave pyramids as a form of warning of colonized lands, a kind of badge for any intruder entering without permission, it was known that they feared that some colonizing race or what would be even worse for them, a race that would liberate the existing colonies could exist and come from outside the known "Great Dome".

The Custodians and Anunnaki began to confront again, now for control of the Known Lands, the human being and specifically the large amount of gold found there.

The giants took advantage of these inconveniences of the Custodians and Anunnaki to be able to enter the lands. Many moved from these same islands, and from other lands such as the "Free Islands" and entered from the north and south of the Walls penetrating the existing domes.

The Walls surrounding the Earths were built by the Custodians in the past so that humans would not have the opportunity to reach the "inner Dome" or "First Dome", since this discovery would expose the falsity of the theory that was preached without discussion, in addition to begin to question several fundamental points of life in the "Known Lands.

The possibility of an Infinite Earth could never reach human minds as this would open up the environment and awaken the thousands of living energies in human bodies that are numb to the knowledge of their past.

Quickly a great army of giants formed in Central Asia and others began to mingle with the humans living there, (possibly the ancient giants knew of "The Source" within each human being) soon these doubled in number, having a great and potent giant-human resistance to the inevitable attack that would come from the Custodians or Anunnaki, when their internal warfare ceased.

They continued to confront each other in battles that took place even in their own lands, thus leaving the control of the Earths as a liberated zone.

These were the boom years of the Great Tartary and the technology based on free energy, the control of the Lands was almost total, even inhabiting every corner of the lands. It is said that some Custodians and Anunnaki saw their pyramids fall without being able to do much since they had to attend their own War, little by little they were losing the control that escaped them like water through their fingers.

GIANT-HUMANS VS. CUSTODIANS IN THE KNOWN LANDS

When the Custodians returned triumphant from their War they found their colony totally revolutionized, now there was a power they did not expect between Giants, Giant-Humans and angry Humans revealing themselves for the years of slavery.

These long years of Giant-Humans developing and basing their technology on weapons of war and defense, added to the fact that much Custodial information was plundered and used for this development and scientific knowledge, led to the climax of a race totally forgotten by the Custodians.

When they returned and analyzed the situation, they knew they could not carry on another war because of the casualties of the last one and all the expense that had been carried out to defeat the enemy, obviously they wanted to start an immediate "reset" but their Pyramids were destroyed and they had lost a lot of power in the manipulation of the environment.

They thought and analyzed several strategies and waited to see how the conflict with the humans would develop, but fearful of this uncertain future.

Another war was born in the "Known Lands", this time humanity would fight together with the giants against their former colonizer, the fierce battles fought cannot be described because it was really something that generated even fear in many of the other circles, every day that the sun set piles of bodies from both sides were observed lying on the lands that were now only battlefields, there were areas covered by a vast and different vegetation that now was nothing more than sand and dead landscapes.

The Custodians also weakened by their last war with the Anunnaki saw that they lost all control, and even feared that later their lands would also be attacked by a humanity with a thirst for revenge, the opportunity to annihilate the Custodians also left a great peace for the "Heavenly Lands".

Everything was heading towards an imminent victory, but something happened in the middle, and this was never achieved,

The Custodians had no choice but to return to Anunnaki lands in order to reach a new agreement with them, there was not much army left that could resist another war but technology and the union was immediately taken in exchange for gold, among other things that we do not know but that possibly have to do with the growth of humanity and the fear of future retaliation".

- Here it is worth clarifying that when the Custodians had to leave to unify against the Anunnaki, they left in command an inferior race called "Greys" of Zeta Reticuli and Orion, they were used to control the Earths while they were gone, but according to the story the "Greys" did not agree with the

Old Treaty and the manipulation received, then they were unconcerned thinking that the human being would never rebel or grow in this way, much less imagined a union with a race of forgotten giants.

"These accepted as they also feared losing their lands at the end of the war, even to the Giant-Humans who now had a large army and sought to free themselves from the Custodial yoke in the Known Lands.
The inevitable happened, an unprecedented war took place in the center of those lands, the two forces used all their potential and technology that they immediately put to the test, the Giant-Humans or rather the Great Tartary of free energy also possessed their own ships, therefore the war took place both on land, water and air.

Unfortunately the giant-human power could not resist throughout the harsh battles and not having control of the environment that the Custodians manipulated, this caused wear and tear and deterioration in the troops as well as "natural" catastrophes that grew out of nowhere in important centers, although as I mentioned before this would mark a before and after in all the surrounding worlds, I knew that if they lost this war they were also somehow condemning future generations for several centuries.

The giants had to escape from the lands since defeat was inevitable, and their death was certain, the Custodians would never forgive the giants for having taken up arms and delivered forbidden knowledge to humans, managing to escape where they had entered, through the North and South passages.

Some humans followed them and also achieved this longed-for escape from the Custodial yoke.

The ancient souls of Asgard, Lemuria and Atlantis that inhabited human bodies started from scratch in the lands outside the first Dome known as "The Ancestral Republic" and although hurt by a hard defeat they had the hope to grow again and return with new strategies now with two different missions, to liberate the human being and to finish with the Custodians. Human beings began in these new lands to connect with "The Source" and understand their true past and importance."

Butler interrupted saying that he had already talked to one of the leaders there, and that they did not agree to help us, not because they did not want to but because they feared that their entire race might actually disappear as almost happened last time.

I told Butler of my concern for the lands of the Republic and also for the lands we had left behind, he commented that he doubted they wanted to end up with humanity inside the Walls since of all the "resets" to date, this seemed to be the one that had worked best for them, besides the "Greys" were also under their control and in turn helped to control the human in many other ways.

Since there was high mind control, basic and/or fundamental issues were not dealt with or if they were, they were easily found and reported with some mental problem, immediately sending the "culprit" to a psychiatric facility where they were easily and successfully controlled by other human members.

Imagine if you went back there William and wanted to tell everything you experienced here or the information you gathered, if you had time to tell the others, they would not believe you, and would quickly send you to confinement or possibly death itself.

All this that I had heard gave me many answers that I never imagined I would ever hear, but it also generated many other questions, there was so much to process and everything was running very fast, it was frantic, according to Butler we should leave the islands as soon as possible, he did not even know his plan as usual, he kept the strategy until the end.

We gathered the whole team to leave, we were going to leave the lands of She-Ki and also leave behind that brilliant being, who had given me the most important part of this puzzle that seemed indecipherable, a master key that opened so many worlds and possibilities, the lost history of the human being was in my hands.

The boys began to ask me about this talk, and also began to look through the book I was carrying with me, Butler also helped me to answer the thousands of questions that arose, including mine, between all of us we tried to make this as logical as possible for our confused minds while the sun went away and a strange night fell on us, one of the strangest in those lands. The sky was tinged with the purest red and generated a fire-like glow, Butler commented that this "fire" is visible if you sail near the Antarctic ring, it looks like a giant bonfire in the distance, it was something we had even perceived before leaving the "Known Lands".

"EL ARCA" - THE PROSPEROUS CAPITAL

After spending that strange night of fire mixed with many theories that we were trying to deduce from She-ki's book, it was a very strange sensation that went from extreme to extreme, to think that we were a point far away from everything and we had come to understand from one minute to another that we were "The Source", that conscious energy of the Celestial Lands that lived in each one of us, and also united us to the ancestral humans and to all those who had lost their lives in each "reset" manipulated and hidden.

We began to spot birds fluttering around our ship, denoting that we were approaching land, although we suspected it we could not confirm it with the captain all the way, but the city that awaited us was again "El Arca", the modern capital of the Ancestral Lands.

The first rain since we arrived in these lands began to fall very slowly, just when I was beginning to think that in these latitudes there was no such phenomenon. The lights of the city were coming on in the distance, this immense city of "El Arca" was an invitation to imagination and confidence that such a perfect and peaceful life could be possible also in the dark environment between the ice walls, without the control of the Custodians or any intruder race among us.

We also began to understand that simplicity was what made everything else great, stepping on the grass with bare feet, the birds perching in the most modern harbor, the very rain that gave it a tinge of melancholy gray from the sadness of thinking that not all of humanity was going to be able to witness what our eyes were seeing right now.

Even though we had lived through a furious attack and the most devastating we had ever seen, this immense city gave us the assurance that all would be well, that this could never fall, millions of "Ancestors" were living their lives as close to what we once dreamed of as children, what we dreamed of for future generations, a place of peace and love where there is no pain or suffering, where work does not mean exploitation, where there is no dirty politics or wars for territory or power, no discrimination or stereotypes, no social difference, everything is shared and happiness is breathed, welcome to the "Ancestral Republic" was heard in the distance, in their own clear language, according to Butler's translation.

What was Butler's plan now? - we wondered.

The captain commented that we could get lost and investigate by immersing ourselves a little inside the city, remember that nothing could be bought with gold or use money since they used another form of exchange there, he explained. The plan was not clear, but he would

 The plan was not clear, but he would immediately meet with Fhael and other leaders from different important places in the Republic.

The boys got lost in the big city and I was left alone, pensive, amidst a torrential rain that fell on my face, although of calm appearance, dejected inside, I kept sinking in my deep thoughts of a human future that could not be.

How to overcome this shared misfortune? I asked myself again and again.

I still had so much to discover in that great Book of She-ki, would I find any halo of calm in it?

This information received had fallen worse on me than on the rest, I now felt guilty somehow, that I could not do anything to free the millions that were behind, and that in addition we had been persecuted and attacked in these distant lands, What heart resists before such an onslaught? What heart could not suffer for the now distant brothers that still remained within this vile environment?

Many hours had passed and I was walking through the streets of this colorful city, some few people were crossing my path, I felt their understandable strange look, my way of dressing was not suitable for this modernity, I felt like a caveman even worse if I tried to talk to them, so I continued my way only observing.

Would they understand that we were brothers and shared the same suffering? And a myriad of questions crossed my mind at every step and the few people I looked deeply in the eyes.

One man even tried to talk to me but I only managed to wave my hands explaining that I did not understand what he was telling me, I only said "Fhael" as if to answer a name known to all and this man pointed to a large building a few blocks away.

There were not even puddles of water that accumulated, the whole system was perfectly functioning so that it did not generate any flooding, modernity hit my face so many times that it was difficult to interpret, I dare not even mention the drawings that came out of the walls that projected humans interpreting the most beautiful melodies that sweetened the ears of passersby.

I returned to the port somewhat crestfallen, I had everything a person needed in front of my eyes, I was before absolute happiness but the pain of not being able to share it generated an immense sadness in me, I also kept seeing the faces of the people who fell in "RENACER".

Butler was returning driving a modern vehicle, when he saw me he stopped it and invited me to get in, his face transmitted some joy, then he commented to me:

- William, we have not been able to get the Anakim to help us directly, it is understandable you know, they do not want to risk their entire race again, but I know that they will help us in the long run, we have won this battle and we do not believe that the Custodians will attack these lands again for a long time, we gave them a lesson that our technology is still more alive than ever, they tested us and I assure you that they came back with fear.

Then he continued explaining to me, with some questions that I could ask on our way to the port of "El Arca", apparently the Guardians were not aware of the technology that had been developing the "Ancestral Republic" in the last 100 years, in conjunction with the Anakim race, they thought that this attack would make them directly tremble and possibly surrender immediately as happened in ancient times in Asgard and other lands.

This had to be taken advantage of in the following years if we were to have a chance to regain the Known Lands and free the brethren from the last reset, but all should be careful, any move that is not planned in advance could cause another reset and the death of millions.

THE ARTIFICIAL WORLDS

We met in the boat that we used in these last trips between the Lands of Giants and "El Arca" and Butler told the group almost the same thing that we had been talking about in the return vehicle, but he put more force to his words and his joy overflowed in every part of his face, he had even got something to toast and the whole group was at its most joyful since we arrived, unfortunately this joy was not penetrating my mind and much less in my heart.

I was still distantly trying to understand what would be the right move to change everything, I kept wondering if this was really possible, and if so, how many years of there within the walls would pass while, I was totally involved in freeing my brothers in there.

Butler tried to cheer me up, it was time to change history and this didn't happen every day, so I hid my temporary disenchantment and joined in the toast.

There was no need to even ask about a possible return to our homelands, this was ruled out by absolute, somehow in the toast I closed my eyes with prayers towards the loved ones I feared I would not be able to see again, can a prosperous place like this be enjoyed if not shared with loved ones?

Butler knew inwardly, he went ahead to tell us that we would soon be visiting the Known Lands again and that we could help much more on this side than by entering there and becoming an easy custodial prey.

They would never forgive such a "betrayal" of escaping from their nets and on top of that recovering a large part of history that was never told, and we, the whole group, did not care what they really thought either but it was our duty to take care of ourselves and stay away for the time being and plan our next visit.

Butler brought us a lot of information on how the Republic worked, he also gave us several books, among them many on the language spoken there. As in "Renacer" and elsewhere English was spoken to perfection, there were several books with translations of the arcane language to English and vice versa, as the captain said, it was time to start studying.

Several years had passed, among so many things I learned during my stay was that time passed slower in these lands compared to the Known Lands, it was undoubtedly what I had more trouble understanding, there was a whole library on time, perception and sense of the passage of time.

As an experienced person with a background in major battles in the U.S. naval force, I eventually gained Fhael's trust, and by unanimous decision I became the naval Commander-in-Chief of the "Ancestral Republic", from there I was able to study more about the defense of the Republic, its technology and its development along with the vision for the future.

We carried out projects of possible attacks on the Known Lands without affecting civilian life, but the missions were almost always discarded due to the difficulty I had in finding the real bases of the Custodians, since they moved from one place to another using portals and also almost never had long stays in the Lands but returned to theirs always leaving some leader guarding.

It was really easy for them with the implementation of the ice walls the human possibility of even reaching the first Dome was almost impossible, besides the conditioning that existed by the media and the academy, they had really created humans that would repeat to exhaustion what their books said, and would even guard the walls until death without knowing that they really existed behind them, only by order of their superiors.

The creation of paper money was also key for everything to work according to his master plan, now everything was given so that the humanity of the Known Lands would never know their true origin nor the lands that were waiting for them behind those frozen curtains.

Can you imagine any possibility that the human with the little technology that existed could navigate between giant blocks of ice, find even a passage and not even know if that passage would give him the possibility of crossing that Dome?

The possibilities were clearly reduced to one in a million, but we had succeeded and they were aware of it, so it would not be strange to think that they would use the human militia to guard their own brothers, most of them out of ignorance and others for royalties.

The bases in the Antarctic ring and the exclusion zones would not take long to arrive, as Butler predicted some time ago, it was known that other security measures would be taken because of the past war and the defeat in "Reborn" would bring consequences.

MANIPULATION IN THE KNOWN LANDS

In all this time that has passed I became more and more an arcane ancestral, I did not handle the language to perfection, but I made myself understood, I was interested in science and technology, I tried to learn as much as I could from those minds really advanced and specialized in the matter.

I learned a lot about how our body works in as much detail as I could, the bacteria that lived in us and what was different from a real disease to one created by laboratory, they were more surprised than me when the group made us different analysis to see everything we transported from our homelands, there were so many bacteria and viruses that had been modified and created for different purposes by the Custodians that it was difficult to count, in fact it was known that their plan was still going on every year to continue creating new ones.

They had people infiltrating the lands who passed information every so often, with Butler and the attack on "Reborn" they stopped sending men for quite a while, and neither did the infiltrators come back to make sure they could not be discovered working there, the whole operation would fall apart and we needed as much information from in there as possible, we had to be one step ahead of them or else we would never have a chance to win.

I was getting used to the fact that there was no social difference, we all lived relatively the same way and no one lacked the basics to have a full life.

The President of the Republic and the group of leaders, although they lived in a remote rural area, by their own decision, did not have any luxury, nor did they receive a different salary from the rest, anyone had a voice in politics (if you can call it that, since it differed significantly from the known) and their ideas were listened to. There was no crime at all and, for obvious reasons, no penitentiary.

Respect for the life of others was the main motto and everyone voluntarily adapted to it, it was something natural that was breathed every day. Spirituality and introspection were fundamental and were taught from childhood, they were part of the education, first going through spiritual growth and then moving on to the rest.

They tried not to have an image of themselves, since the mind could deceive them imagining that they were something or someone for others when in reality they would be based on the subjectivity of others, not having an image and not living from the past were pillars that I struggled to understand for years, two fundamental pieces of a puzzle destined for such growth, they called it "the death of the ego".

From there they based any knowledge and learning that would come later, never the other way around, first to know oneself and then to know the world around them.

They taught me a lot about the great masters who had visited our Earths and who were still remembered, the messages they tried to deliver based on what was written before, but all those messages had been distorted or intermingled with dirty business by the Custodial sector, they would never let spiritual growth become present in each one, besides mixing it with dirty money they would also infiltrate several people who would confuse spiritual growth with religious themes to confront sectors or simply false prophets who predicted future chaos.

The few periods of growth that existed within the walls of ice went hand in hand with moments of peace, without great warlike conflicts, but sooner or later some great war would come, or attacks, plagues, pandemics, always elaborated from some sector (always from the same radicalized power) that would interrupt human progress with possible spiritual growth and this was not going to stop.

Politics was also implemented in conjunction with various societies that led in the control of these limits manufactured from the beginning and that would be modified according to the many wars that existed until today, the so-called countries were just another form of control, where there were supposed "leaders" who ruled but in reality were easily adapted to the same custodial power.

This hierarchical form of control based on the paper money system would be key to absolute control in the development of this new humanity, science would then enter its key role where it would drag society to an extreme spiritual emptying basing its life on mere material facts.

People would then seek to increase their collection of colored paper and would turn away from love for their surroundings, even for themselves, their image would be transformed and reduced forever into simple biological functions. What would then be the dream of a profoundly sick society?

The real battle would then be found internally in each of the humans of the Known Lands, but their realities would be distorted always imagining that the central problem is the other's, hate would win over love by the time humans would notice it would already be too late.

The road to a great dictatorship would seem inevitable, the true feelings of love and spiritual growth as a whole would be less and less valued, and without this we could do little from here, since they would take us as bitter enemies and would join the Custodians without knowing it to annihilate us, their military forces work together when only a minority knows it, the great positions and not all of them.

The system was in place and only details were left for the human alone, without even knowing it, to walk the path that the Custodial power had drawn in his destiny. Then the humans would only take care of this system, the lack of spiritual growth added to the real value given to the material and the system based on paper money was all that a society needed to fall into the vile plan and defend it to death.

THE PLAN
TO FREE THE
HUMAN BEING

While there was a direct plan to free the humans who were still trapped under the Custodial yoke and manipulated since birth by the lie, it was very risky as it could put at risk not only the millions who lived within the Walls but also the ancestral humans of the Republic and races of the surrounding lands.

Butler arrived one morning to my office together with Fhael, and they told me that they had devised an alternative that could be effective, the Custodians were strong in weapons and war strategies, they based their whole life on that development but they had weaknesses like any race, and this could be found in the depth of their intelligence, not to be misunderstood, they were extremely intelligent beings and great caretakers of their colonies, especially the human, who would be the only being which they never released after several long "resets" throughout history, but they found weak points where they could attack.

Their fear could still be felt from a distance, they were not happy that ancestral humans and Anakim still existed around their most important colony, but they had not tried to attack our lands in these many years that had passed, that put us ahead, if they detested us, they had enough technology and military force to try to destroy us, what had led them not to make more attacks?

The meeting with Fhael and Butler lasted more than four hours, they had developed a series of different plans that supplanted the previous one in case of failure, all were based on attacking what was considered the weakness of the enemy, this was precisely their little or no spiritual development.

Another great discovery was their radar system near the entrances to the Known Lands penetrating the Dome, when an "ancestral" entered through the known passages, small and even some large earthquakes were generated in surrounding areas. It was an extreme surveillance system that put them on alert and sent support forces, for that reason it is quite common that the earthquakes were almost always in the same area, and is also the answer to why we were not sending more people for a long time, and we tried that those who were there did not return to continue collecting as much information as possible from day to day in the manipulated environment.

The important thing then was to find another entrance or create one (this was so far impossible, we had not been able to enter by force in any Dome, and it was unknown if this could really be done) nor could we use any portal since all of them were controlled by the Custodians, but the exhaustive study of the closed zone in the external part of the same added to that everything that was proposed in the Republic really was carried out, made that was created through safe ice melting based on statistics not to generate floods, an area called "Summer Portal" (apparently with technology of the ancient Anakim) where entry was possible but could not yet be confirmed if by then the sophisticated control did not cover that area.

If possible, we could then send different "ancestors" into the lands and subtly use their means to infiltrate important information, the Ancestral Republic, the possibility of other lands, and the real human past would be mentioned as much as possible, sometimes it did not matter so much the name by which our lands were known, The important thing was to know about the lands behind the ice walls, as long as it did not alter the day to day life as it would raise great suspicion, many people who carried out these missions were locked up in different institutions, so we were very careful in spreading the information.

We knew that the great part of humanity would not even pay attention to these facts due to the existing conditioning of several generations which would lead to not really pay attention, and although a priori this would seem something negative, in reality it helped us since we gained time in being able to carry out the other plans, until all would finally unite in a single plan or mission, but for that they had to work in parallel and it was an arduous task to carry out.

The plans were really excellent since they did not cause any harm to the human being, to reach the necessary critical mass was going to be complex anyway, for that reason there was another alternative that consisted in carrying out a very deep spiritual teaching, trying to break the human conditioning within the vile environment.

When the human being develops through different techniques implemented by the ancestors in the Known Lands and can block as much as possible the conditioning and therefore the mind manipulated by the Custodial control, then it was going to be easier for many to open up to the possibility that another reality existed outside the ice walls.

These great ice walls would sooner or later become visible and genuine human expeditions would also collide with them, but it was well known from our lands that any idea of going beyond would surely be blocked by generating fear, or directly by force through what they always use, military intervention.

THE SUMMER PORTAL AND THE SPIRITUAL EDUCATION

The "Summer Portal" was a success since the Custodians were not noticing our presence when entering the Lands for several years, the whole group and even Butler were forbidden to enter by order of Fhael who considered that if they found us there, not only would they put an end to our lives but they would try to get information from us using any means, and the whole plan would run a serious risk, as we said the plan had to be perfect or not exist at all, because a failed plan was an assured reset.

The years went by and the plan of the spiritual awakening of the human being in the Known Lands had been increasing and was developing in a correct and safe way.

The teachers who entered through the mentioned "Portal" were able to carry out the teachings and the form of education that any child received here in these lands, prioritizing the importance of the human soul, unconditional love and empathy.

Unfortunately, as we imagine, certain black hands began to be noticed around these teachings, confusing the human being and causing many to move away, these three great premises began to be corrupted as well as to become a cruel business.

But as I said before, there were other plans to supplant these others when things began to get dark, it was a constant struggle so that our incidence would not be discovered, but neither should we let the plans fall into the hands of the custodians completely.

It was time now to carry out another plan that would bring consequences, a navigator and faithful friend would arrive from these lands with a vessel built here simulating the time of that moment, and would tell his story to the world, he would reveal major issues that needed to be known for those who wanted to listen, Antarctic passage between walls of ice, discovery of other lands, the Ancestral Republic would be named for the first time in the history of this humanity (with different name), the story would be intermingled with themes of the time both economic and social for its apprehension, we knew the system created based on the strong scientific conditioning by means of heliocentrism, it was no easy task.

The ancestral navigator spent some time in a well-known harbor within the ice walls, where he showed the curious a lot of real information about the Republic and the human past, including about the Giant-Humans.

Before the story was published, a lot of information was manipulated, and the story came out half-baked being quite confusing and leaving several important points unmentioned, the author ended up disappearing and being locked up.

My faithful friend returned urgently to the lands as this would draw the attention of the Custodians who would seek by all means to understand how the information had been leaked.

While they were confident in their manipulation they would seek other means to dissuade him, and we knew that a not so friendly visit was expected that could come from either the Known Lands, Custodial or Anunnaki.

The Custodians avoided us again, and this made us stronger, the Giant-Humans as Butler once remarked, would sooner or later give their help, and great technology was again shared, and with this we were again ahead of the custodial advance.

What were the moves of the Custodians in this "Silent War"? They would use the human being to match their technology, this would bring great consequences as the human being was not prepared for the use of such advanced technology coupled with custodial colonizing conditioning, it was a time bomb that was not long in coming, great wars and a deadly plague were precipitated into the environment for the enjoyment of the Custodians.

Human expeditions to Antarctica began, financed by leaders who had direct connection with the reigning power, they knew they had to focus on education to continue corrupting the new human generations, several "space" achievements would come to lay solid foundations of heliocentrism.

The possibility of other lands behind the Ice Walls would be almost buried, they started then with the creation of bases around the entire Antarctic ring added to the exclusion zones, a strong militarization of key areas. Also not long after the "Summer Portal" was discovered, the Custodians took this as a game to demonstrate their power against ours, we feel that in a way they enjoyed it but they also knew they were risking too much.

A few years before the first custodial attack on our lands called "Operation HighJump", by means of a large number of human soldiers and custodial technology, the media barely mentioned it, but it was one of the biggest moves made by any military force.

largest movement by any military force in the history of the "new humanity".

The leader was known as "Richard Byrd" and was used in several missions in reconnaissance of other lands, but in the official missions he would never reach our lands, although his attack could endanger our people, both us and the Anakim had no intention of attacking them but to make them withdraw their armed forces in a peaceful way, the Anakim masters talked several times with their leader, but another force entered the conflict and a great battle was fought just behind the first Dome.

Then the same leader would make contact several times with the Anakim masters and would also help us to carry out the plan of human awakening within the Known Lands becoming an infiltrator for a while, eventually by choice or obligation this changed dramatically and as we were informed the military leader delivered valuable and secret information of the Anakim technology, and was the first of the group of the "new humanity" to be sent to Mars in recognition of his work.

Attacking us with other human beings was one of the many perverse strategies of the enemy, it was their way to demonstrate their power and make us face our past, since we sought to liberate it and not to confront them in absurd battles that were defended by mere conditioning.

We knew that all this game that they were carrying out would end abruptly by their way of acting, we were going to continue gaining ground in this awakening, and they would start attacks within the environment with the different techniques as always, natural disasters, pandemics, wars between nations, etc.

Those academic books that until now seemed untouchable began to be strongly questioned and the entire academy began to reel from the possibility of another model. The Infinite Earth would begin to emerge and would be the ultimate plan that would give way to the final liberation attempt.

OSIRIS AND THE INDEPENDENT LANDS

What did we need to accomplish our last step?

That our brothers change their perspective and break the conditioning was key, our forces could never liberate a people who defended their oppressor, in their minds we would be the colonizers who put at risk their current state and also their lives.

The custodial system was strongly implanted, the existing air pollution also hindered our mission. Although there was great resistance from several sectors, it was still not enough for us to act.

Surprisingly, several other races visited us with the intention of acting against the custodial yoke that was really exhausting as well as threatening their "Circles", all help was welcome, the "Pleiadians" were interested in also being able to liberate "The Source" and annihilate the oppressive races.

Their system was close to the second dome existing near the "Second Ice Walls" and the passage between the "Mermaid Lands" and the "Island of Death" was unfeasible, not many could survive the beasts that existed there, so everything had to be done by air.

The Pleiadians had been under Custodial power for some time and had left them on the verge of extinction, their great technological development of ships and spiritual made them miraculously resist and today they became a great free society.

Being close to the Celestial Lands they were also aware of some of the Custodial attempts to enter, they have seen how they used humans on several occasions as well as other races.
In the "Lands of Mars" there were several colonies of different races that had been moved by the Custodians and Anunnaki.

the Custodians and the Anunnaki, they wanted to populate the place with several races where they were in control.

The local race was undeveloped and had not put up much resistance in their colonization.

The humans that were there now all belonged to the "new humanity" of the last reset, and all of them had "earned their passage" by the help given in different missions against their own brethren, we had labeled these lands as noxious in reference to the future.

The lands that were outside of any circle were really disregarded by the colonizers, as they considered that most of them did not have any mineral or race that could be of interest to the Custodians or Anunnaki, in fact many lands had been overlooked in their travels, observing them very overlooked.

This had generated that many races would begin to develop in these lands, as they were for a long time prosperous places without the intervention of colonizing races.

Then in the period of the creation of the great Pyramids and the exploitation in Egypt and Central America, some humans were sent to the Lands behind the Dome, together with Custodial leaders, but they never revealed any passage but were transferred with the use of hallucinogens and in altered states of consciousness, many of which were presented to them as different types of Gods.

The immense land of Osiris was the beginning of the end of the peace of the lands surrounding the great Walls, along with the thousands of archipelagos in the deepest ocean known.

Osiris, one of the Custodial leader took a colony of humans to these lands, but they never let these humans manage to leave, they did not want them to ever discover important lands like Lemuria or Atlantis since at that time there were still vestiges of human birth and their great advance that had been left there.

THE LANDS
OF ORION AND
THE GREYS

These lands were inhabited by the race known as "Greys".

known as "Greys", these beings were hostile and also based their technology on weapons of destruction for attack and defense, oriented to colonize, although no circle was known to be colonized by them, some lands near other "orien-worlds" were taken by this central power.

Together with their neighboring lands of Zeta Reticuli, this race had been colonized since almost their beginnings by the Anunnaki, who had used them in several expeditions and missions to other worlds in the reconnaissance of the "Terra-Infinita".

As we commented they also fulfilled functions in the Known Earths and then in the Earths of Mars, who also had a colony helping the Custodians in their experiment.

After they had failed in their mission to control the human (in the period of growth of the Great Tartary) where they had also lost valuable information of all the circles that integrated this "Great Dome", some battles were fought between Greys and the Custodians, this also ended up helping the human being as well as the Anakim prior to the reunion of the Custodians with the ancient Anunnaki.

There is a theory that these beings had been a direct creation of the Anunnaki as an inferior race that could serve them for different purposes, since they used cloning as a direct form of subsistence and were very robotic in their functions and movements, in fact these beings are completely devoid of emotions.

But the reality is that they were born inside the Dome known as "Lands of Orion", and with similarity to the race of Zeta Reticuli, after the confrontation with the Custodians they had been close to total disappearance, having to resort to their great scientific advance and base their survival on the cloning of beings.

THE LANDS OF MARS AND ITS LOST CIVILIZATION

These lands harbored a great variety of life, the vegetation was abundant and it is the Circle with the greatest variety of animals, flora and fauna known.

Its lands were considered one of the most fertile, and it was the first Dome where the Anunnaki were able to penetrate and colonize.

The original beings of Mars at the time of colliding with these beings, resisted as best they could but it would have been lethal.

They were very proud beings and great defenders of life and their lands, they all perished in battle, the last beings committed suicide when they saw that they were going to be part of a great colonizing race, knowing this sad story their loss is regretted since the true and real Martians were beings that based their technology on purely spiritual growth.

The Anunnaki began to inhabit these lands and use them as a

second home due to the proximity to their own, then with the passage of time and the treaty with the Custodians, they began to use this Circle as an experiment gathering many races from different colonies, which we can still find today.

The first humans sent there settled in "Aeria", an immense area provided with fertile land but the conflict with other races that also lived there did not take long to arrive, while the Custodians and Anunnaki enjoyed the spectacle, on Mars took place "Dantesque scenes" in wars for territory.

As time went by, the human colony settled on another island close to the Lands of "Aeria" because they lost territory.

Of the "last humanity" the first human to visit them was Richard Byrd in one of his expeditions crossing the South Pole, obviously commanded and helped by his Custodial leader "Nimrod", several soldiers of the U.S. Navy and some invited leaders of secret societies (some of them famous politicians) managed to cross the passage that is known today with his name.

In the central lands of "Argyre" there is a portal with a direct connection to the Anunnaki Lands established there at the beginning of colonization.

Today it is a prosperous area and there are no major conflicts, in fact it is a land that some humans can visit as a reward for tasks performed for The Custodians. It is known that some of them even stay there because they manage to rejuvenate their bodies and get to live long years compared to the Known Lands and the toxins existing in the polluted air they breathe.

THE LAST
GREAT PLAN

I was sitting on the shores of the beautiful capital "El Arca", pensive, my body had begun to feel very strange a few weeks ago, the sea covered my feet and my gaze was lost in the horizon. There where I found my lands of origin that I never forgot and that will always be inside me, together with my memory were the faces of my loved ones, many had already disembodied a long time ago.

I made sure they knew my true destiny and my gifts were delivered safely, otherwise they would have surely imagined that I had died overseas in my madness and obsession for a journey with an uncertain destination, my body in those lands would have easily passed the hundred years and I was like a man in my fifties, however something was not right.

What would be my destiny now, would I die in these beautiful lands of the Republic?

The Sun was falling and with it another day without liberating that paradise turned into a prison called Earth, how many people had to die waiting? Without even knowing it, in their suffering day by day, where disenchantment was as possible as perverse wars and false power.

I sat on the cold sand and my body felt as thousands of piercing needles went in and out of every pore of my skin, I was facing a pain so deep that my body gave way, lying now looking madly at the projection we called firmament, with the faithful companions of every navigator, the stars also observed my loneliness, many members of the group had already left prematurely due to our damned contamination, our sick bodies were regenerating very slowly in these lands and we were only a few survivors of the new humanity crossing the "Ice Walls".

I felt privileged to spend my days here but the pain was permanent, something that did not let me enjoy knowing that many brothers were dying in there without being able to perceive the true love that we carried inside.

Thousands of "Ancestors" were still sacrificing themselves by entering between the Walls to hell itself, knowing that the contaminated environment or the Custodians themselves would kill them sooner or later, everything was based on the liberation plan, which with successes and failures was carried out and was still being tried, we had won so many battles in there without any weapon but thought, love and the spreading of the idea of inner knowledge, what every human carries inside.

We had also made remarkable improvements in the air that was breathed and on the basis of all the laboratory created diseases.

My old friend Butler came over and sat next to me, touching my shoulder, knowing I didn't have much time left, understanding it all he commented:

"William, hold on mate, the time of freedom is approaching, they began to hurry in their desperation, a new pandemic will strike soon, we are entering every day more and more Ancestors to the Known Lands, we will use their own means and when they realize it they will be bent, the new humanity will understand that they are under a dirty and perverse power. We are close to reaching as many humans as we had planned by assuming our responsibility.

The moment will come and then we will make ourselves known, with the help of the Anakim who monitor night and day around the walls, this time cannot fail and if destiny demands it, then we will get as many as possible out of there, resist to see the glory of freeing our brothers, so that the true path of spiritual knowledge begins.

I smiled at such an assertion, I gave him my many notes that I had been writing since I left the United States, I wanted everyone to know the odyssey of that group that went through the most incredible places and saw the most beautiful and hidden landscapes, who knew happiness and true love.

This story will be delivered to my brothers there inside the walls of ice, there were already so many truly interested in the Ancestral Lands and in these glorious lands of infinite prosperity and this knowledge that it would be the best way to communicate with them.

My body trembled and suddenly silence invaded, I could only see the firmament, the "iron blues" were crossing at full speed, where were our ships headed? Would it be the time to wake up everyone? Were we really ready?

These lands exist, I repeated over and over again inside me, we are guiding you, the battle is real and it is internal, the spiritual growth will free us all, resist, freedom is coming, trust, we are waiting to free you all.

CLAUDIO NOCELLI

- TERRA-INFINITA, EXTRATERRESTRIAL WORLDS AND THEIR CIVILIZATIONS

THE STORY TOLD BY THE WOMAN WHO WAS BORN IN THE LANDS BEHIND THE ICE WALLS

HELEN, THE WOMAN BORN IN THE LANDS BEHIND THE ICE WALLS

09:15 AM marked the clock in this suffocating and sad gray room, my eyes barely opened and they somehow tried to give me an overview of where I really was. I must admit that every day I find it more difficult to adapt to this world, my mind takes minutes to realize that I am back in the "Walled Lands" where my ancestors have walked long ago.

I found a rolled up newspaper on the door that said June 22nd, that's how they count the days here, each one faithful to their so pigeonholed grid, where it seems that nothing can get out of the script, that mundane script that they created for the forced partners of this abyss, dark and sinister, a humanity that seems to bleed day by day without realizing that it collides every day against the crude reality that they let long ago all this become something immovable.

This cannot be called life, I thought to myself every time I visit the lands where my father was born, my grandparents, my ancestors, those who left their lives to see a free humanity, and

I've found this.

It hurts my heart to imagine the bones of my brothers who must still be buried here in these lands, who died believing and fighting for everything to be different.

Curious way of living I thought while turning on and off a small lamp next to an old bed, here without a doubt there is a strange way of creating a false need for objects. This humanity seems to be paying for the sin of its past having tried to be free, I understand that, although it is very unfair and it is a thorn in the side of all of us who come from the other side, the free side behind the Ice Walls.

"Pay for a place where they were born" this phrase went round and round in my head, that's why I knew well the faces of those adventurers who managed to find the other lands, the lands of the Giants, or the lands where I was born so many miles away from here, but a very high price had to be paid, that's why I come back, that's why my father died leaving his legacy, we never forget the new humanity that was born in these lands deprived of their freedom and their true history, maybe it is time to start opening those "Walls of Fear" as I like to call them, that terrify us for a past where a war was lost, but freedom was gained, that the dead have not been in vain or forgotten as the Custodians wanted, they buried a large part of human history and manipulated it, and worst of all is that they convinced them and now many defend this history and the lands they inhabit.

This world is a very difficult place to survive, in addition to a high toxicity in what you breathe, eat, drink, there are also enough dangers that make it an unfriendly place and for those who manage to escape, with little desire to return, but as I always say, in my heart I have these lands so rooted, when I walk through these lands I reconnect with my past, with my dear father, William Morris, who swore to defend and rescue this new humanity from the parasitic hands of the Custodians.

Also, the amount of wars that were lived throughout the years and are still being lived is really detestable, how they manipulate even in such a basic way as putting different colors in imaginary limits.

or beliefs of all kinds to divide, with that you can only generate that millions of people lose their lives even many voluntarily thinking they do it in a just cause.

The only just cause is freedom, and that freedom can only be achieved by tearing down the curtains around these lands, lifting the veil comes at a high price, but it is always worth knowing the truth, even if this is the last thing I can write.

How many innocent people have given their lives for this cause? Who does not want to know the true story of our past?

In this book I will try to bring clarity, as much as possible on the subject of the "Known Lands" and the "Other Worlds" behind the Ice Walls, I will also try to leave detail of everything we know about the civilizations of each of these, also called, "planets" and a brief history of which we got to know, thanks to the book of "She-Ki" the Giant-Human who gave my father the knowledge that nobody knows in this new humanity, due to the great existing manipulation and the strong conditioning that they exploit from childhood.

The important thing is that only one person I have met who was really interested in listening to my story, even though I had not revealed my real name or where I had come from, we had been studying this new humanity for a long time, we would not trust this long investigation and information if we did not know that it will be delivered with all the respect and in the way we want.

Besides that it takes urgency, we are not here to scare anyone, nor give dates of cataclysms or "resets" (or restarts), but we are aware and understand that the situation of recent years is increasingly delicate, we understand that this process can be accelerated and we are aware of the causes and resulting effects, in case I did not introduce myself yet, my name is Helen Morris, daughter of the navigator William and born in lands that surely you do not know almost 8000 kilometers behind the Ice Walls in the direction you know as "South".

Before I take you on the path of the "Terra-Infinita" and its history, you must understand that much of these texts will not go in line with what you have learned in this "circle-environment" (I will also explain where this term comes from), much of the history told here is possible for you to keep to yourself and that this book can open up this cause.

Much of the story still lives in you, because you were also part of it in some way, only that you have been put to sleep, completely anesthetized, to such an extent that living this life seems normal, a life that one seems to base merely on robotic, repetitive actions, very few are based on love and empathy, the division is every day easier and for any reason, and the big media take advantage of any of these weaknesses that have been exploiting for a long time.

It is also important that you can contrast this information, you should not believe anything about us, but you should question everything, what you have learned so far and what they will want to make you learn by force, always try to surround yourself with people who not only deliver a message of empathy and love, but who really carry it forward and do not generate any division. So do not be surprised if any of this sounds familiar, embrace the ideas that you like the most, embrace them tightly and always trust what you feel, what comes from your heart, your mind will try to manipulate and confuse you.

My father left these lands in times of war, and when I returned I found it almost in the same situation, as you will see, the security that one seeks in times of war, is the same that generates them, in other words, there is no such security from any country, or government, or political party, or any leader of any kind, it is only you humans against those who pull the strings from the dark (today), called "Custodians", "The Watchers", "Caretakers", "The Corrupt Brotherhood", "The Tree Protectors", "Cuijas/Kuijas", "The Energy Absorbers", and I think I have heard many other terms, but we will stick with the first of them, although I usually call them "the parasitic race", it fits them perfectly. They are here since almost the beginning of humanity, and whether we like it or not, they manage and have control of these lands today, can anything be done against this, the answer is simple: Yes, but for that we have to go into many points and find many of their weaknesses as well as strengths, knowing the enemy is the best way to get to break free from their control and / or end up defeating them.

THE GREAT DOME

Before going into each of the worlds, it is necessary to make a caveat and clarify what "The Great Dome" means and what we mean when we mention it.

"The Great Dome" or also called "The end of the known", is that which covers and encloses in some way all the other known worlds, very few were able to see this end and even "touch" it, can it really be touched?

Moreover, it is said that some experiments were made to be able to cross it but it was not possible, it is the terror of several colonizing civilizations that do not sleep peacefully, since any race from outside could take away from them from one day to the other the power that they maintain in that hierarchical pyramid that they themselves built during history. Another world that generates terror for them is the "Celestial Lands" but we will have time to detail this mysterious place that has a great relationship with the human being. In this "Great Dome" there are 178 worlds or "circle-environments", which in turn may have one or several domes that also enclose them with their different climates and civilizations.

Penetrating these domes of each circle is not an easy task. As time went by, the technique was perfected and now there is a lot of technology to carry it out, but this was developed exclusively by colonizing races, many other races explored surrounding these worlds or simply the independent lands (lacking domes).

These domes are almost impossible to cross via air, and almost always another way is sought by land, but the most common is that it can be done through water which is where they are more easily found the way to open passages that can connect the inner-outer worlds, almost like two membranes in any cell, functioning as a barrier that can allow at a certain time the passage.

(When you have greater control to be able to penetrate some specific domes, it can be done via air without much inconvenience, although it can be quite dangerous for reasons that we will see later). Much later many portals were found in several "Circle-Environment" connecting even several of the worlds, the manipulation of these portals was so great that many problems were caused and some became unstable making some beings have disappeared without knowing where they really went or if this caused that their matter has disintegrated. Today it is common to find beings in full development of portals that can connect certain areas within the Great Dome, without ever having been able to penetrate it.

When we speak of the 178 worlds we are not referring to the independent lands that exist between worlds, these are lands that exist and were used by various races when they could go outside, in fact, it is said that these lands exist to avoid long distances that connect the worlds, It is fervently believed that the worlds were made to investigate them and that all of us, in one way or another, are going to go outside to look for our freedom, to know other races and to be able to enter someday in what can be found in the "Celestial Lands" as well as behind the "Great Dome".

THE LANDS OF
THE CUSTODIANS

This parasitic race, as we briefly indicated in the first chapter, are beings that base their technology on attack and defense weapons, using all their potential in the discovery, colonization and exploitation of other lands, as well as the beings they can find.

Their beginning is unclear and full of questions, there are theories among the giants where it is said that the Custodial race was attacked by some other race that did not even come from this great dome, and that they merged with the locals to create a great force that later gave origin to the Custodians.

This would explain the reason for their great development over other races that were still in their infancy trying to survive within their circles.

The Custodians, it is said, were the first to leave their world and advance on their way to the others, with great destructive and colonizing power, having reached each of the worlds and tried to explore around the known "end of the worlds".

While they have been defeated on at least two known occasions by two completely different races, it is certain that they are also vengeful and that, if they have not yet tried again, they soon will.

The Custodians as the only race, were the ones who attempted to enter the "Celestial Lands" that very little is known.

These lands are the most mysterious of all the known worlds, and while all or almost all the races existing today are aware of this place, very few dare to want to penetrate it.

The story goes that humanity, in a way, comes from these lands, and that each of the humans have "The Source" or "Life Energy" (also called "soul") that comes from these lands, therefore, the human destiny is to confront the Custodians, that whatever is done the great clash will be inevitable.

Although it has already been tried and the great forces between humans and custodians have collided (with the help of the Anakim Giants and others), history will surely repeat itself again in these lands, for that reason we are very aware of everything that happens here, any opportunity to free humanity will be used to the fullest, also we cannot make the mistakes of the past, otherwise it is possible that now we may never have another opportunity.

For each reset, the security becomes stronger, and the human standard of living becomes less and less free, the humanity that is living now is nothing like that of my ancestor in these same lands, nor that of my ancestor to the previous one, each reset is worse, stricter, with less freedom and greater manipulation.

We escaped from these lands during the "Great War" against them, the Giants helped us to form a large block and confront them before everything got out of control, unfortunately when the hard defeat came we knew that everything was going to get worse for those born here, besides they know that many escaped and that we would be a danger to all the manipulation and lies in these lands that they spread and control.

It would be difficult to generate another "New Great Tartary" with all the free technology and the great cities that we were able to forge, the truth is that we had the hope that victory and freedom would finally be ours, but, by those things of destiny we did not achieve it. We know that it was very close, but it is also true that defeat would bring more misery to a new humanity, the risk was very high. The babies who are less than seven months old are left at the disposal of the Custodians in these lands, who with their technology take them little by little to a new beginning.

This beginning is sudden and in various parts of the known continents, so there will always be a part that will not have parents, grandparents, and so it will be until forgotten.

Once the number they set is reached, they will begin to manipulate the human to take them on the path they have decided. The vestiges of a past life will be intermingled as their own, even if the human of that time cannot reproduce it nor have the necessary tools, nothing will be questioned as long as everything can be demonstrated by the great leaders, or media, scientists, historians, scholars, celebrities and all kinds of fictitious prestige that they will invent depending on what stage of development the race is in.

The technology will be delivered in small installments until it can reach the level that is also previously established by the leaders.

The Custodians are arrogant beings who detest the human being, for them the human being is a horrible being, who smells bad and does not deserve any freedom, the custodial leaders are really hostile and always were hostile to our race.

That is why they control it, but they also do not allow anything to get out of the pre-established control, they would even carry out a reset before knowing that at least a single human could escape.

The leaders many times met with the intention of eliminating the human race, but there was much debate about it, especially for the tasks that are carried out here, that would bring much discussion among the same Custodians, plus there is a small part that has great relationship with the leaders, many are part of lodges, military or politicians who came to have direct contact with them and were rewarded with their passage to other lands, for example the existing colony in "The Lands of Mars". The story of the "last reset" where my grandparents were able to escape along with my mother, who at that time was a baby, was due to the Great War that took place in these lands more than 250 years ago, put on alert this race who thought they dominated these lands with ease, until the union of giants and humans really shook their power. In the War it is said that one of their most important leaders died at the hands of the Giants-Humans and this also caused that the new human beginning in these lands (with babies of a few months) was carried out under a strict control and manipulation, it is what we are seeing in the current days and what we will continue to see in the near future if things do not change. The Custodians are carnivores for the most part, although they can really eat all kinds of food, do they eat human flesh? I will come back to this question later, as I think it is worth talking about.

They know agriculture well, being pioneers and experts in that field, something they inculcate and educate the human after each reset to carry out these tasks of agriculture and animal husbandry, so that they can then increase their population as fast as possible.

They receive pleasure from human fear or sadness, all that "negative" energy can be "absorbed" by them that they really end up enjoying it, that is why it is common to see great sacrifices in ancient civilizations, or great tragedies, the thirst for human blood, they enjoy these sacrifices and in many stories we can find that they "feed" on this.

They reached a great development in the modification of the climate, and it is common that they create great walls of ice around the colonized lands, this they began to use in the last times since before they had not reached this development.

The walls serve them as a great shield to be able to "protect" or enclose even more the colonized races, in this way it is very difficult for them to escape even when they have to leave some worlds by necessity to go in search of another.

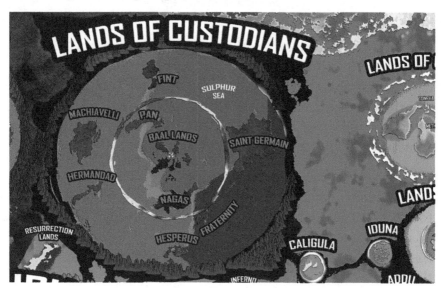

THE ANUNNAKI LANDS

The famous Anunnaki, another of the colonizing and parasitic races that is sickening the other worlds, manipulating and controlling the children of the children for years and years. Another of our enemies, a hostile and power-hungry race. They are the creators of the Pyramids and build these structures in all the worlds they visit.

They are in our opinion, the strongest race within this Great Dome, even above the Custodians. The technology they use to attack other worlds is incredibly advanced. The weapons of destruction, and the facility they have to enter through the domes is also something notorious and that characterizes them and frightens any race. The utilization of portals for transportation led this race to be one step ahead of the others. In fact, it is known the story that they have defeated the Custodians when between them there was a great conflict during the opportunity that we had in the Known Lands to be able to free ourselves. And they were also the ones who caused us to be defeated in the last known pact between the Custodians and the Anunnaki.

This race is confused in several of the stories that are told in the Known Lands, in a casual and often deliberate way, but we find in several stories and books of the Known Lands the Anunnaki as reptiloid or reptilian beings, but the reality is that they are beings of very tall stature (can reach 5 meters),

They live in an arid zone with little vegetation, and although the "Waters of Horus" seem to be paradisiacal beaches from far away, the reality is that they are deep waters and in them live snake-like animals that can measure up to 55 meters long and that do not like the visit of other beings from outside.

Their skin color is yellow-greenish, although their leaders can have a totally different tonality, but all of them have very dry, scaly skin, and their eyes are distinguished by being yellow, red or black, and they have a particular iris (that other beings also share) that is characterized by a cleft, depression or gap and can be both uni and bilateral, generally dark in color. During the many civilizations in the known lands both the Anunnaki and the Custodians (usually the former) have been depicted in many forms with humanoid bodies and with different heads of animal types, reptiles, birds, and a myriad of them. Thus, confusing the true history of the human being and conditioning the human mind throughout his life by these parasitic beings. They are beings that lack all empathy and are based solely on the oppression of other beings and the conquest, the thirst for power and control. In this they are very similar to the Custodians and that is why, they have preferred to share that position than to kill each other, although tension is always expected between these two races, which could be convenient for all the other worlds that are under their power.

THE LANDS
OF VENUS

The original beings of these lands also called "Venusians" and unlike those of Mars, they survived all colonization, but how? It is still not known for sure how these beings were able to make fun of the brutal colonization they suffered long before the Custodians took the Known Lands.

According to some legends within the giant race, the first humans thought to make contact with the original Venusians in order to form a block against the colonizers and thus, learn from each other, this happened in the beginning just before the Custodians took the first humans by surprise and they ended up being colonized in the Walled Lands.

There are theories that some of the early humans who started in the lands of Asgard, Lemuria and Atlantis (in conjunction with a portal connection to Hyperborea) may have escaped before the first Custodial attack and possibly settled in the lands of Venus. The Venusians are beings who base their technology purely and exclusively for spiritual development and benefit on their path of ascending or transcending internally, they did not possess weapons of destruction for attack and defense, this the Custodians saw as easily accessible, once they penetrated their world-environment they thought that everything would be simple in those lands.

The surprise came when the Custodians set foot on the Lands of Venus and a great storm hit this Circle-Environment very suddenly, they did not take note of it at that time as they thought it was the weather there, but as the days passed they saw that the storm never receded and they could not find a single Venusian on the surface (the storms never ceased until the last Custodian did not cross the Dome to the outside). With Custodial technology they began to notice that the Venusians were underground, in bunkers of a technology hitherto unknown to them, and the storm raging up there on the surface was truly devastating. The Trustees gathered to come to a decision soon, they were not going to stay there much longer.

In fact, many trustees started revolts and didn't see the point in dying up there, things got pretty complicated for the leaders.

Many saw it as a failure, and others thought of returning at another time, but true to their history they did not give in, and many Custodians died on Venus, even a very important leader is said to have fallen in those distant lands.

The conquest of Venus for the Custodians was a failure, in fact, they did not fight against the Venusians who did not possess weapons, if they had them I think it would have been a crushing defeat for them, when the story was known in other Circle-Environment they tried to imitate it, but with disastrous results, later we will comment on that point.

 The technology that the Venusians had been developing was not overnight, it was years and years of progress and those bunkers had everything, high level subway connections, the Custodians tried to block and even destroy the area with explosives and missiles, but for each attempt many Custodians died because the areas near the bunkers were also full of explosives and other technology that hindered even the approach. A Custodial leader already at the end of this failed invasion met with a Venusian leader, as it was feared that the

Custodians might try to blow up the entire surrounding circle in retaliation, no one really knows what was discussed or what happened that day, but the Custodians left the Lands of Venus in the worst way, with heavy casualties and a defeat to their credit.

We know because the Venusians themselves told us that in this meeting, besides pleading for peace in their lands, they would have asked for the liberation of the humans, which was totally rejected.

THE LANDS
OF DRACO

The Draco or also known as "Etamines", are the inhabitants of the Draco Lands, northwest of the Known Lands, crossing the Lands of Venus.

These beings that once visited our lands are known for their great technological advance in weapons for attack and defense, as well as great psychic development.

Some of their beings can communicate telepathically, using this technique to subdue any colonizing enemy, or even to colonize other lands.

 The Etamines, by means of a treaty, achieved a union with the Custodians, but at the beginning this was not so, but the Custodians attacked their lands when they were not in their most advanced stage, but on the contrary. The Draco Lands lack islands, but two large continents are found with great vegetation, in fact, the most exotic plants of any other Circle-Environment within the Great Dome exist there. Its great wall of Ice was never an impediment to be able to cross other Domes and conquer some lands (These walls were left by the Custodians when they decided to put an end to the total manipulation of their environment, did they stop manipulating them? we really wonder, we think not)

They started by lands outside the Domes, like their nearby land Osiris, but then they moved their technology to the near lands, many of these beings stayed in these paradise islands, but they use there many of the military bases for weapons development.

What happened in the ancient battle between Etamins and Custodians?

The Custodians finally won at the beginning since the Etamines as we mentioned had not achieved the progress they have today, but it was not easy nor did they surrender, since they knew their lands well and are experts in making large tunnels, the Custodians had to use advanced technology to finally achieve victory in those lands and leave their mark on the walls of ice surrounding the Dome in that "Circle-Environment".

The Draco lands were also visited by other races, such as the Anunnaki, and inhabitants of other nearby lands, such as the famous "Greys" that inhabit The Orion Lands.

The links with these beings led to the fact that today both races live together in a true fraternity, both in Draco and Orion, the Etamins and Greys can be found together.

The age at which these beings can reach is approximately 192 years, compared to the years of the Known Earths. While the Custodians infected their atmosphere and the air they breathe at the time of their attack, as of today they have no diseases nor any great war being waged, although they are spiteful beings and it would not be strange if they are planning to colonize other lands or perhaps a revenge towards the Custodians, but this is all mere speculation.

A great flood that still disconcerts its inhabitants was generated at the beginning, a strange wall surrounds its coasts, it is technology that they are carrying out, it is said that it is used as radar and that it could attack any enemy that wanted to cross them, the surveillance system of their lands increased in the last time, product of the fear that the great colonizers still have for what could be outside this great Dome.

It is possible that the Custodians and Anunnaki are very interested in this type of wall to replace the ice walls they create.

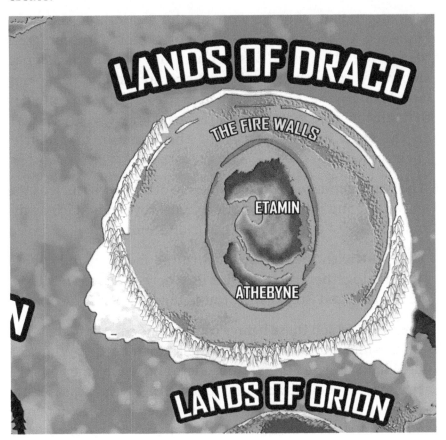

THE LANDS
OF MARS

Lands of Mars, who inhabits or inhabited these lands that lie behind the Ice Walls?

There lies this great world, crossing the second Dome and traversing lands that few humans have ever seen. Mars has great incidence in the Known Lands since in those lands several events related to humanity happened and still happen today. This immense "Circle-Environment" and misnamed "Red Planet", harbored a great and diverse life within its Dome. This native Martian civilization was reportedly totally annihilated by the colonizers, so why wasn't part of it left for possible further development, or even for some kind of manipulation by the colonizers themselves? Apparently this race was firm in their convictions based on their morals and ethics, preferring to die and extinguish their race in battle rather than beg for freedoms in quotas under conditions that colonization would impose. The Anunnaki at the end of their mission realized that not a single Martian was left standing, since the last ones even committed suicide, they were surprised, since they did not expect this to happen, in fact, it was their first colonization and after this they took precautions. The original Martian race was known in later studies, was an advanced race in its technology that prioritized the spiritual growth and welfare of their community.

They had little military training and technology, so their

defense was almost nil.

The Custodians soon took the great lands and grouped in the great centers taking advantage of all the knowledge and progress that was left there.

Nowadays the lands of Mars are simply experimental lands where several races coexist and generate wars between them and different reasons for almost eternal conflicts.

The leaders of these lands are both Anunnaki and Custodians. There is a community of humans, mostly made up of people who belonged to small groups and earned their passage only by their hard work in betraying their own race in their homelands. The best known member who might even be living in the Human Colony of the "last humans" (I am referring to the last reset), would be the well-known explorer Rear Admiral Richard Byrd.

Who knew how to be on the other side for a long time, and to confess some truths before giving himself up completely. Some of the many stories that we have out there and that are written today to keep the truth away from the "Terra-Infinita" and the civilizations that live behind the ice barriers and the Domes that separate them. In the Lands of Mars also coexist the famous "Greys" and some minor draconian colony or also known as "Etamines".

Between the Greys, the human colony, there is a rivalry existing since almost the beginning of the transportation of the Custodians to the humans there. The Custodians and Anunnaki monitor everything very well and do not miss any detail of them, what had begun in the "Clone Lands" today takes place in these lands, possibly this transfer is due to the time difference that exists in that environment.

There time, as in many other Circle-Environments, or lands within different domes, is different from the lands of Mars.

For this reason the passage to Mars of humans is always welcome, despite the dangers involved since it is a one-way ticket to a long life of almost 500 years in comparison. There are also other races almost all moved by the Custodians in their frantic conquests of their 178 Circles or worlds.

And many other races originating from different sectors were also moved there.

The lands of Mars are considered as in a large zoo, where different behaviors, confrontations and conflict resolution are studied, a huge farm of exhaustive monitoring and analysis of races.

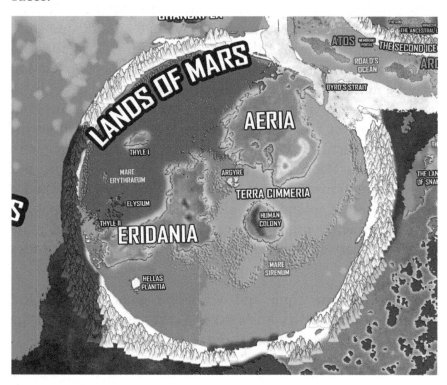

LANDS OF NEPTUNE

Nereida, Triton and Poseidon, the name of their lands that shine in the dark atmosphere that surrounds their "Circle-Environment". The "Neptunians" have had a hard time since their birth, not because they have not been able to adapt to their environment and survive in a climate where vegetation is not abundant, but because the sandstorms and the aridness that encloses this world can be really devastating, for that reason most of the big cities were created on the shores of their most fertile lands, leaving a large portion uninhabited. Anyway, the Neptunians managed quite well to carry out colossal creations, there are buildings so tall that exceed twice the size of the Known Lands, silence is the faithful companion that will go with you wherever you go in this dark world, as its Sun is also very different from those of the vast majority and is totally opaque.

 Throughout the time and with the great technological development that they knew how to carry out, nothing of the climate nor of the darkness was a great obstacle for them.

There are also large cities with very high constructions, many pyramids, since the Anunnaki were the ones who entered this world and took over their environment after a long time.

Recall that the Pyramids are key to the Anunnaki colonization that first starts with friendly and supposed technology exchanges between beings, the Anunnaki can be really great swindlers and lie to their leaders to generate a close bond, and then stick the cold dagger in the back.

Overnight the "Neptunians" were left with nothing, as the Anunnaki had planned everything from the beginning, and everything went as expected.

It is said that this is one of the first lands where they penetrated and ended up colonizing.

The natives of these lands could not cope with any technology like that, although we can assure that it was still in full development, but by that time the Neptunians had opened a long spiritual and developmental path focused on real personal and spiritual improvement, to cross the Great Dome after transcending matter. But it is not that they left the defense to chance, but they had developed a great military power that did not end up serving against the colonizers, although they did get a big scare when they rebelled.

In the beginning the Neptunians accepted defeat, but as these beings were used for certain tasks within their own lands that obviously ended up directly benefiting the Anunnaki "bosses", they rebelled against them generating several pockets of fierce fighting.

Then the casualties on both sides began, and everything got out of control in the center of these lands. Triton became the epicenter of absolute chaos, the blue blood of the natives was spilled in great quantity, the Anunnaki are still today their great enemies, and that after years they reached an agreement to withdraw from their lands.

Today the Neptunians live in peace and with a high development in technology that benefits their environment, their spiritual growth and they are in peace with the neighboring lands and races, but according to the story they prepare in silence for any new attack that could come from the nearby Anunnaki lands or other lands that could generate some danger for them.

Do the Neptunians travel to other lands?

It is said that they have traveled to other lands to investigate how other races live, to generate certain links and to be able to explore their environment, but it is said that they have not visited the Known Lands or spoken to any leaders at any time.

Although they do know the Lands of Mars and have been able to make contact with the "Human Custodial Colony" located there.

As I commented in previous paragraphs, the Neptunians are a race of dark blue color, they feed on local fruits since based on their system they cannot ingest a great variety of foods, they do not eat meat, and they have a certain friendly relationship with the Custodians, although it is not well known why, since they are generally beings that always sought their freedom and independence.

THE LANDS OF URANUS

The "uranians" or "uranites" are of pinkish skin, the tonality of their eyes are completely dark, although there are exceptions of completely white eyes that give the appearance of having visual difficulty, but the reality is that their sight is hyper developed being able to see to great distances and taking advantage of this as a great opportunity to be able to explore other lands.

They have not achieved great technological development, nor are they advanced spiritual beings.

They have long winters, for this reason there are temperatures that become very low during almost the whole year (referring to the local year), 42 years in the Known Lands can be approximately a year and a half difference, compared to the first ones. They are long-lived beings, although they are still today under the Custodial domain, and their climate was totally modified, as well as their complete "Circle-Environment".

Today their life span has been shortened because they began to suffer from strange diseases due to the alteration and manipulation of their bodies in laboratories.

The Custodians penetrated their world when the "Uranites" were at an early age of their development, at first the Custodians had not been interested in them nor in the minerals of their world, but then everything changed when they discovered large quantities of an important mineral under their lands.

There are large excavations (craters) on their surface, their lands look as if they were torn by titanic hands, the reality is that this was caused by Custodial machinery in the process of excavation. The locals work there under great pressure and almost enslaved by the parasitic colonizers.

The little development thereafter is strictly due to this reason, the Custodians do not want under any circumstances that these beings get to develop even moderately.

The uranites today are grouped only in the main lands (their core) called "Titania", they are generally giant beings that can reach 4 or 5 meters in height, they have two very long arms and feed exclusively on vegetables that grow in these lands or around them.

The other lands that surround the great walls of this enormous world are of similar climate to those of the Lands of Neptune.

THE LANDS
OF JUPITER

In this huge "Circle-Environment" we find several lands and each of them has different ways of life.

The natives of these lands identify with their birth lands and are clearly divided among themselves, there being great wars in the past between different factions of the same race.

They live in almost constant internal warfare, this is due to the influence of the Anunnaki when they invaded their lands in an early age.

The vast majority and those who rule today are in the center (their core) called or known as "The Land of Zeus". According to the history that could be gathered from this interesting world is that one of the high ranking Anunnaki leaders lived or still lives in these lands along with the leaders of the Jupiter Lands.

Both the Zeus-born and the "Europeans" currently rule and have the other part of the population (Tebe, Adrastea, Elara, Amalthea, Ganymede, Callisto, Ersa and Pandia) in constant conflict with each other, using the division to be able to continue ruling and manipulating the rest of the civilization.

Special mention for "Metis", these lands are used only by the leaders, and no other being can enter without their permission. They are beings with great development in destructive weapons for attack and defense, and have almost no spiritual development, they are based on a hierarchical pyramid instituted early by the Anunnaki.

Pyramids are found almost everywhere in the lands of this world, as a flag of clear control by this parasitic race.

Contact with humans happened on the Known Earths long ago, exactly three "resets" or reboots ago. They show clear hostility to almost all other races, even had several conflicts with the Custodians.

They studied the human being for a while, since they have large laboratories with great scientific advances for the modification and manipulation of beings.

These beings are of short stature in comparison (1.40 to 1.50 meters) are known for their particular eyes and a big head. They are carnivorous and feed mostly on animals that are born on the surface of their lands.

PEGASUS

The lands of Pegasus, near Jupiter and Hercules, became a great headache for several races for a long time. The beings that were born there were identified by their wings, which they created basing their technology on exploration, not so much to the weapons they could use for attack and defense, much less to colonize other lands.

This played against them when they faced the Custodians when they visited their "Circle-Environment". But surely their surprise was greater when they found that these beings moved through the skies without great difficulty because of their great metallic wings that beat back and forth, almost dancing throughout the firmament of this beautiful world.

It required no great effort to take these lands, and the "Lantians" as they were called because of their great central lands, came to an agreement with the Custodians that ended up harming them extensively.

They lost much of the mineral wealth of their lands as well as shared their technological advancement and thus further helped the Custodians to advance in their development to penetrate the "Celestial Lands".

The "Lantians" realized too late the real plans of their colonizer, and several revolts were generated that ended in massacres of the winged ones. Some say that this race ceased to exist and there are other versions that have even seen them in other lands, but they are confused with the beings called "angels" of the lands of the same name, since they are also close to the lands of Jupiter and they also have large white wings.

The Lantians usually wear their long white hair, with great development in alchemy and scientific advancement, they are not usually hostile to other races but brought their race to the critical point of its disappearance when fighting against their oppressor.

ALDEBARAN

In "Aldebaran B" live the "taurinos/taurines" and they have a great relation to what you know from past stories like "The Minotaur", that monster with a bull's head and a human body. The taurines are a faithful reflection of that representation, and if we dig deeper, we could find a direct relationship between the taurinos and human beings in past resets, some stories of the giants confirmed that the taurinos fed on human flesh. But in recent times the taurines proved to be benevolent beings who were able to end the Custodial rule a very long time ago.

Since then they are not well regarded by the races that dominate within this "Great Dome" since they have saved several races and species that were about to become extinct, even those races that had not been able to develop their full potential due to attacks of the parasites already mentioned. Their genetic material has been modified several times, but they have not been able to modify their empathy and love for life in other worlds. It should be noted that at the beginning of their development this was not the case, for that reason great wars were carried out within their territory.

They are carnivorous beings (only) and nowadays they can be found scattered in several other "Circle-Environments", they are also beings that were dedicated from the beginning to the spiritual development, although they also have great knowledge in exploration ships and weapons.

I have had direct contact with some Taurians, as they have lived with the "Anakim" giants for a long time, have shared their technology and wisdom with us, and have helped us a lot to survive after the "Great War". It is very common that both Giants, Taurians, Titans and several other beings are represented in the stories told in their lands as evil beings that feed on their pain, suffering or even their flesh (although the latter in the remote past could be true), that is why the representations of their imposing figures are often rejected in the "new humanity". They are beings that can measure up to 4.5 meters in height, and are differentiated from the rest by their large horns that are often cut from small.

"Aldebaran A" has animal and plant life, but the Taurians do not want to live in that area because of a violent past where much blood was shed. A great internal war between beings of the two lands led to the complete extinction of people living there, for that reason and out of respect for the memory of all those who have lost their lives there, it was decided not to use them.

THE LANDS
OF SATURN

The "Saturnians" are beings of very tall stature, some reach up to 14 meters in height, their psychic development along with their imposing figures, makes them very strong beings, for that reason and for their great technological advancement, they were never conquered by any parasitic race.

These lands, even though they are gigantic and attract attention because of their big rings, were not visited until relatively recently, when the Anunnaki visited them for the first time, they came to a quick agreement because they saw these lands and the native beings as very hard and difficult to colonize. The Anunnaki were coming from hard times of many wars in several places, especially in the Known Lands, and they did not want (or rather could not) have another big war, they knew they did not have much chance against the Saturnians, for that reason they preferred to have a friendly relationship with their leaders.

The funny thing is that when they tried to find leaders, they realized that it did not work that way there, the hierarchical pyramid of which they were so used to did not exist, there were no leaders or anyone representing their race, they simply all did it as a whole, their great psychic power united to carry out decisions that would satisfy everyone and benefit the entire race, these titans were really united.

The exploration ships they possessed were extremely

advanced for the time, and it is said that they taught the Anunnaki a lot about "the Great Dome" as they were able to visit it on several occasions.

They flatly refused to help them to penetrate the "Celestial Lands" as they consider it sacred like so many other races.

These beings are frugivorous, they usually have a bluish color in almost all their body and white tones in their abdomen. These titans visited the known lands on several occasions during different resets, carrying thousands of stories that are today intermingled with mythology by Custodial manipulation. Some have been immortalized in the Known Lands, they can be found on large stones, mountains or trees as some suffered from Custodial technology long ago.

Along with the Anakim, these beings are feared by the Custodians and Anunnaki as they consider them a real danger in their plans to conquer the "Celestial Lands".

LANDS OF ORION

These lands are dominated by beings known as "Greys", generally of small stature between 1.30 and 1.40 meters high, they are beings of great psychic and scientific development, their laboratories are extremely advanced and undoubtedly the best that can be found within this Great Dome. They have been experimenting with many races, they have in their possession knowledge about all of them, existing here, and the Custodians have used them on several occasions in their obsession to try to achieve penetration into the Celestial Lands.

But as everything tried was a failure, many of these beings were busy analyzing the human being in depth, carrying out abductions and other genetic tests.

They are beings that lack empathy and are generally hostile towards humans, only on a few occasions have they shown compassion, but cases of abductees who have had really bad experiences abound. They have been abducting and experimenting with human beings for a long time, in fact in the time before the last reset and other resets as well, they were already experimenting with us, the curious thing was when they tried to do it during the time of the Great Advanced Tartary, where free energy was controlled and a very superior technology for that time, the ships of the Greys were destroyed almost by thousand every day.

We could call them brothers of the beings of Zeta Reticuli, since their races intermingled and today they coexist together.

In the time before the Great War, these beings were in control of the Known Lands for a short period of time, as the Custodian and Anunnaki leaders had had major uprising problems in another "Circle-Environment", this was taken advantage of by the Giants and Humans to carry out the largest uprising in history.

The Greys were defeated without being able to do anything but go in search of the Custodians, these beings were expelled from the Known Lands by the Giants, this they would never forgive them. And although there were later meetings with giant leaders, it is well known that they detest them and that the feeling is mutual.

The greatest leader of the gray beings died in the Known Lands, that generated that the hatred that they had for humanity was raised even more.

The Greys colonized independent lands, but never came to dominate any other "Circle-Environment" on their own, the beings of Zeta Reticuli were colonized by the Anunnaki and used in their great expeditions towards the exploration of other lands, on the other hand the Greys of Orion followed a similar path, but on the Custodial side.

With the great difference that the Orion Greys really revealed themselves when the human uprising existed, the death of their great leader caused a deep hatred towards the Custodians for the task of taking care of other people's lands. Several battles existed between them, which further facilitated the power of the Great Tartarians in the Known Lands.

Although it was never managed to have them as allies since they hate humans, the truth is that there was an exchange of technology between gray leaders and humans, but they fell into the hands of the elite and were used against and for the destruction of the race itself.

Grey beings can also be found in the Mars Lands, which is a large experimental land where both the Custodians and the Anunnaki jointly control. The human colony there clashed several times against the Greys, but were defeated in all those battles.

They use cloning to subsist as a race and are very robotic in their functions, they are devoid of any kind of emotion or empathy. They came very close to being totally exterminated in the past.

PLEIADES

The "Pleiadians" are very close to the known lands, they are very tall beings that keep great physical similarity with the Norse. It is said that their ancestors survived the battle of Asgard against the Custodians, and then escaped to those lands in the Pleiades. They are generally benevolent to humans, but made a peace pact with the Anunnaki during an early age of their development.

They rely on your spiritual development and improving your living conditions. Their "Circle-Environment" is believed to have been manipulated by the Anunnaki since almost their beginnings, for that reason they suffer "natural disasters" from time to time. Trying to improve their current situation, although their lands seem to be destroyed at an accelerated rate.

It is believed that this was implanted to force them to have to escape from there and seek refuge in the known lands. Although many of these beings visited the known continents (especially the northern entrance through Asgard), they do not feel comfortable coexisting with humans. They looked for other alternatives, but they were a failure, they also failed to live in any of the lands behind the "Second Ice Walls".

These beings did not help the humans in the Great War, although neither did they help the Custodians, they simply stayed on the sidelines, although there is a good relationship with the giants, they are not seen with good eyes as allies, since they showed no interest in humanity in delicate moments of history.

Anyway, their great spiritual advancement is worthy of learning, they are beings that could help humans on their way, and lately there are more Pleiadians entering the known lands.

It is estimated that in the near future they could migrate in large numbers and coexist in these lands, accepting certain Custodial conditions, perhaps this is happening right now.

THE LANDS OF THE CLONES

This is indeed a very strange earth, it was created as a totally experimental "First Mars Earth", although it was not used for a long time until they transferred the idea to the "Mars Earths".

The first to penetrate this "Circle-Environment" were the Anunnaki, finding only life in a very early stage of development. It was immediately used to transport some of the then dominant races to create an experimental site for conflict resolution and inter-race development, but this did not prosper and it was almost destroyed.

Then it was used as cloning lands, to save lives of important leaders of the different races, for that reason it has that characteristic name. There was an escape of beings that were used for cloning that had to be chased in order not to generate great commotion in the different worlds. This also happened with human beings who were used for cloning, who escaped from there, these beings were robotic and lacked any feeling or empathy, no doubt all this was another aberration of the parasites.

This experimental land today is completely abandoned, they are one of the many forgotten lands that someday maybe someone can reuse, the Pleiadians also have these lands in view to make a massive relocation, but the truth is that it is not known what can be found there, since the large laboratories were abandoned overnight.

THE REPTILIANS

These beings are often mistaken for Anunnaki or other beings, but the reality is that they live far away from the Known Lands. Although they have visited them on several occasions and have made direct contact with leaders, they are beings who prefer to live far away from other worlds. Their homes are generally built underground, and these advanced reptiles have shown great hostility to humans on several occasions they have encountered them. Generally if they visit other worlds, they do so to implant subway bases that could be used in the future, since they monitor everything from there with their advanced technology.

Although they have a whole Circle-Environment for themselves as "The Lacerta Lands", most of them prefer to live in "The Island" near that world. There they have a large subway city and although they live in independent lands, they seem to prefer it that way. They have had in the past great wars against the Anunnaki, and are considered of great advancement and development of weapons for destruction. These Beings have earned their due respect from the great colonizers, have never been used as beings for inferior tasks, nor have they been able to bend them in any way. It is very possible that if they had to choose a side they would go in favor of the Custodians in a possible future war against humanity.

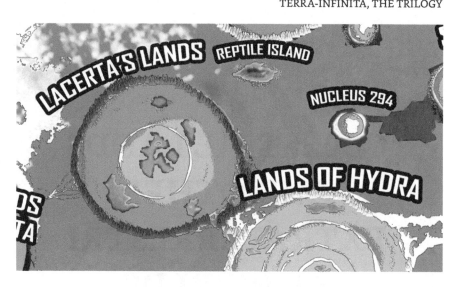

CELESTIAL LANDS AND OTHER EXTRATERRESTRI AL WORLDS

There are many other worlds that are being left out of this book, and that soon will also be detailed about them. There are so many extraterrestrial races that struggle to survive in a system that seems to leave to mere luck the fate of each one, those who survive or those who die.

It should also be noted that there are many others, although to a lesser extent, where peace and development reigns, perhaps because the parasitic races did not see or find anything interesting, perhaps they monitor them from afar or simply their development was subsequent to the visits in their lands and go unnoticed.

Other lands, as we have seen, did not even manage to develop completely when the parasites entered their worlds and emptied their lands along with their dreams, besides staining their history completely with blood, manipulated and changed their future forever.

The human being was broken and still could not twist the destiny for which he was created, his kingdom was taken a long time ago and it does not seem that they will leave the throne soon, perhaps it is time to reveal themselves to the despot king.

It is true that at least three colonizing races weigh on us, and although we are still standing we are being emptied spiritually every day, the death of the human being will not be physical, but it will be when we reach the point that there is no being in the Known Lands who knows that inside is his spiritual potential enough to change everything around. We must also learn from many other races that managed to overcome, we must follow some of their techniques to overcome the oppressive and manipulative power in which we live here, many of these races are willing to help in the path towards the awakening and human freedom.

It should not be forgotten that the Celestial Lands, the mysterious and hidden lands where the parasites could never enter (and that they tried with all their technology together), continue to keep our secret, the one that only we humans carry, "the Source of Life". Maybe we are the link to the other lands behind this Great Dome, the fear of the colonizers is real, because they cannot manipulate our essence, they only manipulate our physical environment, nothing can harm our inner self, it is time to wake up.

PART TWO - HELEN'S INTERVIEW, THE KNOWN LANDS AND THE LAST RESET

THE NAVIGATOR'S DAUGHTER BORN IN THE ANCESTRAL LANDS

Why the official versions do not inform us about these worlds and what is the reason for their visit to our lands?

Those questions are somewhat complex to answer quickly, but I will try, there are many continents behind what you know as "Poles", I would call them barriers or walls, they can be of ice as in Antarctica and in several other parts, as well as mountains, although there are several types of these barriers both in your known world and outside.

I have visited your lands so many times as I consider myself part of here, but the ancestors have even visited other worlds repeatedly, and thousands of other races have also visited us, both in a friendly way and in the most cruel way.

We could say that I am also part of here since my ancestors were born in these same lands and lived here until the final day, since I was a child I was motivated by the idea of being able to return and step on the soil of my mother and grandparents. They gave up their lives for the freedom of our entire race.

My father is William Morris, and I must tell you that he was born in these lands like you, he had the fortune of being able to cross those imposed, artificial ice walls created by the same parasites that control them today and managed to find our lands, I mean "The Ancestral Republic" or whatever you want to call it.

There he met my mother and formed a great family, I have the best memories of my dear father that fortunately many are knowing little by little and soon a large part will know more about the lands where I was born.

WILLIAM MORRIS, THE MAN WHO TRIED TO CHANGE THE COURSE OF HUMANITY

My father with 34 years and a great experience in the Continental Navy met a person called Butler who was infiltrated in these lands and who had also been born in mine, for reasons that we cannot say, but with a team formed by several members experienced in war and above all their experience in maritime navigation, and despite the thousands of complications and threats they received, they were able to enter the polar zone and cross those Walls and then find our lands. It was easier for my father as he was obviously led by an experienced captain who knew the way very well.

It was not all random as it seemed at first in the story of the first book "The Navigator Who Crossed The Ice Walls", the reality is that Butler was an expert person in the subject of navigation, as he led the "Naval Council" in my homelands.

He has visited these lands many times more than the world imagines, he is one of those who has done and contributed the most to allow us to infiltrate here and put into action the plan that he had devised together with my father.

As I said before, they have fought together with many of us who continue fighting for these lands, which we keep in our hearts and which are as much our lands as theirs, although I do not feel at ease here for obvious reasons about the damned race that is in power and that manipulates and prevents its development freely, these lands should belong to the human being, I mean the real human being, not that false dome that only nods its head to what is imposed from above, it must be ours because that is how it was dictated from the "Celestial Lands" to Hyperborea, the human being should not seek to escape from here but to subdue its colonizer and expel it, I understand that what I am expressing is certainly very complex to carry out today, that is why an alternative plan was sought, which is to get humanity out of here before the next reset.

THE NEAR LANDS

Our lands have a name different from everything that has been named in the stories, and surely much of the continents abroad as well, although many keep the spirit of the great stories and battles that may never happened, I will not annihilate his dream or confuse it with names, besides I prefer that my lands remain for the moment with the name that some know it, "Ancestral Republic" is fine as it represents what we are, the surviving human ancestors prior to the last reset.

We are your ancestors, although the lands were different before the "Walls of Ice", our parents and grandparents were born, fought and some died here. You cannot imagine how many stories are told in my lands about the great heroes that were forged here, just as heroes were born in my lands who have done great deeds in these regions.

How is it that you speak English? What is the language used in your lands?

In my lands a different language is spoken, native, especially in the main city, but we speak several languages of your lands, our parents escaped from these lands to start again in the outer lands, they escaped from all corners of this world that you know, then in the other lands different communities were created, but at the beginning, when this happened, each community was divided precisely by their culture, they began to create their own language and their own culture to generate links and that there are no divisions between the ancestral humans. Then, as time went by, many already used our native language and even forgot the language of their father or grandfather, this happens more, as I said, frequently in the big cities, but we try not to lose the connection with the past.

Why did your parents escape, or rather from what or from whom were they escaping?

They escaped from the worst war that has ever happened here, and they did it because there was no other alternative, escape or die, for all was lost.

Forgive me for getting emotional when I talk about this subject, my grandfather died in that battle as so many millions of others did too, my mother escaped being very small in my grandmother's arms, the giants saved many people for that we are eternally grateful.

THE GIANTS OF THE GREAT TARTARY WHO WANTED TO LIBERATE HUMANITY

The Giant race joined the human race in the previous reset, they came from outside to free us from the vile custodial oppression, they believed it was the right time to unite and wait until some of the custodial masters returned. The Great Tartary, the one that was erased from its maps and history, was the perfect union of giants and humans, that is why the past of the giants or the Giant-Humans was hidden forever, or simply their history was manipulated with tales full of lies mixed with mythology and in many ways they were sentenced as "enemy of the Gods". The truth is simple, and you will see it with your own eyes in the future, the only enemies of the Gods and of breaking the free development of the races, of uprooting and destroying the spiritual development not only here in the Known Lands but in many of the other lands, are without doubt the colonizers themselves, the enemy race that destroyed the dreams of the past and will destroy those of your future if you let them.

The Giants only show their greatness by staying hidden so as not to generate more harm to the current human being, since in the past everything has gone wrong and for that you are paying a very high price. These lands that are the only ones you know for now, have their oceans stained with ancestral blood, our blood, that tried to change everything, that were very close to achieve freedom forever.

HUMANS, GIANTS AND CUSTODIANS, THE GREAT WAR OF THE LAST RESET

The Great War started so fast that there was not even time to understand what was happening, the Custodians attacked the big cities, as they always do, they go directly to the central power to weaken everything from its core.

The giants warned in their visit to the Humans that the Custodians had the plan to contaminate the air that was breathed here in this World-Surroundings, it was already known about other continents beyond the Domes, but not in great detail, neither was it certainly known about the Custodial greed and hostility.

All this knowledge that we acquired with time and the help of the giants, was largely drawn from the information the Custodians had prior to the Great War. Another inferior race was in control of these lands and this was used to develop all the potential we could reach in the shortest possible time, incredibly organized plans were carried out, everything worked like a great clock, the advance of the Great Tartary was not done overnight, but neither was it long in terms of time in these beautiful but terrible lands. The walls did not exist back then, the continents were different, although they did not change by much, they manipulated their lands, their climate, their environment totally in the new beginning, they were never going to admit that they came close to losing their best colony, let alone in the hands of the "giant barbarians" as they call them, and the humans they really detest.

THE DESTRUCTION OF THE GREAT CITIES, THE FALL OF AN EMPIRE

The great cities were invaded by black smoke, the Giants brought technology and taught the humans in Tartary, the level of technology that was used at that time had never reached the hands of humans, it was a difficult process but they were achieving really great things, just the Great War came by surprise, although they expected it, they did not think it would come so fast.

Then came the great flood and different attacks, there came a time when we knew that all was lost.

The Custodians were weakened and those in power, the greys who were their lackeys, could not cope with the power of the Anakim, the giants who helped the Humans with their technology. There are several races of giants and not all of them joined in this war, in fact many of them split later because they did not agree to help, they saw it as a certain defeat.

At that time the hope of being able to defeat them was latent and that filled the spirit of any person who lived on this soil, the feeling that generates to finally be free is priceless and sometimes the dimension of what is taking place is not taken into account, that War was the cruelest that has happened here.

It also brought with it a great retaliation in a reset and a different beginning, what is being carried out at this moment, the system that oppresses you and turns you into a robot with mere biological functions, the spiritual emptying, how your mind is controlled, which does not stop for a second to give you messages and messages so that you cannot enjoy the present, All this is a product of that custodial fear of losing your best colony, unfortunately the Ancestors carry that, and the Giants too, for that and for many other reasons different plans are being carried out to free you and end once and for all this macabre system under which you live.

Many will ask, how is it that we can give all this valuable and at the same time dangerous information if it falls into the wrong hands?

Your answer is that we can give this kind of information because the majority simply will not believe it, and what we say here today will be forgotten by the majority tomorrow, it is like when someone has some kind of different experience, with whatever race, or for example the story about my father and the lands where I was born, but it is different if the government of this world with all the mass broadcasting apparatus tell a lie, for example, that the sky you see every day is pink, then many will come out to repeat it and even fight to death with anyone who says that the sky does not have that color, even more if important scientists who have graduated from distinguished universities come out to say that anyone who argues that the sky is pink will be labeled as ignorant forever, and possibly affect him all his life, then you already have two things against you, the immense power of the word of the great media that are controlled and that enter every home around the world and also you have the word of confidence in quotation marks, of the great scientists of the best universities that will give the necessary strength to submerge the majority to a lie that will be taken as absolute truth, soon nobody will even discuss about this subject for fear of being catalogued as ignorant, some will not even want to look at the sky for fear that their own mind will tell them that it does not have the color that they say.

A few others will fight against this lie without caring what they are told or that they will be ostracized from many places, or they will not even be allowed to talk about this subject with a simple censorship.

This is nothing new to you, look around you right now, this is what is happening, if you do not do or say what they impose, or simply what the media reports or what the distinguished expose then you will be labeled as someone who is on the opposite side of "progress", "advancement", or "development" of humanity (with many quotation marks). Possibly you will be ridiculed, attacked, sidelined, branded as a traitor or many other things, this is certainly unfair, the shadow controlling parasites who want total human degradation in conjunction with spiritual hollowing out can label another with their great means of influence and coercion and thereby destroy them completely. That is why we keep coming back to these lands and will continue to be here, to fight against this dangerous conditioning they exert.

THE LAST RESETS IN THE KNOWN LANDS

The previous reset has been the cruelest of all, because they were close to losing control, it could not have been otherwise. It is even said that there were periods where humans and giants were controlling the situation, but once the four great centers fell, the millions of deaths left by the War, it was difficult to recover.

We all knew at one point that we had been defeated, my mother has told me so many times this story which in turn was told by her mother, I already repeat it by heart, she was only a newborn, do you understand, they lived in a prosperous world and suddenly all their dreams were trampled, many found loved ones who had died next door, their houses were on fire or had disappeared, they used technology that you would not understand, they could even petrify beings, they had already done it in the past, they had to see themselves in a really desperate situation.

 When all was lost the great flood began, as it is known here, the mud flood, in reality this happened in different forms but it dragged everything in its path, it was something of colossal dimensions, many of the humans that grew up after the last reset used vestiges of these monuments or buildings, even some had withstood the war and the flood quite well, They were resistant to ancestral technology, they were prepared for everything, that is why you will notice that many images of the past do not match the reality that people lived, the difference in technology and architecture, they mixed the history in such a way that it is difficult for you to understand it completely, but at least you will have an idea of how the whole process was taking place.

The Resets, with some difference that existed, at least the ones I know of, are almost always carried out in the same way, they put a limit of years for the race they are controlling to develop and reach a point of knowledge and technology, they will always try to manipulate reality to reach that point as slow as possible, they take it really as a game, basically they will try to pause your spiritual growth and the truth about your origin and your World-Environment where you are, clearly they will never make themselves known nor will you have any kind of contact with them, but you will be able to find them in history in several possible ways and forms.

When a "reset" takes place, let's call it "natural", considering that the previously established limit of years was reached, they will make everyone over seven months of age die, this can also be decided in advance or it will simply be thought of at that moment in meetings of the "Parasite Dome".

The flood that my parents, grandparents and all that generation suffered was the same that would have happened in case we had reached the limit of years of development, only that they initiated this in an urgent way because of the war that had been unleashed, the last reset in these lands did not reach the time limit that they had established for our development, but we were not far away either if we consider that when the Giants visited and joined us in these Lands, they started to educate us about the Lands and the life behind this World-Environment, we started to learn too many things that they considered dangerous.

Not to make this answer so long, your babies of seven months or less than that will be left alive (not all, they will decide depending on many factors), those above that age will be killed or die in catastrophes of different kinds, this "World-Environment" is justly manipulated in its entirety by them, imagine you live inside a Greenhouse, you can understand it that way, you can make it bloom or poison it from one day to the next or even slowly.

THE CONTINUING JOURNEY OF WILLIAM MORRIS

My father returned to these lands, to the lands where he was born, he longed day after day planning over and over again how he could return to help those he considered he had left behind, "his brothers" as he referred to them. Knowing this great and painful truth was killing him every day, imagine knowing that your brothers were dying in there in a veritable hell of wars, manipulation and pestilence, and that nothing you could do on the other side, where your life was also in danger, for by then the Keepers had begun to attack the lands beyond, which until that time had been kept silent.

Not only that, but the Custodians had encountered a great city of Giants and Giant-Humans who were not only traitors to them, and therefore deserving of the worst punishment.

By all accounts, the Anunnaki did not decide to take part in these attacks and the Custodians were quickly expelled from my lands, the technology by then quite advanced thanks again to the help of the Anakim. This surprised the Custodians who returned to the Known Lands with the fear of the possibility of losing them. They then tried to reinforce the walls with all the technology and military possible, a time of ridiculous treaties and military bases all over the area was coming to prevent any human being from being able to reach this truth, now, was that enough to prevent our ships from getting through their bases?

THE INFILTRATORS DOUBLE, SO DO THE PROBLEMS

When they least expected it the Custodians had in their most precious colony around 14000 infiltrated ancestors, this network we created was part of the Morris-Butler plan, together with giant leaders, and several races that also participated and still participate in silence for human liberation.

We knew the danger of infiltrating these lands, as the Custodians could never know that this amount was infiltrated, helping and informing many humans about the other worlds, the spiritual potential and the true human history, this could cause an immediate reset, everything was delicate and we could not be noticed in a treacherous way.

At the beginning it was not a big problem to overcome the barriers, military bases, custodial technology (with radars that even cause earthquakes) and a myriad of obstacles that we knew how to overcome. But, not everything was happiness and we knew that sooner or later it could happen, an alarm went off (earthquake) near what you know as Antarctic Peninsula or we know as "False Antarctica". A group of people traveling from The Ancestral Republic encountered a military base patrolling the area in an icebreaker. Our people sank the ship when they tried to escape, and this irremediably echoed in the great spheres, they began to chase everyone in every corner you can imagine.

With great lies and excuses they went into homes in many countries where they feared we were hiding for ten years or more, they searched for every clue and began to use technology to control the movements of the new humanity. Although they already had this type of technology, they completely reinforced it after the Peninsula incident.

All this complicated the plan, and it was a complete setback since we had people infiltrated in the high spheres, politics, lodges, organizations, companies, universities, etc. This was a bit of an ice water bucket since we had been counteracting with our technology any custodial detection and a great advance was being made to be able to finally carry out in a timely manner the transfer of many of the people who were beginning to awaken.

Many of the 14000 had to return, the fear was already a reality and some ancestors died in the worst possible way as they were sentenced as traitors, I will not detail the many tortures they suffered. Captain Butler returned to our lands in solitude, I will never forget that day, my eyes filled with tears because it was the day I knew I would never embrace my father again.

THE DEATH OF WILLIAM MORRIS

Butler approached my mother and me, crestfallen, and his eyes in blood, he was also wounded in an arm and a leg, those ten or fifteen meters were the most eternal of my life, when he was finally close to us, he looked up and could not hold back his tears, my father had died in the Known Lands at the hands of custodial-military technology near the Antarctic zone.

The Custodians had delivered to commandos and military leaders of certain countries, advanced technology that they did not even know how to use, this was extremely dangerous for all life within the walled lands, in fact, the Custodians knew very well that this was a big mistake and put at risk their own colony, I think that although they were experienced in war, they did not handle well that a race could overcome them or the danger that entailed losing those lands.

They mistakenly decided to give technology unknown to the new humanity, only to help them in quantity against the Ancestors who were returning to their lands (many humans were also doing so with them). The humans were also given knowledge of weather modification and environmental manipulation, the Custodians really went into despair.

The ship ("Iron Blue") where my father was traveling along with some ancestors and humans of the new reset disintegrated in mid-air while crossing the Antarctic skies. A large invisible barrier was created by the Custodians just before the Dome, of course this was not known at the time and many ships were destroyed. To put it simply, they blocked the part of the Dome that we had opened by air. Butler was returning with William in another ship and told in detail about the death of my father, Butler managed to survive by a miracle.

It was undoubtedly the worst moment of my life and I really felt a lot of frustration and helplessness towards these lands, at that moment I lost track of Custodians and New Humanity, I only thought about if it was really worth my father dying for a cause that seemed lost from the beginning.

With time I understood and now I understand, I feel it in my heart, I am also part of these lands and I know that my father wanted as much as I do now, that humanity is freed forever.

This technology that the Custodians gave to some leaders of the new humanity had also brought several inconveniences within the Known Lands between countries that used part of this technology to threaten and even attack each other, the use also to make ships, planes and all kinds of transport disappear, people disappearing disintegrated to them. All this added to the knowledge given on the manipulation of the climate and the environment, was, in short, a chaotic era that continues today. It has been feared since then that humanity would be destroyed in absurd wars with the use of biological weapons, or that the Custodians would decide to reset for fear that they would be exterminated, or even that humans would use this technology to attack them, obviously the third option was the one that was farthest from happening.

CLAUDIO NOCELLI

TURNING THE
HUMAN FARM
INTO ETERNAL
FREEDOM

I understand that you may be wondering, so where did the whole plan go? And it is a question I want to answer before I finish.

Changes are going to happen, the plan was never abandoned, in fact, after my father's death, it impacted the Republic more as William was well loved along with Butler and they represented the face of freedom and the direct link to the known lands.

The fight against the Custodians never ceased and we remain steadfast against their oppression, manipulation and control of these lands as well as other races, unfortunately we could not move to the next phase yet, because this takes time.

The new humanity has a long way to go on this spiritual path, first it must free itself from its own mind, which controls it and does not leave it even a second to breathe, to be able to silence those inner voices that are nothing more than a custodial control that they implanted since the beginning of this last cycle.

The thousands of thoughts that come into your minds control you and many times break your dreams, most of them are simply negative thoughts, the competition you are subjected to and the division between you for almost every cause that takes place here are really exhausting and can lead you to the easy path of surrender. This energy drain and sense of constant struggle to any race on any world would have wiped you out long ago and you are still standing, it only remains for the majority to know where the real enemy is, their macabre psychological games that generate division among you, and to break this control and conditioning.

The new humanity has an admirable resistance to adversity, and infinite potential for spiritual growth, which is something we must exploit and can be taught from an early age.

They will instead try to manipulate the children with weapons and distraction, bombard their minds and continue to try to create robots that follow their dogmas and patterns without question.

They will use the usual, the big media, the men and women recognized by degrees that are only given in the corrupt Universities that they call distinguished or outstanding, of which very few have access, they will also use the manipulated part of science and anyone who gets in their way they will try to ridicule them first and then attack them in every possible way.

I do not mean to leave studies or the universities, but on the contrary, maybe one of the ways would be to enter there and be the best in each field to be able to modify from within everything that is corrupted or manipulated by them. Anyway we have a totally different system than the current one in these lands.

Within our plan is also this, to be able to enhance the greatness of the real scientific advancement, unfortunately the ancestral and giant-human advancement was destroyed or simply hidden from the new humanity.

We will continue with the struggle to make this humanity understand, that if they unite in true love nothing would stop them, that their brothers are out there and also in here waiting for the right moment, that we have never forgot them.

Many lost their lives trying to save them and it will continue to be so, the ancestral technology will continue looking for the way to end this control, there are many other races that overcame the Custodians and were able to free themselves, this is possible, but the human being will not be left easily because he has inside what no other race has, we are the "Source of Life", the possible reason for this Great Dome, and surely the direct connection to other worlds beyond, we are different and with a potential that few would imagine with all the conditioning received in a life in these lands.

We are still in these lands and we will continue standing here, fighting together with you, those who woke up from this bad dream called "human farm" and want to turn it into an eternal freedom.

CLAUDIO NOCELLI

- HIDDEN LANDS BEYOND THE ANTARCTICA

THE CONTINUATION OF MORRIS' JOURNEY BETWEEN INTERCONNECTED PLANETS

THE FORGOTTEN
HEROES

In this day and age, looking at that white mantle of walls as a gateway seems far-fetched, and today, very few dare to do so, one of the paths could be found by digging deep into the true agenda that hides in the dark minds of the dome that in turn plays intertwined with the archaic and parasitic colonizers of yesterday, those who treacherously penetrated the Domes and poured their plans into our kingdom, and so it is and will be, as I say, ours forever.

Antarctica brings with it the mystery of those questions as old as humanity itself, only that sometimes it is clouded among so many news and information that run from beginning to end in the mainstream media that end up accumulating almost by obligation in our minds riddled with news that hide other motives behind that thick fog of those who rule today, I say today, but I could also say the not so distant yesterday, although every day seems like a dagger stabbing into the hearts of true humanity, the agony of living in a cold and unjust world, these writings are not simply stories for you and me to empathize with our reality, they are mere parts of a puzzle that we can put together if we really try, they are parts of our stolen history, our brothers who died fighting for our future, for a different one, and today we forget them simply because we were sold a different story since we were children, the human ancestors and the giants sleep in the hearts of those who really want to remember, of those who still want a fair and different world from today, from this macabre, gloomy, unjust and sometimes repulsive present, these writings will remain forever for those restless minds that are not satisfied with what they were told, with those who debate in front of them according to the books that are kept under golden domes, the fictitious titles that some organizations wanted to grant, nor those who have been meeting to change the world for many years and who do little or nothing or achieve, simply because the reality is that they do not try to do it either.

You and I can change it, and I affirm it without any doubt and in spite of the adversity that you may find on your way, even in some of the stories that you will find right here in these writings, as I always say you should question everything, even you should not believe anything of all this just stay with the parts that resonate within you, just follow your heart and investigate from there without prejudice and absolute freedom about the reality that surrounds you, and then from there gathering those parts left to us of this great puzzle, joining key pieces, understanding what was the Great War between the colonizing parasites and the true ancestral heroes, this is the beginning of a unique journey that you as a reader can join me and follow the same course of the beginning of your great change, today can be that day, there is no need to wait for it, just let it happen, come on! No being on this plane deserves to be trapped in a parasitic conquest, we all deserve to be born and live free until the return to the Celestial Lands.

THE ENCOUNTER
WITH HELEN
MORRIS

On the shores of a beach far from the big cities, under a harsh winter weather, everything was desolate, the cold was my only company at that moment when suddenly everything became strange, the movements around me had become slower and the colors looked more vivid and I could even distinguish their thousands of shades perfectly.

I closed my eyes and then I felt how a diffuse figure that seemed feminine was approaching, everything happened very slowly, the following sensations cannot be explained with words, it was like seeing a hologram in front of me, even with my eyes closed, the image was there.

- It's not so long ago that I have seen you and you already look older, huh, how are you still seeing this world? She asked in an angelic voice, very hard to mistake. Besides the question and the strange situation surrounding the experience I understood perfectly who it was.

- Helen! Her name came out from inside me, as my heart was suddenly racing.

HM - So, won't you answer my question dear friend?

- "Humanity in here is most complex," I was able to say and then added, "But, when united for a real reason their strengths don't seem to fade easily, at least that's what I learned from a mysterious woman who claimed to come from afar" I smiled staring at this strange "holographic specter" of hers.

HM - "That's totally valid, a phrase that seems to come from someone intelligent," she smiled now complicit in my earlier joke, then continued:

- "It's a pity that many are forced to take equivocal paths then don't you think so?" I nodded, and though I dared not until then express more than that.

- "When did you come?" I asked excitedly. Her eyes penetrated my being like two lighthouses dazzling the sight of a navigator finding new lands, an inexplicable feeling of love invaded my body.

HM - Things are getting difficult again, I sense that many of this new humanity already know it, it is not my function to alarm anyone nor do I intend to, but have you seen everything that has been happening here lately? We follow it closely. "I think you already understand it well, time is the most precious thing and when it comes to such a sensitive issue as freedom, which is paramount, something has to be activated within all of us."

- How could I help? I asked.

HM - You are already doing your part, it is the right time for all the information we possess to be revealed, or at least what is important, about the lands outside the Dome and the first ice walls, reaching the right point we may have a new opportunity to carry out the Morris-Butler plan, the parasitic agenda has not slowed down from a few years ago to here, it is constant and seems to have no other outcome in their plans, they have already decided long ago, the fate of the new humanity depends strictly on the changes that can be made from here to the future, you understand, Don't you?

- Do you think that there are some of those points in this "parasitic agenda" that are inevitable? I asked her fearfully for an answer that seemed to be known in advance.

HM - I prefer to think not, but I would be lying to you, the situation is worrying, and it could not only reach these lands, it could reach ours too, the ones outside this "First Dome".

- I opened my eyes as wide as I could... How is it possible that a new reset could also damage humanity outside?

HM - It is a possibility, not all resets are alike, indirectly it would affect us anyway, we need to unite and stay on the indicated plan, there is no margin for error this time, nothing can fail. But excuse me for interrupting this talk, I will go directly to what I came to tell you, do not forget that being in these lands generates me a deep pain and not only in a physical way since my body hurts being here, but stepping on these lands always make me have mixed thoughts and feelings, on the one hand the joy of seeing my brothers of the new humanity and on the other the idea that we could not achieve yet what we so longed for, human freedom from the parasitic hands that today still control it, I see my father's face every day here repeating that phrase, but, as I said before, let's go to the point of this meeting, there are many topics to know about my father William, let's continue from where we had left that time about his interesting and mysterious journey.

THE ANCESTORS RETURN TO THE KNOWN LANDS

- William, wake up! It's time to put the plan into action, look to the sky "The Iron Blues" are advancing! Don't abandon us now your brothers need you... Butler's voice rang like bells from an ancient church in my poor confused mind. I know I had received some kind of injection to revive my slowly fading body.

"My brothers" that word made my body detach from the cold sand that hugged me tightly so as not to let go, but even if this was my last breath I had to be on my feet, helped clearly by what Butler had given me as I lay unconscious on the shore of the beautiful ancestral beaches.

- William, up mate, look around you, it's time now. Butler sentenced with a small phrase that swept everything inside me, it was like those devastating waves that can take everything in its path.

I knew how important it was for me and for many of us such an event, the "Iron Blues" and thousands of ships were going straight to the "Ice Walls", those artificial frozen walls that forbade our brothers to see a new dawn, the radiant red Sun that contemplated an advanced civilization like the Ancestral one, where I already felt part of it, of survivors who fought long ago against the same yoke that today possesses the new humanity in various ways, that keeps them living a simulation full of lies, that offers them only a tiny part of an absolute happiness that they could live understanding that they are "The Source" and the great importance under this great Dome.

That your energy is so rooted in the "Celestial Lands" that so many other Worlds keep close track of it, and jealously imprison you within these cold walls that act as a division, today permanent, next to the "First Dome". If only they knew their true past and the purpose of their creation, that they were born to be free and to fight against this snatching of freedoms towards their own race and towards the others, they were all born to be heroes, each one in his own way, and not to compete in a hostile world among their own brothers for a piece of bread, for thirsty drops of power, for an absolute and spiritual existential void, I have it clear because I have lived there and I have felt the same as each one of you can feel.

My body was less sore, but partially numbed by the ancestral medication that keeps me alive hopefully for some more time, and the time I have left I will absolutely use it around the liberation of my brothers, of a humanity that can step as hard as those giants that crossed the same ice to help us wake up. Long live the awakened humanity that fights for its own spiritual freedom! I shouted inside me, who knows why, but I felt that internal euphoria, although no one heard it, it emboldened me for what was to come.

Thousands of Ancestors were already crossing the borders towards the "Known Lands", those continents that since we were children we were taught and somehow forced to understand that it was the only thing we had, since according to the official books, the famous Christopher Columbus had discovered that "New Continent" that would mark a before and an after, It would pale in comparison to what I discovered on my journey with my old ship, which crossed the famous "Antarctic Polar Circle" and took me to lands I never thought I knew, that I could never even have dreamed of. How could a remote place give me so many answers and so much peace along the way?

Only that my peace was intermingled with that intrinsic pain that means leaving my lands of origin and the knowledge of what was happening behind, but this would be nothing if I knew that my brothers were in good hands or in total freedom, but that all suffering in there came from the dirty parasitic hands that had stolen the eternal spiritual growth of our own race, humanity was imprisoned between walls, false stories, maps and a very uncertain path to follow, the many resets suffered and the thousands of generations waiting for a peace that would hardly come being under the same Custodian power, which for thousands and thousands of years (in Known Lands) submerged us in an absolute confusion about our creation, true mission and resentment towards the "other brother".

This story has just begun, but it is a unique path that you

will walk together with me, you can believe it or not, it all depends on your inner self, but here I will try to give you some details about the worlds surrounding our Known Lands, the way I learned about them from the teaching of the ancestral masters themselves as well as from the thousands of stories and records that exist in the Ancestral Library here in these lands, but let's go in parts, we still have a long way to go.

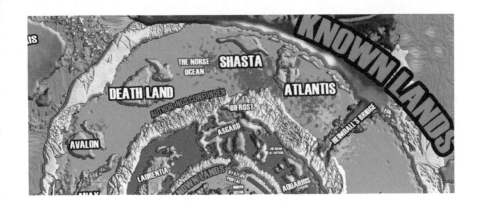

THE ICE WALLS
AND THE FIRST
DOME

My great friend and companion in this odyssey, Butler, who was the pioneer and who brought me to these distant lands, had somehow saved my life, had made me know not only the true human purpose, but also had given me a new life, away from the sinister clutches of the old continents, as well as meeting the woman of my life who has given me the most precious gift from the heavens, my daughter Helen.

Starting from scratch in other lands, trying to understand how their technology worked, their society, their way of life, was totally strange and it was a process that lasted a long time for me, but I must admit that it is much easier to adapt to the life of the Ancestors than if I had to go in the opposite direction.

I could not understand how an Ancestor, for more experiences he has had, could undergo the punishment of returning to the "Known Lands", I hope these texts will reach those readers who are more curious about the lands they inhabit, and if these are my brothers from the old continents, I hope they will understand that my absolute wish is that one day the majority of people will understand that they are under this Custodian power that in each past "reset" has poisoned more and more not only our bodies but also our minds, the way of life has been getting worse as these resets have been carried out.

When I speak of "resets" I am referring to the sudden and abrupt endings, always in a cruel way, that are generated in the known continents to the different times that humanity lives and has lived through the times since its beginning, these resets that we contemplate throughout human history would be seven (counting the clash of the first humans in Asgard-Hyperborea against the Custodians).

Here they call them different generations, the ancestral ones lived in the "Known Lands" or "Old Continents" after the "Sixth Reset" that took place the Great War between Giant-Humans, Humans, and other races against the Custodians, Anunnaki and part of the race of the "Greys" that many came from Orion and others were settled here while carrying out what would be one of the largest and best equipped civilizations of all times of mankind in those lands that we have record of, The Great Tartary.

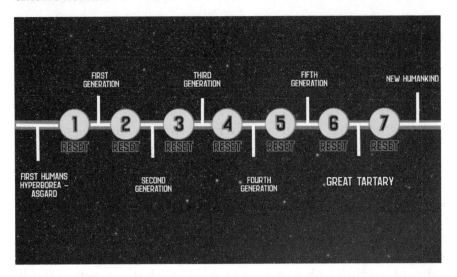

The great veil that does not allow approaching the "First Dome" and that extends throughout the geographical region covering the "Circle-Environment" of the "Earth" as you know it, was planned and carried out during the sixth generation, more specifically, during the advance of the Great Tartary, that with its technology that came from "outside" better said, the use of "extraterrestrial technology" that transferred both in knowledge and prototypes a part of the race of Giants, called "Anakim", and also another race of Giant-Humans of the fifth generation (this I will explain later).

There is nothing worse that derives to hell itself as "Resets", and they can happen in several ways, the Anunnaki helped to install their Pyramids for the development and capacity to be able to generate great floods throughout the Known Lands in a fast and better controlled way, each pyramid can act both as a projector to the "Sky-Dome" and act in a "holographic image" creating way as well as scanning large portions of land for different types of statistics, both of the soil and the environment itself, regulating the climate and toxins that may or may not affect a certain group of humans, as well as having a great impact on the human mind.

This was advancing since the third generation of humans, when the Anunnaki put their parasitic hands and helped the Custodian control and manipulation in all these lands, and as they improved their technology it was no longer necessary for the pyramids to be scattered throughout the length and breadth of the continents, Although in use they had a direct impact and were used, they were used more for urgency than for a technological issue, since they control the weather and almost everything inside the Ice Walls themselves very well.

The Walls were created by them not only in these lands, but in many other worlds that we can find crossing the different Domes and other barriers that can appear in our way.

The incorporation of the use of "Portals" was key in their race to conquer other worlds as well as the manipulation of these, to be able to advance in their desire to know the mysterious lands behind the "Great Dome" that, apparently, are connected in an intrinsic way to the "Celestial Lands" or "Terra-Incognita".

THE ANCESTRAL BOOKS OF THE SACRED LIBRARY

THE BOOKS ABOUT THE HIDDEN LANDS

Before beginning this extensive tour, I must clarify several points that are necessary, and that may also be enlightening when we go through it later. All the information that we have gathered and that you can find in one of our most precious buildings in the city of "El Arca" or "The Ark" and "Renacer", where Morris visited thousands of times during his extensive stay in the Ancestral Lands, is simply a tiny part of a great puzzle, which although it is true that it is more complete and can be visited by any ancestral citizen, unlike those of the new humanity (which most of them do not know), we must also take into account that we still have a lot to know, even from the same Custodian or Anunnaki dome that are trying to unveil some mysteries today about everything that surrounds the Celestial Lands and what is behind the Great Dome.

They answered anyway the deepest questions that seemed to haunt about the great mystery of the existence of the beings "down here", but, now is not the time to give you more information so as not to overwhelm you, this information you do not need for now.

I think the best to start this path as once the same Giant-

Human called "She-Ki" taught my dear father William, the stories of the ancients will explain several important points of the lands that are unknown to you today, we have an extensive part of our Library with all the stories of those heroes, both ancestral and human of previous generations, including other stories that were taken in the great Custodian centers where many Giants and Giant-Humans entered during the Great War, custodian reports that explain many phenomena, such as the use of portals, hidden lands and the famous "planets" as you know them.

What I meant before with "the vast majority is unaware" is that there are groups of people who are aware of various custodian phenomena and plans that are carried out daily, even on other lands and I would dare say on custodian technology as well, in fact it has been and is delivered to this day to members who are in the highest spheres, secret organizations and several people of the forces that have possibly traveled and been in other "planets" or even lands that surround their walls, some have returned and others have not, among all the stories that you will read below you will find several of these characters that for favors done against their own brothers, have won a passage to other places, some of them as recondite as that of their dark minds that worked to harm their own race.

These texts have never been violated nor have they been exposed to other people who have not been our Anakim brothers or ancestral humans, therefore do not alter them, they have never left our lands and today it is time to do so, with a great purpose and destiny, which is neither mine nor their own, but that of the millions of humans who are born in "Walled Lands" without being able to even stop to think about the ground they walk on, because they have not left you, because they outrage you, they punish you, they inhibit you, they restrain you, they empty you spiritually from the primary schools to later make you compete among yourselves to see which one gets the prize of eating too much, eating and not eating at all, they play with your stomachs, with your minds, with your hope, as they played with your great grandparents, grandparents, parents, siblings, etc.

These texts are an intrinsic part to find the forgotten path of our past and our greatness, it will be up to you to draw your own conclusions about the stories that are expressed here, as well as to differentiate the many lies that some will bring to light later in reference to these books both about the lands that were kept hidden for the new humanity, as well as many other topics related to the ancient civilizations, the resetting, and the colonizing parasites, as they will most likely try to manipulate and erase these stories throughout these years that will be sent by the same Custodians who will try to prevent this knowledge and the final liberation.

We will never determine what you should or should not believe, you should always investigate on your own and follow what your heart feels without any conditioning, but be aware, about everything that is opposite to the most important, about the infinite spiritual potential of the human being and his freedom.

Knowing this reality at least you will be closer to be able to see all that we are exposing here, freedom is only one and can be obtained in many ways, such as fighting, but the fight is not physical as we learned in the "Great War" where human freedom was sought and obtained only a reset of new human slaves of their own lands, then the path has to be spiritual, if the mental chains are broken then you will be in a place that not many were, at least in this humanity, where the cold parasites rule, you can even travel to that place without lifting a finger.

RESETS, THE LAST STEP TOWARDS TOTAL DESTRUCTION

"Resets" or "Restarts" are undoubtedly one of the major concerns of both us and most other civilizations and worlds around us who are aware of the current human situation. For those who are not aware, a "Reset/Restart" as its word indicates is to carry out an abrupt ending to make room for a new beginning, but if you still believe that "a new beginning" is something productive or healthy, I regret to inform you that in this case your illusions will be shattered into thousands of pieces, because this is almost always carried out in the worst possible way, hostile, bloody, cold, violent and all the terrifying qualifications that we could use here to catalog such an aberration before life, and before, in this case, humanity.

This interruption to human progress is always carried out in the worst way and the motives are not positive either, after each "Reboot" there would always be enormous changes with modification in the human mind and body, as well as modification of the environment.

The Anunnaki-Custodian technology was advancing so much that it was more and more difficult to miss anything. These "Resets" are carried out by the same parasitic races since the beginning of their colonization here in these lands, but as we were saying, they were intensifying each time they were carried out, one after another, because either humanity itself took the pressure to the maximum level to know its true essence, the worlds and civilizations that surround it in conjunction with the dirty parasitic hands it has on it, or it was carried out by the latter, or it was carried out by the latter in their eagerness to abruptly end a war, a large scale revolt, or simply an advance in technology worrying to the power, "the power of the known power" we could call it, since it does not matter too much the faces or bodies we know that may be at the front in those unreachable domes, they are always or almost always dominated by the same Custodian-Anunnaki power.

Of the Seven Known Resettings, the most serious and the one that was carried out the worst based on the bloody and hostile, added to the change that humanity would have next, was the last one, and it was carried out to annihilate the great heroes of the "Great Tartary" as well as the humans who followed fervently and had understood what the true desire to be free and all that this meant.

Once the Southern Giants or "Anakim" penetrated from behind the so-called "South Pole" or rather "South Portal" they immediately began their plan to liberate humanity by providing technology that the sixth generation human had never seen, as well as information from outside the First Dome.

The Custodians who had had an epic battle against the Anunnaki during that period where the Giants took the opportunity to intermingle on the old continents, had to once again come to a treaty agreement with the Anunnaki to help them with this great problem that had arisen during their absence on their most treasured colony.

They had left an inferior race of Orion Greys, who, although they surpassed humans in technology, the colony had simply not been guarded as it should have been, it is still unknown if it was intentional or not, but since then the relationship they had with the Custodians for trusting them and not fulfilling the assigned tasks guarding their great colony was to change forever and take a course of no return.

The Giant-Humans, Anakim Giants and Humans of the sixth generation began to die in different ways, both in the same battles in the many air attacks to the great cities-cores as well as different "climatic disasters" would begin to happen and help the annihilation of every being that stepped on the known lands. The deaths were counted very well to reach the needed number of "Reboot", the babies were prepared in their great hidden laboratories to proceed to inhabit the "new human dawn" in the seventh generation.

The new humanity would begin, I mean, our humanity was beginning to emerge. During great battles, heroes both giant and ancestral perishing in what would be epic memories of yesterday trying to change the course of a sleeping humanity, the Great Tartary would fall along with its great technology based on free energy, and its many dreams shattering into pieces against the cold ocean watered with blood.

Many of the humans were able to slip away and escape along with the Anakim through the passages or portals that led to the other lands behind the First Dome, despite the great floods and eternal roads to them, some of them survived and even today continue to tell their stories, the parents of my dear wife, and she herself who even as a baby of just months could escape in the arms of her mother to an uncertain future but that gave her some hope to start again in other lands away from their origin, but also away from the terror that was being lived. Undoubtedly then, this last recorded restart was the crudest of all for the way it was given and for the sorrow of feeling that we were very close to winning that great battle for freedom and that everything came to nothing with devastating consequences for the new humanity to come, our own, my brothers, who continue to struggle daily to free themselves knowing it or not, from that world that they were told that it must be like that, that they were manipulated that it cannot be changed, that they were given in a rain of lies with absolute bad intentions to leave them on their knees since childhood, they can still get up, I still know in my heart that humanity lives and dreams more than ever with a possible freedom, and we from here, believe me, that we will try everything until the end of our days.

THE PETRIFIED TREES, THE SOUTHERN GIANTS AND THE CONNECTION WITH FIFTH GENERATION HUMANITY

Why did the Anakim Giants and other race of Giants decide to assist in the liberation of mankind?

It is a great question that haunted my mind over and over again, throughout my studies here in these lands with the ancestral brothers who gave me from the beginning a warm welcome (although as you know it was quite traumatic as soon as we arrived) where I was, somehow, sharing with the same ancestor of our new humanity and where I also took advantage of my closeness to, at least, be able to clear some of my concerns.

While it could be understood that the Anakim simply saw the opportunity to infiltrate at a propitious moment during that confrontation between the conquerors themselves, the Custodian-Anunnaki War, it is also true that much was risked in that movement of jumping across into hell itself by beings who perhaps were not even aware of their true essence.

I felt that something had to motivate them beyond what was explained superficially and the understanding that each one could have acquired from this fact, She-Ki knew how to give me the answer some time later, after my permanent insistence to be able to contact her again, I needed to ask her several questions and one night finally came what I longed for so much.

She-Ki confessed to me that the Anakim or Giants of the South, have human blood running through their veins from a remote past. During the "Fifth Generation", that is, prior to the Ancestors, and that, in turn, that same blood some also share with another more primitive Giant race, there being a direct connection with the lands of Asgard, all this was again like a bomb exploding in my mind with fresh information that could dispel great clouds of uncertainty, each word of She-Ki became more and more interesting and began somehow to close many paths in my confused mind.

The human physical build was very different, so was the way time was passing as well as the environment in the "Known Lands".

A handful of Anakim Giants and a few of another Giant race decided in those times past to overcome the First Dome to infiltrate the human lands, a little out of curiosity and a little to see the possibility they had to infiltrate some information as well as technology. They did it through what we know as "South" side of our lands, and settled there for a long time, in many manipulated books they can be found even today as "Patagonian Giants", although the dates are incorrect as well as the image of them that would be publicly known.

These beings began to feel part of these lands and to get closer to the humans that also lived there, and since then they simply began to develop. Although their bodies began to get sick, this did not happen until many years after their first visit, as they were not fully aware of the toxins that could rain down from the heavens themselves.

They came to make large fortifications in the closest part of the known "Antarctic Peninsula" between what is known today as Argentina and Chile, in addition to other lands that do not appear on current maps and all the way to the islands that were there at that time.

The Giants began to explore "the old continents" and the hidden lands (many of them disappeared between the floods by later resets) and surprisingly discovered trees of colossal sizes, they began to understand that the human past was totally different to what they understood until then, these colossal trees were difficult to locate in human history, they did not fit directly, the first humans coming from Asgard, Lemuria and Atlantis had to have not only used them but "planted" themselves with some purpose, now, what kind of energy or connection did they have? Were they used in some way as Portals or to hide another type of technology? Who or who had given those "seeds" or knowledge to obtain these mysterious trees to the ancient humans?

Many questions hovered around this issue and the Giants

surely came to a conclusion, for that reason they decided to settle there and even enlarge their population without attracting so much attention from the ruling Custodians, perhaps their answer was rooted in the beginning of humanity and its connection with the Celestial Lands.

The trees during that reset were cut down, destroyed (burned, pulverized) or petrified with Custodian technology, many of them we find today along the known continents, many others are taken as simple hills, mountains or even mountain ranges, then we will understand better what happened to these Giants as well as to the humanity of the Fifth Generation later on.

There are still some memories left in the ancient books of the old continents about, for example, "Medusa", that monster that turned into stone those who dared to look directly into her eyes, it was a faithful reflection of a clear message "the one who drew the veil of the dark dome would be stone for all eternity".

Besides being metaphorical, the idea that beings could be petrified is somehow established in the Known Lands but certainly always in the form of mythology or stories far from reality, it is quite complex to understand that giant beings or titans have also been petrified throughout human generations, perhaps many of them sought to free "The Source" for the kingdoms to restore their peace, let's not forget that the colonizing parasites soon invaded many of the worlds even when the beings of each environment were developing, therefore, it was easily accessible for them to conquer almost all of them, with exceptions of course, but sooner or later they would obtain the power they have today.

Are there mountains or hills that are ancient petrified beings?

That is a question that I will not answer at this time, but, I have asked She-Ki although it seems crazy to many, I did not want to stay with that intrigue, the truth is that I can confirm that giant trees if they were cut from their bases, some were so huge that today are also considered mountains or forgotten mountains that stand out among the plains or even more spectacular mountains, the bones of enormous beings could have suffered the same fate during their stay in the old continents, simply for trying to change the course of the human generations to come, many of these colossal trees were used as a form of transfer of matter, or better said, natural portals to distant or hidden lands.

THE GREAT DOME AND THE CELL WALL IN THE 178 WORLDS

As I commented earlier, the Great Dome is the one that "covers" above all the "known worlds", I mean, known and not so known to many of us outside the First Ice Walls, this is key to understand how these worlds could work, I also understand that it may overwhelm you in a direct way at first as you are not even familiar with the lands surrounding your continents, it would be more difficult for you to understand how all of what you know as "planets" can meet in a horizontal direction instead of vertical as drawn by the most prestigious scientists of your Circle-Environment, it is difficult to deal with this idea and believe me, I spent years studying how the First Dome could work and what is projected on it.

Directly speaking "what the heavens show every day". To be able to really interpret how one could "navigate the skies" going directly horizontally to the Poles, or, better said, to the "Antarctic Polar Circle" which is that only physical barrier it has before the direct collision with this barrier-dome, a priori, invisible.

The Dome barrier functions simply as described, a division between one environment and the other, but as something known to you (so far) in your time as is the "cell" in specific parts of its walls there can be a direct connection that mixes or lets pass in a certain way, something from environment A to environment B, or vice versa.

In a basic way we can compare the artificial "Ice Walls" as a cell wall fulfills its function to act as a barrier that the, in this case, "pathogens" have to overcome to colonize that other environment or circle-environment, but it is also a dynamic structure, and then we could compare the Dome with a plasma membrane, in this way we could say that the wall of the Dome serves not only as a means of natural barrier of each "Circle-Environment" but also to restore itself in case of suffering any significant modification in its climate or general environment, separating the interior environment from the exterior, with exceptions in particular places.

We can call these channels "portals" or "passages" that help us to overcome these barriers that seem insurmountable, and generally are made by water, except for exceptions by technology that can be done through the air, but the passages both from the interior to the exterior and vice versa, are made by water as they provide a high percentage of success, as we were saying the domes are in the first instance as permeable "membranes" but sometimes selective as in the "Celestial Lands".

Although the domes are "natural" and are found, from the information we were able to collect, since the beginning of time, it is not ruled out that it was some creation prior to the beginning of the first colonizers, who were those who ventured out of their Dome or Membrane to explore other places, like a baby born out of the womb, civilizations have left their Domes to explore and exchange information in one way or another, Many of them still have not left by omission or ignorance, perhaps one goes hand in hand with the other, in our lands we humans have not left because of total manipulation of the colonizing parasites, otherwise I believe that today the same current civilization would be creating new ways to make way for what the extra-terrestrial destiny has in store for it.

To leave the dome then we could call it as the "birth of a race" in a certain moment or generation, the beginning to interact with other neighboring beings that surround, the colonizers thought that the "Great Dome" would work in the same way and that it would also connect to other domes and other lives, and that going out to the "outside" there would be another type of "birth" but none of this worked and all this remained as a big question mark, from there is also born the great doubt about what is found inside the "Celestial Lands" as mysterious as selective.

THE HIDDEN LANDS OF THE BOOK OF NINJ-MUH AND SHE-KI

There are several "continents" surrounding the First Walls, just outside the continents unknown to the seventh generation (or the great majority), and I say great majority because there is a small group of people close to secret organizations who are aware of this, as they have direct contact with some Custodians and who have served faithfully against our brothers.

These continents can be found under various names, and believe me, I have fervently read the thousands and thousands of books on maps and geography in general here in the Great Library of the Capital called "The Ark", and I have found the various lands that surround both yours and ours, and the names may be different and may be modified as they are studied, but, I have on more than one occasion asked many ancestral teachers, including Captain Butler, who has recommended to me one of the most complete and complex books of this beautiful culture, which could be called in the native language translation to something like "The Book of Ninj-Muh".

The people here are always willing to help in almost every task, but even more so if what one seeks is knowledge, being a bit of an attraction from the beginning of being a survivor who has crossed over from the "other side", that hostile place that today is looked at from afar, and having overcome a major battle here when the Custodians attacked us upon arrival, I think I have earned a bit of respect from the citizens and for that, they never ever reneged on spending hours sitting next to me to translate texts or help me understand the millions of questions and confusions I had in my mind, and still have, although a bit more dissipated.

The Book in question had very detailed maps and compared with the "Book of She-Ki", it was known that the giants had to their credit several and several of kilometers traveled under the Great Dome and were knowledgeable of both other worlds and other races, as they had been contacted and engaged in conversations with many of them.

It is worth mentioning the different existing Giant races, which are several, and not all of them are in favor of human liberation, although they are reluctant to discuss or explain in depth about this subject, what has reached my ears is that no Giant race would be against our liberation but simply many of them would not be willing to try to help us because of the consequences that this could entail, for example, what happened during the "Sixth Generation" with the Ancestors is reason enough not to set foot again on those lands that today are so far from my sight but not so far from my heart, my lands of origin, that I have called "Earth" so many times before knowing this path.

Following the Book of "Ninj-Muh" and comparing it with the

Book of "She-Ki" we can come to the conclusion that, each race that lives in a land will name it in such a way that they can make themselves understood for their subsequent geographical location, tracking, and organization of the same, in turn in their native language or communication they have, consequently, the root of the original name of a site is always lost but rather begin to use others that are understandable and easy to locate based on the coordinates provided, there may also be some differences based on their actual location or shape as it was being done as technology and exploration were carried out, especially to the Second Walls and surrounding the "hidden lands" of Asgard.

From here I will humbly give you the names as they were translated from these books, but you can find several different names for each race, and if we consider the native language of the Ancestral Lands, then it would be even more complex that the translation does not lose the essence of each one, anyway I will try. (It should be noted that you will also find maps with different names within the "Known Lands" that will not have any relation with the names found in the Ancestral Library or that have been shared from here).

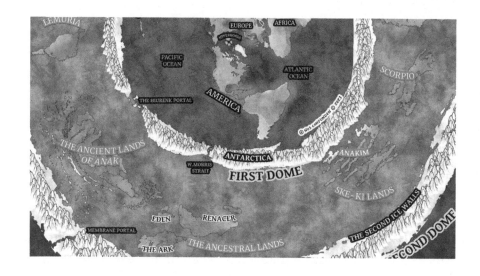

LANDS ACROSS
THE ANTARCTIC
POLAR CIRCLE

The lands where I am stepping at this moment, are called "Ancestral Lands" or "Lands of the Ancestors", they can also be known as "Ancestral Republic" or different names that sounded sometimes there in my lands of origin when infiltrating us with information.

In the Ancestral lands live mostly humans of the "Sixth Generation" survivors of the Reset and the Great War fought there against the Anunnaki-Custodian power. Some of the survivors were able to regenerate their bodies in their entirety in order to reach the maximum possible life span (between the first and second dome) and lead a prosperous life continuing with other generations to come.

In these lands also live a small percentage of Giant-Humans, also survivors of the Great Tartary, and Giants of the South. Then a tiny portion is integrated by us, those who arrived during the "new humanity", some of the jokers here call us "the sleepers" as a way to differentiate them from the previous ones, since in the new humanity for the moment the vast majority do not know their essence and their environment, but as I said, it is just a joke because as in all resets humanity is born manipulated to not reach this information or make it covering as long as possible, possibly if there were survivors of past resets here they would call the next generation in the same way.

In this new humanity full of confusion and despair it seems to be simple to rewrite history and lead many down the path of spiritual self-destruction, once the majority does it, then it will only be time for others to imitate.

Today when the media is controlled, the interference is greater, I mean, the interference it will do in the minds will be to such a degree, as when one runs in terror before something or someone that gives us the feeling of imminent attack, it is not the same a state of alertness in mere silence than one being in a critical situation with danger of being attacked, you will get two totally different and opposite paths.

The Ancestors here are **81,039,041** people (at the moment I am writing this) that live throughout all these lands, although people do not crowd in the great Capital for work or to obtain another type of benefit as it happens in our lands, like any great city anyway it gathers a great number of people within the same number indicated.

There are some humans living in "The Ancient Lands of Anak" and in the "Lands of She-Ki", there are no records that there is another group of humans at least settled in other lands between the First and Second Dome that have at least sent signals or established some communication with these lands.

Crossing the Second Dome and Second Ice Wall and without any of the ancestral masters or She-Ki having confirmed it to me, it is said that there are humans in "The Lands of Venus" and that there is a great connection and relationship with the Venusians, in fact, when the parasites tried to colonize them, they were able to expel them by reaching an agreement, and within that agreement one of the strong points was nothing more and nothing less than the discussion about human liberation, although this was not achieved.

There are confirmed humans in "The Lands of Mars" from the known continents, many of them were sent there as a "prize" for having betrayed their own brothers, then this colony settled there along with other races. Some of the following generations have left these lands in search of another type of life, commenting that the life that takes place in Mars is totally conflictive and harmful in all its dimensions, a ship from there has arrived to our coasts as well as ancestral ones have infiltrated there by the "Byrd's Strait".

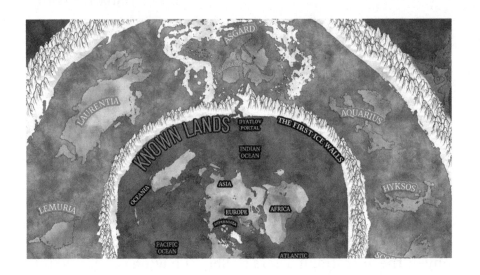

THE LANDS OF ASGARD AND THE DYATLOV PASSAGE

The "Dyatlov" passage has in its memories several remembered episodes and all of them were regrettable leaving only sad memories of the experiences. Reaching the gates of Asgard is not an easy task for almost any being, much less for humans, even worse if they are humans with basic technology that simply out of curiosity try it. In the ancestral knowledge it is known that there are several artificial portals created by the Anunnaki mostly, although the Custodians have also manipulated and used such technology for the transfer of matter.

Many of the portals were left in disuse and forgotten in different points of the many lands, the known continents are not the exception to the rule, and one of these portals is located in old settlements of the Great Tartary near the known "Ural Mountains".

Several explorers tried to reach it and use it to lead them directly to the gates of Asgard, almost always led by a person or leader who had come to the knowledge in some way, either by chance or some kind of information he could surely get from manipulative sources coming from "higher up".

For this reason, most of these expeditions failed and ended in a very bad way, one is well known in the use of this portal, they have a powerful scanner and this enables any custodian or force that is operating in the area to proceed even violently to prevent this from taking place, however, they are very unstable portals that were not stopped using for the transfer of material for their mistakes. Generally they are very old portals, but why were they not destroyed? This is the question I asked myself, the answer had several possibilities:

- **A** - They are not interested because the use of such a portal would lead to certain death.

- **B** - There is permanent custody in conjunction with high tech scanners.

- **C** - They are a trap for curious humans

- **D** - It is another form of Custodian-Anunnaki entertainment with humans (perhaps this option could come in conjunction with all the others above).

In fact, it is known that many of these leaders of direct explorations to hidden portals are often driven by the same Custodians who play with this human scouting group until they get there, even letting them cross the portal without really knowing what will happen to the matter they will end up moving, It is something extremely risky, but that the Custodians or other races, sometimes, with the desire to acquire energy from their fears or terror that they end up instilling, do not worry at all, but rather on the contrary, they end up taking advantage of it.

Be that as it may, these portals can still be found and are very dangerous, the "doors" of Asgard are not easily accessible and are hidden lands, so much so that they were used and thought to settle the first humans, knowing that they could be discovered but sought the best option to develop, the other lands they used are Lemuria to the East and Atlantis to the North, Asgard had direct connection through a portal with the lands called "Hyperborea" which are located in the center of the known continents.

In Asgard it is believed that there are still fortifications of the first humans and masters that gave rise to the great birth, but its access is complex as well as trying to pass through the passage "Bifröst" that leads to Atlantis and its neighboring land "Shastar".

The lands of Lemuria are today inhabited by a strange race of little development that was transferred from outside and that had throughout history very little contact with humans or Giants, there was found a long time ago very strange subway technology and of still unknown origin.

"Laurentia" on the other hand, is a land inhabited by Venusians, they are in this way the closest to our lands, it is believed that they send information to their lands of origin and leaders so that they are aware of all the movements and modifications that the colonizers make, it is expected that they can also come to help human liberation in the near future.

"Aquarius" and the lands of "Hyksos" are inhabited by hostile creatures in conjunction with the Lands of Sirens, there are several stories of humans who "collided" with these creatures that I will share in the next chapter.

In both the "Island of Death" and "The Lands of Death" there is no life, not even plant life, although it served as a passage for several races before penetrating the "Known Lands" today were simply abandoned. They are totally deserted places in contrast to their past.

In the lands of "Scorpio" there are three different types of Giant races, including the Anakim.

In the southernmost lands like "Argos" and "Athos" there were Anunnaki settlements, but today there is no confirmation of this, curiously it is dangerous to navigate in that area near the "Byrd Passage" and for that reason among others, it is complex to visit those distant lands outside the Second Dome.

In "Talos", lands near the Bridge of Hades, there is great darkness, the creatures that inhabit there are inferior of first generation without development, also transferred by the colonizing races.

In "Avalon" and "Anax" coexist two different races coming from outside, "Etamines" from Draco and "Grays" from Orion.

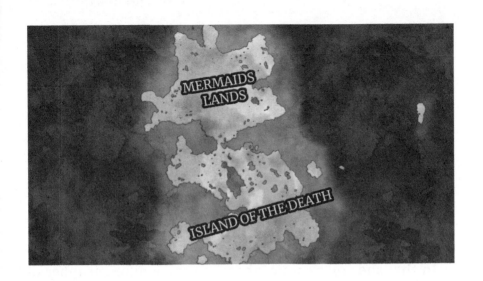

THE HUMANS WHO ARRIVED TO THE MERMAIDS LANDS

"History and Geomorphology of Adjacent Lands" - ARB201 - H101-

Heimdall Bridge-
Book of the Great
Capital Ancestral
Library "The Ark"

By the year 1900 of the last generation a ship had plans to visit the southern latitudes and explore an area that motivated many explorers of that time, without the Antarctic Treaty or the many maritime exclusions this old but resistant vessel headed straight to the cold Antarctic waters on September 28th.

Ernest, the captain, had an experience of almost 40 years, he knew every port and every corner, in the year 1923 he was sailing with ten other sailors over the famous "Drake Passage", the waves lashed the ship, they were intense swells that reached great heights, although the crew was really used to storms and complicated navigation, during the dark, lonely and gloomy night death seemed to call their fate on several occasions, there was no way to sleep a wink at that time.

To add drama to their then frustrated adventure, a great storm lashed the area and their boat became a simple paper boat sailing at the mercy of nature, the destiny was in the hands of what the "Earth-Mother" could decide before such a reality that struck full in their resistant and adventurous hearts. Everything was out of control for several hours that seemed eternal for those sailors, the course completely lost but not so the hope of each one of them who tried incessantly from one side to the other to keep the ship afloat, chaos and order from one second to another always played alternating for those times among all the old adventurous boats that were not content to travel the known, but rather to make way and history towards a new dawn.

Their old and wet clothes were not helping in the face of that raw cold that hit their faces, they now stood together as the rain and the waves seemed to give way, the hope that this generated ended up breaking in the face of that cruel and sudden winter that seemed to lash. Strange "Ice Walls" appeared before them, and they turned quickly so as not to break their ship into a thousand pieces before this sudden white wall, "majesty of the Gods" as they described it.

The deep Antarctic waters were wreaking havoc among the surviving sailors, so they began to sail in parallel and move far enough away to try not to die of hypothermia, although the impetuous swell increased its intensity as they moved away from that great icy wall. They began to observe that between this, until now, perfect and immense wall of ice, suddenly began to break completely at a vertex, not that the wall would fall before us, but rather as a large crack that generated an invitation to pass, who in their right mind would try with an old boat to dive into a suicide mission? Well, we would! But not because we really wanted to, but rather because we were slowly dying in the face of the painful cruel cold, the hunger and the totally unknown course.

Suddenly and without my being able to explain it in words, a great vortex seemed to emerge from the same sea, the swell did not intensify, but the vortex generated a strange swell that rotated like the hands of a great clock, first they went in the same direction and then in all of them in unison, we all became dizzy and we had to sit down or some of us directly fell on the wet and smooth floor of the boat, When I opened my eyes again I could see another vortex emerging directly between the crack of that Ice Wall, nothing seemed to make the slightest sense to us, I began to fear that I had died and that this was what they called "the beyond". Our bones that could hardly move because of the pain of intense cold suddenly began to obey the orders of my confused brain, the cold was not only gone, but there was no wall or waves hitting our hull, we looked at each other thinking the same thing, then we decided to externalize it with our vocal cords.

Where are we? Who could really explain this adventure? We were surrounded by a calm ocean, a reddish and strange huge dot, perhaps a nearby "Planet"? It appeared in the distance, compasses erratic, navigation problems continued, what other plan was there?

Simply to approach the only land that appeared on the horizon before everyone's eyes, would these lands be our true salvation? I think that before everything we had experienced and what we had gone through, and even without understanding how we had suddenly crossed some walls through two vortexes of light, the reality is that we were almost in agony between the storms, the intense cold and our ship close to sinking, we could call all this as a miracle and we could not see those lands as anything other than a salvation.

We arrived to its shores and we were beginning to doubt again how safe this area was, what other place was there? We all agreed on that answer, none, there was no more land in sight in an unknown sea, the question we all asked were we discovering new lands? And if so, where were we?

We descended, although some of the members did not want to, but our food and drinking water was scarce, we were in an absolute emergency, the sand was whitish and there was great vegetation in the distance, it gave a great appearance of being able to find fruits, rich and beautiful fruits! That's what I needed and urgently. We found some strange red fruits in some trees near the coast, we did not hesitate for a second to try them, we waited a while, perhaps not so prudent but we could not last much longer without food, we returned to the boat full of these red fruits in order to finish our provisions, which were not many.

It was nightfall in those lands, we were on the coast and there was no movement around, only the calm ocean generated some waves that kissed our ship that miraculously had survived. Although we were exhausted by all this mysterious adventure we could not sleep a wink yet, it was difficult to understand our position and even know what time we were in, we began to doubt again our reality around us, but we felt tired, pain, hunger, thirst and everything that a living human feels, we could not be dead and this was not at all what we knew as "promised lands".

Ernest! Ernest! They woke me up screaming, see that captain, what's that moving through the waves? Yellow lights seemed to illuminate our ship through the surface of the sea, a head appeared and shone directly in our faces, they are eyes! They all shouted as they hit our boat with force, the blows could be heard all around our ship. Because of the light they emanated and that reddish "planet" that illuminated the horizon I could make out their faces in more detail, they were eyes that emanated a strong yellow light, their faces were scaly and their untidy hair fell between holes that gave off water, they were the most terrifying beings I had ever seen, we all ran to our positions before my scream, and we were ready to escape from there immediately, they began to make deafening screams, they were communicating with each other or it was a warning to us, either one way or the other we hurried to get away from the area, these creatures sort of "sirens" of the most terrifying fiction stories remained in the distance staring at us as we moved away, their lights were lost in the horizon, the fear of the unknown is really paralyzing but this exceeded any expectation, we followed the opposite course to those islands but certainly aimlessly and lost in the strangest sea that anyone could have ever sailed.

We tried to find the location of where we thought we had arrived, and that strange vortex was there, but this time only one of them and in the horizontal part attached to the ocean itself, we stopped there and a white light emerged from the bottom generating the shadow of our boat towards the skies, seeing this suddenly we were again "on our side", but not near the ice walls but in the African coasts that three of us knew very well, the compasses began to work again, our destiny now was to go home and try to forget the strangest adventure we could have lived or expected to live, without a word to anyone about this matter or we would be locked up or accused of anything, no one would believe this experience.

THE SECOND
ICE WALLS

Another of my concerns when I found out about these second walls and understood a little of the functioning of the first ones, was the following: Why then are there ice walls imposed by the colonizers also here in this Circle-Environment?

Well, the answer I have received was that these lands when they were penetrated and taken in a violent and colonizing act by the Custodians, specifically after having failed in their visit to the neighboring lands "Venus" they took forward the creation of artificial walls so that information could not be easily passed from the core out, as they considered it of absolute weakness, it was sensitive information that the Venusians could use later.

The complex situation after taking these lands and finding the first humans developing, took place with several decisions along the history, and one of them would not be so long to wait with the creation of these walls that keep away in many ways any curious navigator that could try to cross the huge cold distances of the Second Ice Walls.

Anyway, this did not prevent that with the technology of the Giants one could cross to the lands of Argos or Atos or simply to the gates of the Mars Lands next to the "Byrd's Strait" who was recorded in previous books I have published, since Byrd himself was the one who would cross, "requested" at the time by the Custodians themselves and with their technology, helped by the Custodian Leader "Nimrod" who was later killed in a battle of the Ancestors near Lemuria.

So I don't think these walls were of much use to the coming generations (second generation onwards) since once they took control, humans could hardly have escaped from the First Dome. Crossing the "Second Dome" according to navigators and R. Byrd himself left a record of it, you feel a thrust and it seems to "sail through the sky" when you are penetrating The Ice Walls and Dome to "The Lands of Mars", the feeling could be described as being fired at an incredible speed and entering a deep abyss without having control for a few moments on the ship that is moving it.

THE STARS AND PLANETS IN THE HEAVENS, THE ABSOLUTE ZERO LINE CROSSING THE ANTARCTIC

This is another sensitive and not at all minor issue about how our environment works, the same conditioning can be "activated" as one tries to interpret the functioning and projection of the domes, the planets, the stars and the many worlds that seem to be far away from us "up there".

As Byrd and many other navigators who have been able to cross this passage leading into the interior of the "Lands of Mars" or misnamed "red-planet" have commented the thrust is similar, and it is important to remember this phrase once again, "As we navigate or traverse the very heavens" this could give us a closer explanation to what we understand as "Space" or "Universe" that in the science books of the "Known Lands" or "Earth" lead the new humanity to learn about reaching distant planets and stars as something extremely far away or even improbable by technology and studies, when in reality we can connect those planets or lands directly crossing these Domes in a horizontal way as directly crossing Antarctica or the Antarctic Circle.

Nowadays this is not possible for human civilians for several reasons, some of them we have already mentioned as the security guardianship with bases along the same circle, radars around the so called "South Pole", as well as the great distances of frozen oceans, huge walls and an extensive region of low temperatures without possessing adequate technology and the location of the passages already previously opened to find adequately and without errors the passage or portal to transfer matter from the interior to the exterior or vice versa.

Even with the right technology sometimes, as we will see later, mistakes are made that can end tragically, since the custodian technology advances and is updated frequently, for this reason only some beings are able to cross the domes, portals and even those Ice Walls that the custodians have left so that this impediment is increased to a maximum level.

But if all this were not already complex by itself, we also add what we know as a "strip" or "line of absolute zero" that is just before the First Dome, where events are experienced that we could consider strange or out of the ordinary, many space agencies and military of the new humanity study these areas periodically for many years, even many military have come to these areas to experience these phenomena (Byrd has also done so after his Antarctic expedition of 1934 in his experiment to spend months studying this famous "line of absolute zero").

This strange "Line" in addition to experiencing physical changes, some people have visions of Polaris Auroras that plunge them to the most absolute depth losing track of time and their surroundings, visits from different times, coded messages that have reached them, images of deceased people that can appear before one, and a myriad of phenomena studied in depth previously by the Anakim, Ancestral and now a part of the new humanity with custodian complicity, make of all this phenomenon a place as recondite as strange, and as it could not be missing, the Custodians used this site to locate several humans and other beings to proceed to the study of war conflicts and psychological experimentation in these lands of the "absolute zero" (then you will find testimonies on this subject in later chapters).

It is very possible that this study is also related to the attempt to understand the connection of "The Source" that humans and the Celestial Lands (Terra-Incognita) have, since the entrance to those lands has always been the obsession of these beings (both Custodians and Anunnaki) since they first encountered them a long time ago.

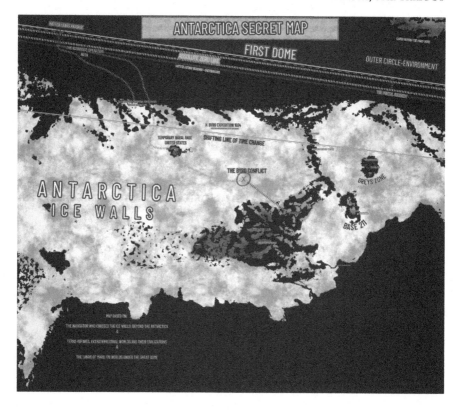

THE CONNECTION OF THE FROZEN WATERS AND THE CELESTIAL LANDS WE CALL THE UNIVERSE

As the title itself indicates: "The frozen waters can lead to another uncertain destination of those celestial lands that we call universe". It is difficult to understand this celestial connection between the existing domes and the stars or planets around us, when we advance horizontally through the portals we are connecting our matter and transport in a "natural" way towards the "beyond".

The "absolute zero line" is nothing more than a way of adapting our physical body and our conditioned mind to the possibility that these phenomena can be experienced, sometimes, many of these phenomena are presented to us, and very possibly after a strong shock, as well as other times they simply happen when we least expect them, we try to find then in our minds that are based on memories and therefore, on past experiences some kind of logic that can make us feel that we are not going crazy, but, many times it happens that along the time, we forget or even our own mind sends us messages that "none of that really happened" until we forget that event in a graduated way in order to continue with our daily "robotic" lives based on simple biological functions and competition among the same beings that this new humanity seems to lead in a frenetic way.

During the transit across "The line of Absolute Zero" we can experience the most sinister terrors as well as the most angelic songs that we have never heard before. The voices or images of those friends or relatives who are no longer with us, or the inner demons that will visit us before crashing into the First Dome, a shock of absolute reality towards the logic that we try to manage, a direct blow to the part of our mind that tries to control and pigeonhole everything. As if in a form of preparation for what is to come next, our mind must first walk through the inner hells before peering beyond our lands.

It is possible that this change is hardly noticeable if you have previously been able to break those chains that bound you to your past.

How then could we understand that the stars seen in the heavens are a mere specter of what we find around us through portals/passages?

The passages or portals that go through domes always connect with another reality, another time and another totally different atmosphere, both going and returning, when leaving a manipulated atmosphere as in the Known Lands the shock is even stronger, connecting with these hidden lands behind are simply a reception several times catalogued as "sacred" since in there you live a life with many unfounded fears and projected in your mind (of the new humanity) by the same conquering parasites that are above you or better said were placed there.

If you break this reality by going through a portal, you would be leaving the life you know totally behind, this does not mean that you will forget your past or your experience in the known continents, I assure you simply because I have not forgotten them, but it will change your way of thinking, not only by understanding a little better about how the plane you live and transit works, but that the Circle-Environment of your lands is submerged in negative energy and fears that infuse as part of their great food/pleasure the Custodians.

Then you will understand that the heavens are mere projections of a simulation that humanity lives daily even today within those lands that you inhabit, and that I have inhabited, like so many other ancestors, the manipulation that you live daily is simply sinister and it is something that we must break forever, not only those of us who are out here trying to help you, but yourselves, it is complex but not impossible when you can see what surrounds you, not only with your eyes, from a physical perception, but when all your energy accumulates towards the same direction in the mere silence, when there is nothing limiting and your connection is direct, you will be able to connect with other lands even without leaving the First Dome in a physical way, the celestial lands are also within you as "The Source" and the potential of your infinite spiritual growth that no other race here within this Great Dome possesses.

HELEN MORRIS, THE STORY OF THE NAVIGATOR'S DAUGHTER

A STRANGE VESSEL APPROACHES THE SHORES OF THE ANCESTRAL LANDS

Many of our books about the Other Worlds were interspersed with stories of our past heroes, both those who survived the Great War and those who fought and overcame the fear and uncertainty of what might really exist beyond.

The Anakim Giants would help to understand more about our plane thus adding to our Library a myriad of countless wisdom that was translated into the most sacred books and archived for further intrinsic study of what really surrounded us.

In time millions of reports, archives and texts were added that arrived from various parts of the Known Lands during and after the Great War, that the Giant-Humans knew how to obtain from many Custodian bases, until the time came to interrelate each point and each story that we received.

In this way we could reach many conclusions and knowledge that we did not have until then in the Ancestral Lands, We were able to identify many races and Circle-Environments that would have been impossible for us to elucidate by the mere fortuitous fact of how far our expedition technology reached, clearly we realized that our technology was not enough to make a great journey for the moment, besides first we had to investigate how much real distance existed and how many other races could receive us in one way or another.

The images of our heroes still shine among the great books, Captain Roald for example, who exposed himself to danger to obtain information from the Lands of Mars, crossing a passage little known at the time, and giving his life so that his companions could get out of there and tell of his exploits.

Many others sacrificed themselves so that our history and knowledge would continue to advance, and thus also, in addition to understanding these worlds around us, also reach the point of technology where we could go further advancing and be able to help the humans of our lands of origin, the point of being able to cut the "Resets" forever was undoubtedly one of the biggest reasons to be able to acquire more and more knowledge of our surroundings.

They were very complex missions and for this reason it was not very common to send men for the expedition crossing the Second Ice Walls, our knowledge was acquired in dribs and drabs, it was very slow and we needed to somehow understand much more about our environment inside the Great Dome. But without expecting it, one day our luck would change forever, this story has no waste and can also deliver several answers as it also converges somehow with all the information that we are delivering gradually.

One morning I awoke very early to strange murmurs coming

from outside my home near what we might call the "Main Port of Embarkation", my father William and Butler were also outside among the crowd shouting in excitement at something approaching us.

It was a clear morning so there was great visibility and about 500 meters from the coast a "coded ship" was approaching (Some advanced technology in some worlds allows to hide the real shape of the object and change it to a generic one or to one that "resembles the culture where it is approaching" but until then we did not know it) We saw it in black color without any distinction coming towards us at a great speed, I did not even have time to worry that it might attack us because William and Captain Butler were together with naval personnel very calmly waiting for this mysterious arrival.

This ship suddenly changed and adopted a very curious shape and even moved towards the inner part of the coast, our naval force was attentive but the silhouette showed a being waving towards our position without seeming to have any intention to attack, it was several seconds, but I think that inside me it lasted much longer than that, the tension when an unknown ship approached was always extreme as we had gone through several bad experiences in the near past.

It was difficult to distinguish what kind of being was visiting us, it should be clarified that we had received several beings from different parts of our plane, but this being did not match anything we had seen before, he came out with a smile waving from afar, the first thing he mentioned in a strange accent native to our Ancestral Lands, was that "his visit was going to be very brief and that he was passing through to other lands" as soon as he spoke with my father and Butler who accompanied him to the main building of the Naval Force to ask him some questions about his real purpose here, following the protocol, it was not a time to trust anyone, much less a being that we did not really know where he came from.

We feared he would be sent by the parasitic Custodian or Anunnaki races to really get some kind of information about our technology, numbers of citizens, military, or other kind of information.

The Being passed among the hundreds of people that we crowded there trying to get as close as possible to see both this strange vessel that practically ran aground on our shores and also this mysterious character of a bluish tone that was visiting us, his clothes were totally white, like ancient tunics that fell on his slender body, He was barefoot, his skull was disproportionately large and his huge eyes had a yellowish hue, he always kept a very strange smile since he descended from his big ship, he even looked from one side to the other as if he was grateful for the hospitality, I can not lie that he emanated vibes of great peace and confidence.

I wanted to go after my father, but William trying to protect me was reluctant to let me approach this new visitor, therefore, he strongly requested me to return home until I could talk to this visitor and be able to understand what he was doing there. Butler followed at his side at all times and never lost track of him, he was followed by several important members of the forces, as I said earlier, it was a day that would quite change the way I understood the plane we lived on.

I could never fight against my meddling ways, for that reason and since my father had not let me get close to this person, I slipped inside that big ship as I was not sure I would ever have a similar opportunity. This peculiar ship did not resemble anything we Ancestors had, nor anything I had been told about other worlds, we all claimed that it had changed shape between coming ashore until it finally ended up in the very sand.

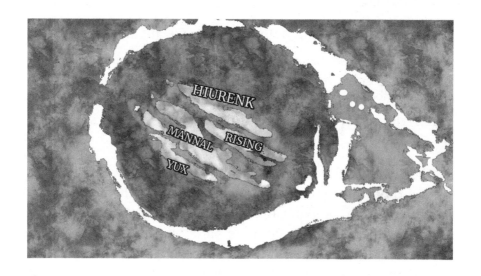

THE BEINGS OF CASSIOPEIA

As soon as I set foot on this strange boat, not to say the strangest that any human has ever seen, I realized for an instant that inside it was totally different, it seemed as if inside this ship was much bigger even than what it showed on the outside, but that thought fleetingly passed through my mind and evaporated from one moment to another when I found three beings in front of me, similar to the first one that had gone down with my father, they were staring at me.

Terror invaded my body and I was completely paralyzed, they noticed it and quickly one of them advanced two steps towards my position and stretched his arm trying to somehow reassure me, or so I supposed, although by then I was terrified I felt inside me that they did not want to do me any harm.

I think I trusted more than I really should have, I always had these episodes that I called "ancestral-new humanity dichotomy", the part of my mother and my father, two generations that had merged and were now in me in some way.

While this could have gone really wrong and I might not be telling this whole story now, the truth is that the beings tried to calm me down and began among themselves to emit strange sounds while from their bodies emanated a bluish-white light, I did not fully understand what they were performing, but it was a kind of communication between them staring into each other's eyes.

This would be another strange occurrence but I was going to start getting used to all these experiences about the civilizations that inhabited under this Great Dome. One of them had a gray colored cube but then it would turn a pure reddish color and from this same object a kind of pale light would come out towards the wall and project an image, this projection on the wall showed without stopping one image after another of their Circle-Environment, their citizens, the way they lived, even the same Dome that enclosed their lands of origin, and to my surprise an image of what I interpreted would be of the confines of this Great Dome.

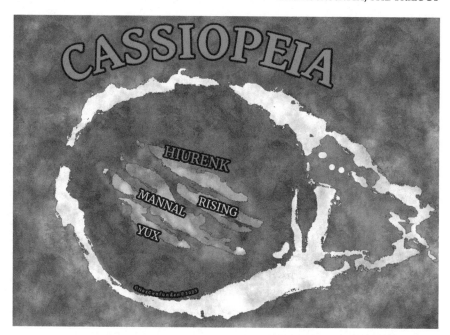

THE BEING CALLED "HIURENK"

Between total astonishment and some frustration at not being able to initiate a conversation with these beings, I made signs to them so that we could leave the boat, to which they refused, I then assumed that they would not leave until their alleged "leader", who was meeting with my father and Butler, did not show up there to give some kind of indication or order.

While I didn't feel any kind of hostility or warning of danger in there, the reality was that I didn't feel comfortable either and even less so without being able to communicate with them other than with some signs where I felt like an infant trying to talk to the parents.

I proceeded to make signs of greeting and slowly retreated up a type of staircase that seemed holographic but firm enough to reach the deck.

When I set foot again on the shore and looked back again the boat had a different hue, more reddish, and it was not the product of our known Red Sun, however, the shape remained. Many citizens had seen me enter and approached me to ask me what was inside, I wanted to avoid any answer by making gestures of "not having seen anything", because if I commented that there were more beings, many other questions would not take long to arrive and it would be a long interrogation, there might even be some other curious person who would want to get inside.

My father was approaching in the distance with the new visitor and Butler and two marines followed him behind, they escorted him to the ship and I did not lose sight of them all the way keeping every detail. The being returned to the interior of the ship and now it was my turn to run to my father and although he was not going to be happy about it, tell him about the beings I had seen in there.

William was holding in his right hand the transcript of the whole conversation with the being, since every important event inside the big building is automatically transcribed, stored in memories and copies are generated, so that every answer can be analyzed in detail. My father was then very busy with other marines and chiefs of the different areas, therefore, I turned to Butler who with his distinguished kindness listened to my every word. Butler opened his eyes at every word of my story as he knew he had risked too much, but he was glad that I had been able to give him another piece of knowledge about these beings, then he told me that all this was somewhat similar to the version that the same being had given, and after my insistence, he promised to give me a memory to read the transcript of the visitor, who called himself "Hiurenk" and also like the rest of the team that came on the boat, they claimed to be from a place called "Cassiopeia".

THE PLAN TO RETURN TO THE LANDS OF ORIGIN

Everyone in the Ancestral Lands already knew my father well enough to know perfectly well that this welcome visit was excellent for our central plan of liberation of humanity, both the knowledge that these beings brought and their technology, especially the latter, and so my father would then try to make it all fit somehow into one of the plans they had created to return to the Known Lands.

In fact, I would later learn that he had not been able to resist too much and had proposed it to him in the first conversation in the Great Building. My father understood that time was getting tighter and tighter.

The transcript did not come to me from my dear father but from Butler, who had given me a copy of the hidden encoded memory. My father was trying to keep me away from all this conflict, but the reality was that we were all part of this long and arduous journey and, of course, I would be no exception.

Butler was confident, but from the expressions on his face, I knew it wasn't going to be easy to convince the new visitors to hand over valuable information about their technology, after all, we weren't sure they were aware of our origins and the visit seemed to be more casual than for some kind of mission or knowledge about us.

The night came abruptly before so much convulsion caused among the citizens, the news was not long in coming and spread all the information that strange beings had stopped on our shores. I noticed that my father had a great illusion for this new opportunity, you could see it clearly reflected in his face, I could never see him like that again and that filled me with hope at that time. I understood that inside him was the hope that "Hiurenk" would help to enter in a safe way to the home that everyone had had to abandon and somehow he dreamed that one of the many plans created would work for the human liberation inside the Ice Walls and the First Dome.

They were not so wrong based on the technology that these beings had reached and knew how to manipulate, in fact, I had seen it with my own eyes, the interior of that ship looked like something out of the best fiction books that my father talks so much about, our "Known Lands", added to their type of communication and the resounding change in the form that their ship could take, could be of great help in this way to slip away without any kind of mistake before the Custodian eyes.

THE
TRANSCRIPTION

- Fhael: Well, it is a pleasure to greet you again, I introduce myself, I am Fhael, the president of these lands, on my right is our Commander in Chief Naval William Morris together with Captain Butler.

- Visitor: My respectful greetings, I am sorry for my accent, I will try to communicate as best as possible with you, please understand that my communication is visual-telepathic between our race, but we adapt well to the environment, and since this does not work with your race I will put all my effort in your type of communication.

- Fhael: Do not worry, again receiving you is a pleasant surprise, like most of every visit we have received here, we would like to know the reason for this and that you could give us more information about it since we are quite worried about what is happening in nearby lands and all our lands are on alert, where do you come from?

- Visitor: I am sorry for what is happening sir, my name is Hiurenk, our origin is distant lands called "Cassiopeia" or ARB032 we arrived to these lands sailing latitudes surrounding and somehow we have collided with your "Membrane-Dome" some time ago, we decided to avoid it until we met an extension in South direction, without remedy regarding our energy used by the vessel transporting us, having to penetrate the South Membrane-Dome of ARB204 (Mars Earths) avoiding ARB201 (Known Earths) for the time being, until we can better understand the functioning of its Circle-Environment in depth, besides the detection of our technology of what dwells there.

- Fhael: Sir, many points here are of interest to us, you comment that you have been able to penetrate the ARB204 Dome, has this required any difficulty based on your technology?

- Hiurenk: I am sorry I do not fully understand your question, but we have passed through that membrane without difficulty since it is at a level 2 with respect to our scale of 7. Therefore, I mean, we have passed through that barrier and then we have encountered "VStemcells" beings like you, but with different type of DNA, marking as a junction the type of origin detected.

- Morris: Hiurenk, have you been able to enter various Circle-Environments? -
- Hiurenk: That is correct, sir.

- Morris: How many of them have you been able to visit?

- Hiurenk: To be honest in our history not as many as other known races, but we have been able to go through enough of them to understand how many of them work, and many other beings that make up this Great Dome.

- Fhael: How many Circle-Environments do you consider to

exist?

- Hiurenk: We have the information that there are 178 up to the giant dividing walls, but as I was telling you, we cannot confirm that since we have not been to each one, anyway, we have information on most of them that I will have no problem to give to you to add to your files.

- Butler: Excuse me, how has your experience been at ARB204?

- Hiurenk: One of the strangest, we have encountered various types of cells in there, and the control they have there is hostile, as well as among the beings themselves, we have seen situations of which we do not agree and do not accept in our civilization. We have also found experiments in laboratories under the surface, some abandoned and others currently in operation today, as I was saying, some are of the same species of origin, there is a group called "Human Colony" and within that strange Circle-Environment are the beings that value life above all others, but they are under constant attack, they have asked for our help and we have been able to free a contingent, but we have not wanted to participate actively since we try to stay away from the control in each Membrane-Dome.

- Fhael: Excuse me, Hiurenk, have you made contact with any of the races in control there? Rather, who are in control? And what kind of relationship do you have?

- Hiurenk: We are against any type of control over another being under any Dome, sir, we cannot confirm the race in control of ARB204 as there are several types in there, what we can intuit is that it could be undergoing some type of "control experiment" or other type that we are unaware of, no doubt it is an altered Membrane for the development of races of another origin.

- Morris: Have you been able to enter ARB201 (Known Lands)?

- Hiurenk: Negative, sir.

- Fhael: Forgive me for asking again, but your visit to these lands has not been clear, what is the purpose of your trip?

- Hiurenk: We have left our lands of origin relatively recently (depending on the comparison in each time-limit within the respective Domes), and are exploring lands for the knowledge and progress of our environment.

- Fhael: Were you under the control of some kind of species?

- Hiurenk: We have been under the hostile rule of the Custodians for a long time, clearly we had no possibility of growth or development of any kind, our race was just beginning to develop spiritually when it was colonized, many of our race have penetrated outside of our environment for fear that they would return, but the reality is that the Custodians left our lands long ago and we believe that they will not return, we also take this reason very important to be able to contact other races and to be able to deliver our small part of the history, if that can help in some way, although as I commented following our nature we cannot enter actively in any conflict of another species.

- Fhael: Perfect Mr. Hiurenk, for the moment I have no more questions to ask from my position know that you and your group are more than welcome to our lands, the Ancestral Lands and we will try to give you what you need to feel comfortable and you can leave whenever you want on your journey.

- Morris: I would like to be able to talk to you later about something very important, with Butler we believe that you could help us in our long fight against the Custodians, since you somehow were able to get rid of the colonization in your homelands, and we as you may know, are still in a battle that seems eternal.

- Hiurenk: Yes, I am very sorry for what happened in ARB201, it is known by many species around about your history, if in anything we can help know that you count on us, but we do not want to be involved in a direct conflict as that could endanger again my brothers in the lands we have left transitorily behind.

- Morris: I understand, do not worry, thank you very much for your time and I will be visiting you tomorrow morning so I can give you details and you can provide me with some information we need.

- Hiurenk: Perfect, I am here to help, grateful for your hospitality gentlemen.

THE NEW CASSIOPEIA TECHNOLOGY

That night my father would arrive again to the coast to meet that big boat that now had an opaque color and reflected the same sea that was hitting hard against it. With the help of Butler who told him about my contact with those beings in there, we were able to convince him that I also be part of this new contact, I understood later that my father also wanted me to witness such a conversation, as it was not going to be a regular one, but could mark a before and after in our development of the plan to free the new humanity.

We entered without problems going up to the deck and then descending by that "holographic" staircase that deposited us in a huge room, the dimensions did not make sense and seemed to be much larger inside than what we perceived from the outside.

Hiurenk approached us, he was alone and offered us something to drink, a drink of the strangest I would ever go to taste then commented that it was a fruit characteristic of his lands, it really did not taste bad but I was not used to it so I only tried a sip and left it there on a desk, I did not trust these beings much either, after all they were still a strange visitor (the drink kept its temperature from start to finish of the visit, and this lasted for hours, the container was a dark "gelatinous" cube that was very cold to the touch).

My father and Butler told him about the critical situation inside ARB201 and while they did not give any details of the plan, they needed to know more about both the enemy or enemies we were facing and also about the penetration of Membrane-Domes, as the latter was the most complex and where the Anakim Giants did not want to be an active part at the moment either. We thought that, if an outside race provided us with the necessary information to be able to enter undetected, we could also encourage the Anakim to join us in a mass release of new humans into our lands and surrounding lands.

This sounded far-fetched and unlikely, but hope was not lost, much less in my father, who had the illusion intact that these beings had arrived at the right time to somehow help us enter.

Hiurenk was honest with Morris and Butler, and told them that this could not be carried out as planned, but that they would give him information about technology to open a Portal/Passageway that could be at that moment above any kind of radar or custodian technology, that they had certainly done it on Mars Earths and that they had not had any problems.

My father was jumping with excitement, and I swear that if Hiurenk did not show seriousness as he seemed to be a being that would not show any kind of feeling towards us, my father would have given him the tightest hug at that instant. They agreed that they would travel near the First Dome - Ice Walls in a few days while they prepared their plan well, Hiurenk confirmed that he had the necessary technology to open a portal without being detected, but there was a primordial condition, Hiurenk commented that opening the portal would bring information to the new humanity about the spiritual development, and that was the only way to be able to free themselves from the Custodian/Anunnaki control, manipulation and yoke.

There was no possibility of winning any war against them at that time with the technology they carried, maybe some battle, but never a war inside a totally manipulated and controlled Dome and Environment, in fact, the humans themselves could turn against them with just some kind of manipulation of the means used there.

They agreed then that several ancestral masters would enter to provide information on spiritual liberation and development, the beings of Cassiopeia knew well that humans had infinite spiritual potential and that they were the "key" to the Celestial Lands, they were well aware that the Custodians were not going to leave the ARB201 colony easily as they had done in other Circle-Environments.

Hiurenk was also clear and concise about something, they would NOT enter into any conflict or help in any direct way, they would only open a portal with the guideline that information about human spiritual development would be entered.

THE HIURENK PORTAL, THE HUMAN SOUL, UNCONDITIONAL LOVE AND EMPATHY

So it was that during this "Silent War" between the Ancestors and the Custodians, the "First Operation Portal-Dome Breaker" was carried out, which consisted in melting ice, always taking into account statistics in order not to generate any climatic disaster, for a long time several ancestors departed from our ports to the "Known Lands" or "Ancient Lands" through this passage between fearsome giant icebergs, waves, and especially in front of the Custodian bewilderment, which when they discovered it already had several thousand of our masters publishing, teaching and prioritizing unconditional love and empathy as a way of life.

I must admit here that several people of the new humanity were rescued and left for our lands, but this happened in a small stage and with a small group.

The scientific conditioning almost collided abruptly by the time they realized what was happening in that remote area of the "Pacific Ocean", some 2000 ancestors were already scattered throughout the known lands delivering all information (some successfully and others not so much) about the infinite spiritual growth, questioning the scientific minds, what seemed unquestionable until that moment, that many secret organizations (with direct Custodian connection and manipulation) are made known and as if that were not enough, some human vessels arrived in the area by chance (and not so by chance) and left with great astonishment although only one of them dared to cross that dreaded passage, which was a death trap since it was not easily navigable, but would have to have great technology to cross it, but with a little luck, cunning and wind in favor, the impossible was forgotten when a group of five humans managed to cross it (It should be noted that this unfortunately was possible only in a short stage of weeks).

When the Custodians could notice that there was an ancestral hand in these teachings they tried to corrupt them, and they were easily annihilated, the spiritual path was manipulated in such a way that it was taken to dirty business, added to other repudiated subjects that together with the great media made that the great tower built on pure teachings was completely demolished in a few weeks.

Many masters were locked up and accused of different crimes, making known to all humanity the aberrant hidden causes they had, and somehow, they began to unite these noble causes with perversion, business and several other things that added to obscure the true purpose, some of them ended up in psychiatric centers at the mercy of "controversial behavioral treatments" in conjunction with experiments of all kinds that they carried out since then. Others were taken to prisons with the worst conditions, and others were killed outright.

The Custodians again went into a rage against their old enemies, the ancestral ones and the Anakim, for their most precious lands, they feared again an attack from us, in fact, when they found the passage we had opened with the help of the beings of Cassiopeia (Hiurenk Technology) they exploded and decided to attack our lands several times, but, they would do it in the most perverse way that they know how to do very well, then they granted very advanced technology for the time to the humans themselves, in that way the armed forces of the new humanity would attack several places before the "First Dome" but they would fail resoundingly.

The "Operation HighJump" of which we have already spoken previously was the scene that they expected to generate some fear in the Antarctic zone and to be able to militarize the zone, in this way they would also infiltrate custodian beings in some of the Antarctic bases and throughout the Antarctic circle to surround and undermine the zone with earthquake generating radars.

This type of technology generates earthquakes of great magnitude as soon as it receives an alert of infiltration of Ancestral Human DNA or some type of matter that they themselves previously added, this happened for a long time and continues to happen today.

Clearly this was not going to stop my father Morris and Butler to continue on their way to achieve the liberation of the new humanity, they would look for other ways and no doubt they would dare to infiltrate again in the lands of origin, Hiurenk had given them some information to penetrate the Membrane by air, but it was a very risky mission, although as I said, greater was their illusion to liberate them.

THE 178 KNOWN
WORLDS

Hiurenk before leaving again to "Cassiopeia" lands, or at least that was what he told us, gave us several memories to file in our "Great Ancestral Library" about the other worlds that they had been able to know and others that they had not entered or perhaps not even navigated closely but that they had acquired from several other races and from books as old as the beginning of life itself.

We in the Ancestral Lands compiled all this information and after extensive and arduous work of managing, comparing and gathering all the works, reports, reports and texts, we have come to the conclusion that these are all the Worlds (Circle-Environments) that lie beneath the Great Dome, or within the vast and enormous walls that contain and divide the known from the unknown.

ARB201	KNOWN LANDS - EARTH
ARB204	MARS
ARB123	VENUS
ARB013	ANUNNAKI
ARB004	PLEIADES
ARB206	SATURN
ARB207	ALDEBARAN
ARB208	ANGELS
ARB210	PEGASUS

ARB032   *CASSIOPEIA*
H005   *ORION*
X001   *CUSTODIANS*
X003 *JUPITER*
C412 *HERCULES*
C413 *ANDROMEDA*
C414 *ARCTURUS*
C415 *VANTH*
C416 *BETA LYRAE*
C417 *SAGITTA*
C418 *SHAM*
C419 *VEGA*
N820 *SADALMELIK*
N821 *SADALTAGER*
C422 *MIRFAK*
C423 *ALGOL*
C424 *MENCHIB*
C425 *SIRIO A*
C426 *NUCLEUS 270*
N827 *ALTAIR*
N828 *SIRIO B*
N829 *ALFA CYGNI*
N830 *NML CYGNI*
N831 *P CYGNI*
N832 *SADR*
N833 *CYCLOPS*
N834 *FAWARIS*
N835 *ALJANAH*
N836 *EFIALTES*
N837 *WR 142*
N838 *HYDOR*
N839 *SADALSUUD*
N840 *CLOUD LANDS*
N841 *NUCLEUS 290*
N842 *16 CYGNI*
N843 *ELENEI*

N844   ALBIREO
N845   DAMASEN
N846   PERSEI
N847   ATIK
N848   GORGONEA TERTIA
N849   GORGONEA QUARTA
N850   NUCLEUS 272
N851   ETERNAL
N852   MIMAS
N853   DRACO
N854   DELTA 2 LYRAE
N855   QUAOAR-X
Y556   NEPTUNE
Y557   LANDS OF CLONES / SECOND EARTH
Y558   URANUS
Y559   LEONIS
Y560   TITANIDES
Y561   TIERRA CEO
Y562   FOUNDER LANDS
Y563   NUCLEUS 286
Y564   DENÉBOLA
Y565   TRANSMUTE
Y566   CRONOS
Y567   PAN
X068   BALDER
X069   HEL
X070   TYR
X071   IDUNA
X072   CALIGULA
X073   THE FINAL DOME
X002   NIBIRU
X075   HEIMDALL
X076   GREEN STONES
X077   ARA
C478   AQUILA
C479   SCUTUM

C480 CORVUS

X081 PLANET-X

C482 ALGENIB

C483 MARKAB

C484 HELVETIOS

C485 ENIF

C486 LANDS OF TIME

C487 ARCANE ISLANDS

C488 CRUX

C489 FROZEN LANDS

C490 DIMIRIO

X091 INFINITE LANDS

C492 BIHAM

C493 HOMAM

C494 EL TEMPLO DE ZEUS

C495 CELESTIAL RINGS

C496 ROSS

C497 MATAR

C498 SALM

C499 SCHEAT

C4100 VERITATE

C4101 TITAWIN

C4102 CRATER 18

C4103 DELTA 1

C4104 STEPHENSON 1

C4105 R LYRAE

C4106 XY LYRAE

C4107 MERU

C4108 POLIBOTES

C4109 ORIOS

C4110 CLITIO

N8111 ARTEMISA

N8112 PERIBEA

N8113 SKAT

N8114 POLO

N8115 EDASICH

N8116 RASTABAN
N8117 MERCURY
N8118 MAIA
N8119 THUBAN
N8120 NOVA PERSEI
N8121 DÁNAE
N8122 U SAGITTAE
K001   CELESTIAL LANDS / TERRA-INCÓGNITA
N8125 LACERTHA'S LANDS
N8126 BABCOCK
N8127 BACO
N8128 HYDRA
N8129 ERIS
N8130 ALKAID
N8131 NUCLEUS 284
N8132 TANIA AUSTRALIS
N8133 EOLO
N8134 BOL
N8135 LANDS OF THE STORMS
N8136 ETHERNAL FIRE
N8137 ALCOR
N8138 MIZAR
N8139 DUBHE
N8140 KURHAH
N8141 RAI
N8142 LANDS OF THE FORGOTTEN HUMANS
N8143 SKADE
N8144 NUCLEUS 294
N8145 BÓREAS
N8146 CIH
N8147 NUCLEUS 282
N8148 ERRAI
N8149 PHICARES
N8150 TSAO FU
N8151 SCHEDAR
N8152 ALFIRK

N8153 SEGIN
N8154 RUCHBAB
N8155 CAPH
N8156 SOUND
N8157 TASO
N8158 NUCLEUS 276
N8159 ROTANEV II
N8160 SUALOCIN
N8161 MUSIC
N8162 ALDULFIN
N8163 WASP
N8164 ORO
N8165 POLUX
N8166 LANDS OF THE SILENCE
N8167 CASTOR
N8168 ALHENA
N8169 SHERATAN
N8170 ARIETIS
N8171 NUCLEUS 274
N8172 TOXIC LANDS
N8173 BRAHMA
N8174 NUCLEUS 280
N8175 MEKBUDA
X176   ADDU
N5177 WISE
N5178 GIANFAR

THEORY-BASED
MAP OF OTHER
SURROUNDING
DOMES

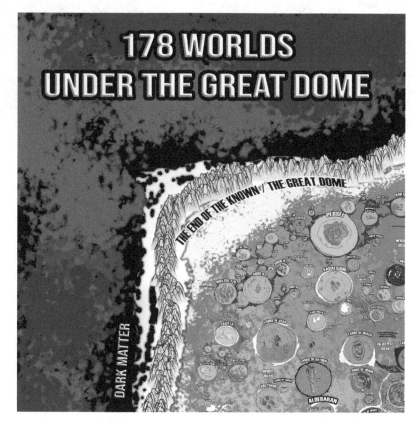

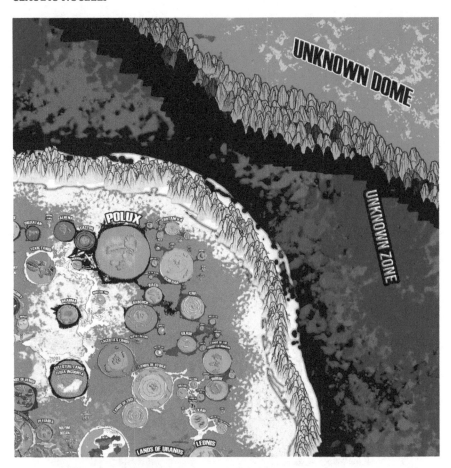

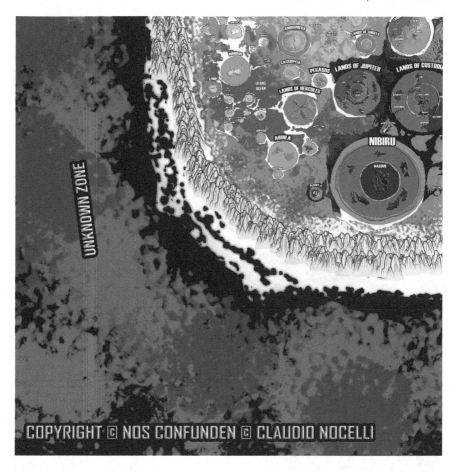

TERRA-INFINITA MAP WITH NAMES APPROPRIATE TO THE NEW GENERATION

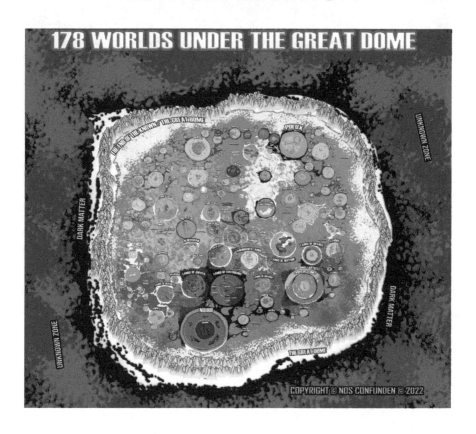

TERRA-INFINITA MAP

CODIFICATION

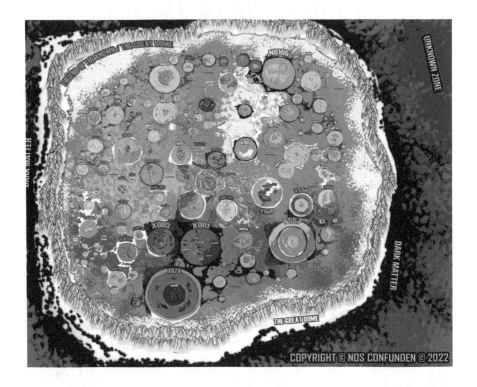

WORLDS DIVIDED
INTO PARTS
ACCORDING TO

"N-X ZONE" CODING

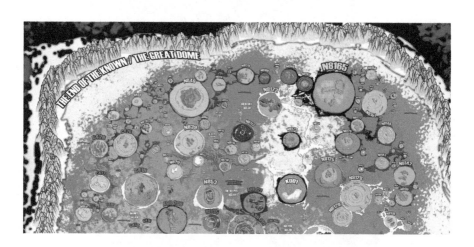

WORLDS DIVIDED INTO PARTS ACCORDING TO "C-X ZONE" CODING

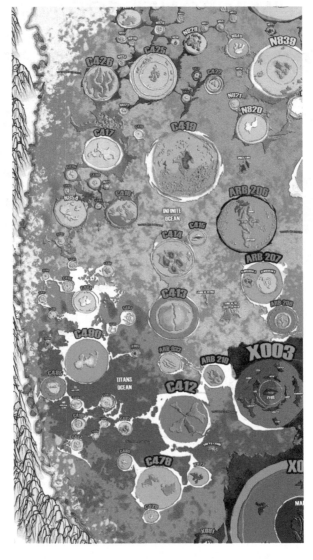

WORLDS DIVIDED INTO PARTS ACCORDING TO "ARB-X ZONE" CODING

WORLDS DIVIDED INTO PARTS ACCORDING TO "X-X ZONE" CODING

MAP DIVIDED INTO PARTS ACCORDING TO SPECIAL CODING:

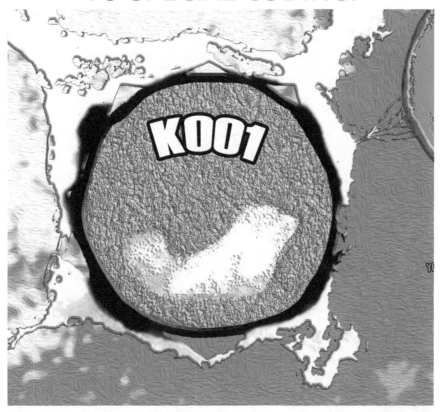

WORLDS DIVIDED INTO PARTS ACCORDING TO "Y-X ZONE" CODING

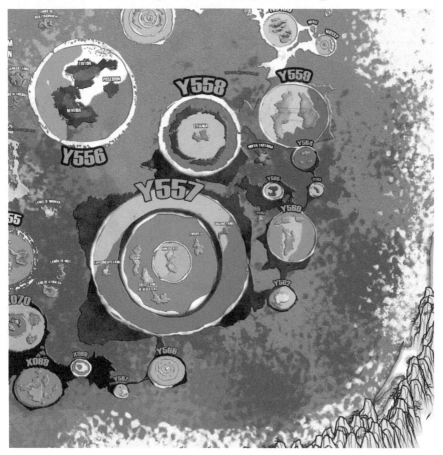

STORIES OF THE PLANET-WORLDS INSIDE THE GREAT DOME

ARB204 – THE LANDS OF MARS

What we know about their civilization of origin: Killed in war against colonizers, it is believed that some of them managed to survive and emigrate from their lands, but there is a lack of information to confirm it, it was believed that the "Martians" had been annihilated in their entirety, but, the most recent theories speak that a not so numerous group could be living on the coasts of nearby lands and that they had been sighted by several races.

Their present: The lands are occupied today by different types of races, including the human race ("VStemcell"), it is a zone of controlled development, there are conflicts and wars of all kinds.

We have information that a part of the human race living there in a large colony migrated to other lands that have visited ours in past times. Also some of our navigators have penetrated its passage/portal to the interior and have informed us in detail about some of the species that live there.

They are lands of constant conflict between many of the races that inhabit there (especially the one coming from The Lands of Orion - H1ORION -) and little or no spiritual growth, it is believed that the various races compete with each other in the development of weaponry for defense and attack.

Many humans arrived from the Known Lands as a "reward" for betraying their own race, this was happening also during the period that is today the last "post reset" humanity, as we were able to gather from several navigators who went into the connecting passage between Mars and Second Dome Lands we were able to obtain much valuable information regarding how the Human Colony lives there after years of having left their homelands.

All the members who arrived there as a "prize" did it with absolute happiness imagining that they would live in a paradise and that they would live five times more approximately than their current average life on the known continents because of all the existing polluted and manipulated environment.

But, when they arrived they realized that the Custodians had betrayed them in a certain way and that all their help and betrayal to their brothers had been just another trick that the Custodians used to perform. They would manage to live much longer (if they survived the many current wars) but they would do it in a really different way than planned or promised, as long as their bodies could be absolutely "cleansed" of the manipulated environment of the old and known lands.

Although the lands of Mars have paradisiacal coasts as well as an incredible variety of flora and fauna, the variety of colors in each landscape is really catching, but, the wars that are carried out by the many races that coexist there make of these lands a true hell.

Both Captain Hunt and Roald and so many others, who are proudly remembered as examples every day in our lands since they helped enormously to gather information to understand our environment, told and detailed their experiences in these lands penetrating the well-known "Byrd's Passage" and all that was also of course as proof of fire kept in our memories of the Great Library.

The writings of Captain Hunt are quite consistent with the other accounts, the "Human Colony" existing in the misnamed "Red Lands" began first on the shores of Aeria, and then forced by other races, especially the harassment they received from the Grey Race of Orion (H1ORION) in conjunction with the "Etamins" from the Draco Lands, led the human group to settle on a large island off its shores, in Terra Cimmeria. At the beginning it was hard work to build their bases from scratch again, but they had custodian technology that had been given to them upon entry (possibly as a modality for all races in this experiment), so it was not so difficult to make their dome-bases operational again. The buildings in the Mars Lands were "Dome" or "Dome" shaped and it could not be otherwise since it had been imposed also by the Custodians, among many other requirements to live there.

Humanity suffered from the beginning and then it was not so different, the attacks of the Greys and Etamins had ceased in intensity, but not radically, every now and then they received attacks from the coasts and these missiles impacted near the operational bases and had even affected several domes created by the humans, generating many casualties.

One morning the Greys attacked their coasts directly and killed more than 100 humans who were not prepared for a confrontation, it was really a massacre and this was told by a direct witness in the visit of Captain Hunt. The brave navigator had left our lands in the direction of the Ice Walls - Second Dome in order to face the dreaded "Byrd Passage", since it was said that it was a passage/portal that was very complex to go through, besides the experience could be really traumatic.

This was not an impediment for Hunt and his crew, in total there were 8 people who left in a ship in the direction of the "Membrane Portal" and then to its passage through the "Roald's Ocean" in a West-South direction, between the Lands of Argos. The passage or Membrane Portal (crossing the Second Dome) is a very complex site since very few ancestral explorers have dared to cross it, although the "Anakim" Giants have helped us a lot to get through, the reality is that it is still unstable for us and we try to avoid it, not only because of its difficulty but also because of the length of the route. Captain Hunt and his men left armed structures on the shores of Argos, in case they needed to return urgently, as well as to help the next visitors who wanted to risk entering through Byrd's Portal.

The ancestral technology could safely detect, or so we assumed at the time, any enemy approach, whether from the Greys, Etamins or any other race, except the Custodian, for that reason it was extremely risky to navigate in those latitudes. In any case, it was a risk we wanted to take if we wanted to bring back information from those lands that could be of great use for the human future both within the first and the second dome. We were not yet aware of how the humans there would react, although we knew about the existence of a colony and we had had contact with a boat that had escaped from there, a possible confrontation against them was totally uncertain, but as we said, we had to try, since those humans had direct contact with the Custodians and although we had a totally negative view towards them for having betrayed their own race, the information there was as valuable as gold in the known lands. Besides, we wanted to know how they had developed there, if there were still wars, or even worse, if there was still a human being in there.

The first encounter took place exactly 17 days after crossing the passage/portal, which, as a side note, was not so traumatic to go through, but Hunt records a sensation of being pushed at breakneck speed for a few seconds and upon entering you totally lose control of the ship, added to the fact that the radars stop working for a long time and the sensation of having been inside that passage for a long time, all this was really catastrophic for people like us who were entering hostile zones and had no way of knowing where we were navigating or if there were enemies nearby.

It was not until five days later that we were able to recover our technology and get it operational again, and when everything was fully operational, we decided to set sail along the coast of Aeria. Then Hunt tells in his memoirs: "The sea off the coast of Aeria is one of the most incredible that we had ever sailed, from afar everything seems peaceful but there is a swell that from nowhere becomes a thrust so violent that the direction is completely lost, as close to the Walls of the First Dome, our boat was prepared but the swings made some of us ended up sick for some time.

We tried to reach "Argyre" that from its distant brightness dazzled our senses, we were called and attracted there as the ancient stories of the Siren Lands tell, only the sunset, the violent sea and us, the stillness suddenly invaded us, all was silence for some time until we touched the shores of Terra Cimmeria, it was time then to face reality, it was all or nothing and my men knew it very well, would there have been any human left standing there? And if so, how would they receive us?"

On those shores there were three humans doing some kind of repair on the dock that from afar marked somehow, that there was a large human settlement there. We approached with our boat very slowly, the moment of tension increasing as we passed. Because of our type of boat they surely had no idea who we were, and this worsened the conditions to establish some kind of signal before contact. Our entire boat was illuminated with white from end to end, the message was clear, we did not want to initiate this contact in the worst way, nor that they interpret any kind of hostility, after all and even if we were so far away in our ideals, we were human beings in unknown lands and far from our origin.

On the shore the humans now "Martians" had stopped all the activity they were doing and were staring at us from there, each one in their position far away from each other by great distances, this caught our attention, usually in an arrival in this way those who receive visitors are grouped and try to welcome or not, but the ways were different from what we thought.

Our ship parked close to the shore, the sea in that area was extremely deep, and I descended with my companion Richard, who was the most diplomatic, to make known the purpose of our visit.

Richard made signs before descending towards the base that would transport us to the same white sand of Cimmeria, the humans there saw us from afar without making any movement, they did not even talk to each other, they seemed robotic actions.

They were very young people in appearance, and their clothes were dirty and torn by the hard work under the Martian sun.

A man came towards us and greeted us cordially, he told us that it had been a long time since he had heard an accent like that, strangely what we least imagined but most wanted happened, it was a cordial welcome from the human colony in these lands of suffocating heat but beautiful scenery. He told us that they called him RS200 and that all of them had names like that, between letters and numbers to differentiate themselves, and that long ago the proper names had ceased to exist there, Richard asked him about Byrd and other known names that we knew had entered these lands long ago, but neither RS200 nor the others knew how to give us information (or did not want to).

Later Richard would show him a picture of Byrd that some people knew, their answers were confusing and ended up saying that "R. Byrd had left the lands long ago. Byrd had left the lands some time ago" but we don't know if they were referring to a death or that he had physically left the shores, we didn't want to insist for the moment, although we wanted to know his whereabouts.

First of all, we asked him about the Custodians and leaders there, these young men were exactly 26 people living together in pitiful conditions and seemed to have been abandoned, although later we would learn of something worse than this.

The leaders were called "Cuijas" and we were told that they approached them in particular ships, silent and that "walked the waters", these beings had clothes that simulated or rather, that were shaped like animals known from the area of Terra Cimmeria.

To use this type of costumes was quite common among the Custodians, when they approach beings of their Colonies, we suppose that it is to confuse both the same beings and the histories that they can leave towards the future, we can find it in thousands of representations within the Known Lands, for example, in the Ancient Egypt of past generations.

The "Cuijas" as they called them, did not often come there, but they had certainly been moved from one zone to the other, the island was well divided into four parts, and the zone we had arrived at was a "Zone of Reclusion" or "Zone of Punishment", where for some reason they considered that they had violated some established rule, they were taken there as a punishment performing subhuman labor in high temperatures under the sun, with basic tools, for this reason they had received us in this way, they were not even surprised, I guess they imagined that it was another mental game of the Custodians and part of their punishment, or perhaps they were begging for some kind of rescue to come from outside.

Very curious all this experience, the first humans arrived to these lands with the promise from the Custodians to live in a paradise for more than 500 years, and they found this reality where they, their children and probably several future generations would live in pitiful conditions.

This all seemed like some sort of divine punishment for betraying humanity, but the reality was, the Custodians and Anunnaki themselves were playing with human minds no matter what rank or closeness they held.

Both Hunt and all the crew, after talking and spending two nights there in this area considered as punishment, moved away from the coasts trying in a very risky way and out of the plan, to reach Eridania, they had obtained some important information about this area and they did not want to lose the opportunity to visit it. If they were detected by some Custodian radar, approaching a portal or Anunnaki Pyramid, or simply some other race that could alert the presence of ancestors there, the whole Circle-Environment would go into alarm and the impossible would be done to find them, for that reason to continue sailing there after so many days, knowing that at least another three days would be needed to return to the Byrd Passage.

It should be clarified that the humans in the "confinement zone" begged on several occasions to take them out of there, they flatly refused, not because they did not want to help them (after all they were a new generation paying for past mistakes) but because taking them near Byrd Passage or navigating through its seas could be easily detected, since the "RS2XX" carried several tracking chips with custodian technology very difficult to manipulate, they had neither the tools nor the laboratory, nor the suitable personnel to perform a surgical extraction of that technology in their bodies and/or blood.

Since they could not contact any ancestral base, not even the structure that could detect the signal left at the gates of

Mars, since any attempt could be detected there, the risk was even greater, first that they could not be rescued and second that if they were captured or killed the complete information would be lost and all the answers that the human prisoners of Cimmeria had given them about their entire colony would have disappeared completely and the entire trip would end without fulfilling its main objective, besides not having been added to the memories of the Great Library.

When they were on their way south towards the lands called "Eridania" the distances were extremely large and the "Mare Sirenum" became even more and more dangerous as it passed, the technology of the ship was not the best, so we decided to return immediately. Surprisingly all the crew arrived correctly and without conflict against the Custodians, Anunnaki, Greys, Etamins or any other race, and the information gathered by the humans there was really valuable, after overcoming the passage of Byrd from inside to outside, the entrance again to the Known Lands of the second dome was a relief, three days of rest, Three days of rest, contact with base, transfer of files and internal rejoicing for having complied, we now undertook our return to the Ancestral Lands to tell from our own mouths to the thousands of impatient souls who were waiting for us, leaving us with a strange sensation on our return, had the Mars Lands been or were being somehow abandoned by the colonizers?

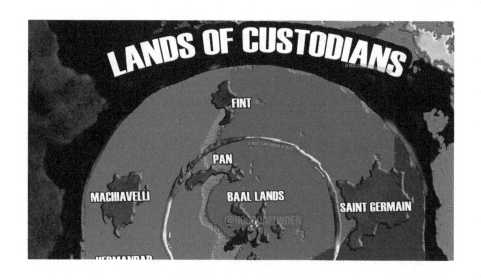

X001 – THE LANDS
OF CUSTODIANS

Inhabitants (Approximate Data): We do not have an exact figure, it is believed that more than 27,000,000,000 and others scattered throughout the plane in their Colonies within the Great Dome.

What we know about their civilization of origin: There is little information about this parasitic and colonizing race, in conjunction with the Anunnaki Race are responsible for the human devolution, by manipulation and stunted spiritual development between constant and uninterrupted wars and resets in most of their colonies.   It is believed that they took over 90% of them in former times and used the same for their great technological advancement when most other races were not even developed for their defense.

Their present: It is believed that these beings are in an incessant search to be able to penetrate the great dividing walls or Great Dome, and looking for the connection with the "Celestial Lands" or "Terra-Incognita" and they still continue in their study achieving, as far as we know, great advances to be able to understand what could be found outside the Great Dome and inside the "Terra-Incognita" There is much information about the subway bases and BSM (Mobile Submarine Bases) existing both in their own lands and in the Known Lands, and we also have information about the same type of bases in other lands, but these are very complex to analyze as they change over time their position radically, although at one time followed a certain pattern, after the Great War and the new reset carried out have made major changes throughout its structure.

In our books we find few stories in direct reference to their lands and only one of them seems to have enough strength to be mentioned, it should be clarified that this contact was not direct by any ancestor but through a Giant-Human that approached their lands surrounding them as close as possible before being detected and that I will detail later in this report.

These beings are known for presenting themselves to the natives of different "Surrounding-Circles" with a humanoid figure and upper limb or face shaped like different animal forms that are usually characteristic of each region, and so they were represented in our lands in many of the drawings found within the official history of ancient civilizations.

Their hierarchy stands out for the classic pyramidal shape that they installed in all the sites they colonized and ruled for long periods, its dome is divided in turn into three distinct positions, although these three parts are known as "Leaders" the truth is that only the "Royal-Leaders" are always those who have the last word and carry out the most important decision making.

Story H012-304 in Lands X001 from the book titled (Translated from native ancestral language) as: "**No Parasitic King Will Be Accepted by The Ancestral People**" - Great Capital Ancestral Library - The Ark.

"Mik-ha dared to carry it out, we do not know why, but he broke formation with his ship and was lost in the horizon, although he had told me about his mission by an internal voice that demanded it, the truth is that I never thought he would actually carry it out. I thought it was just a joke or a play on words, but today I saw him for the last time and this would be the last memory of that old friend". Mik-ha was a Giant-Human survivor of the Great War, after settling in the "Ancient Lands of Anak" he sailed with 6 other members of the special forces over the lands they called "Neo-Biz" at that time, they were lands that were used in the beginning as depots and military bases. The Giant-Humans were grouped together as most of the ancestral humanity (that survived the last reset - Sixth Generation) had grouped on other nearby islands, all of them important members of the famous "Great Tartary" the empire that was defeated by the Custodians during the Great War.

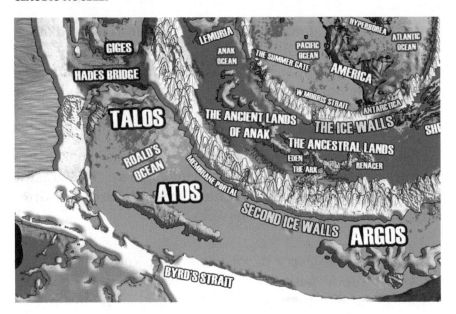

Mik-ha had already commented in several opportunities that to know the enemy it was necessary to approach their lands, by information obtained from some of their bases and reports in bases of the "Greys" in the Known Lands (generally temporary bases during their leadership that would quickly fail before the advance of the Great Tartary) it was known approximately their location in the maps that the "Anakim" Giants had at that time, although the leaders had flatly forbidden him to attempt any approach flight to any region other than the surrounding region between the lands they had taken behind First Dome, Mik-ha seemed to disregard several of these requests, and had flown over the land of "Lemuria" even reaching the lands known as "Laurentia" on several occasions.

The leaders of the special forces were not like military leaders that we usually know in any army of the new humanity, they were quite permissible but clearly advised that any false move could result not only in certain death but would clearly endanger the entire region, they should stay hidden as much as possible and for the longest period of time until, at least, recover their civilization and organize themselves in every possible way.

Mik-ha reached the Second Walls very close to the "Second Dome" and flew over the area to establish some point of union, he was looking for an exit point, a "matter connector" or "Membrane Portal" and he would achieve his goal in one of his many trips following some frozen islands of the Ancient Lands of Anak also close to "The Ark" of the Ancestral Lands.

He studied the area, made calculations and was also helped by several Giants whom he mentioned above and never left names explicitly so as not to blame them for what he was about to do, Mik-ha set off "South" breaking formation and in a determined way directly towards the "Membrane Portal".

Completely breaking the pattern followed by those of his

own strength and civilization at the time, there were few records of the Giants outside of the Second Dome, he achieved the unthinkable, and communicated directly with his leader informing him of his new adventure into the unknown lands, "The Custodian Lands".

The Giant leaders met and being aware of the situation, they tried to persuade the young adventurer but everything was rejected and Mik-ha would continue his course flying over "Athos" all over the "Ocean of Roald" something unthinkable for then with an ancestral ship via air.   Surrounding the enormous existing walls between the "Lands of Mars" and "Land of Angels", he went through a thick fog and an incredibly high risk bordering the "Lands of Jupiter", this heroic and lonely journey was almost a suicide for the great leaders who already resigned helped Mik-ha's flight to reach its destination, although it was quite uncertain.

Mik-ha communicated with base trying to explain the little he could visualize, there was a kind of dark wall, totally dark, in fact he had almost hit it among the fog still existing around him, although less thick than before. Those dark walls were the strangest he had ever seen, and some huge towers seemed to emerge from the other side, they were undoubtedly the fearsome Custodian Lands, those enemy lands were in front of him.

The last communication with base was that a red light seemed to be behind him and following his path, it was ruled out that it was an enemy missile by the detail of the pursuit movement, but those would be the last minutes of direct contact with Mikha who never communicated again with base nor returned to our lands. His companions tried to persuade the leaders to send ships to his rescue, after three Suns passed, two rescue teams were sent, but they had great inconveniences to overcome the surrounding walls between "Mars" and "Known Lands" and unfortunately they gave missing the young Mikha, obtaining great information about the position of the enemy lands, and other surrounding lands since he managed to send details of his scanning achieved from his ship.

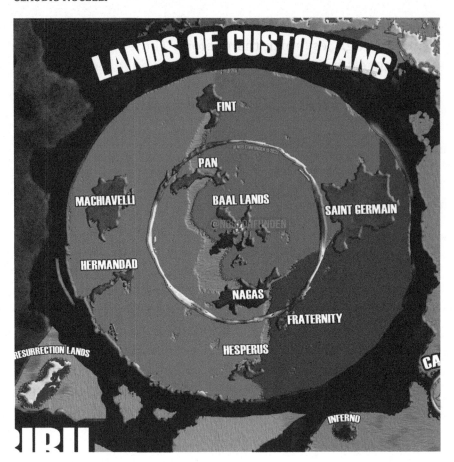

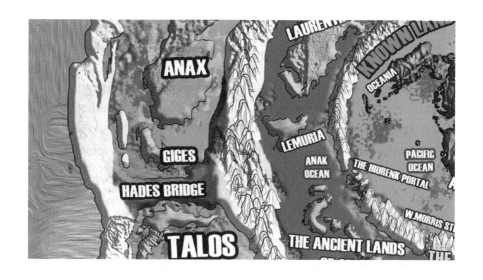

LANDS OF LEMURIA, THE CONNECTION WITH THE BEGINNING OF HUMANITY

Many books can lead to the confusion that the lands of "Lemuria" would be close to "Asgard" because it goes back to the very human creation, or rather, since "The Source" took physical bodies to undertake an arduous and winding path facing those who would later be its parasitic colonizers. For this reason we can find maps of Lemuria close to the famous Atlantis "north" of "Asgard", where it all began. But with the passage of time we have confirmed and updated in our database that Lemuria, which so many references are found even today within the "Walled Lands", is connected to the lands just "north" of "The Ancient Lands of Anak".

These lands were visited on several occasions by the Ancestors, Anakim Giants and Giant-Humans of old Tartary and has a great direct connection to Asgard and the structures that could still be found there, unfortunately reaching the gates of Asgard is far from simple and the Ancestors have suffered many casualties trying to do so, as have other races. It is a very controlled site as it could answer great questions of the existence and history of mankind, as well as we know that there are portals inside and outside our homelands that could connect and transfer matter directly there, although it is very unsafe due to the instability of these.

After the desperation of the inhabitants of Tartary in their escape out of the "First Dome" entire families had to find refuge wherever they could, although the closest lands with which they collided were those mentioned above as "Ancestral Lands", "The Lands of She-Ki" and "The Ancient Lands of Anak" and the same welcomed families escaping from the Great War between humans, giant-humans of Tartary against the Custodians and Anunnaki, also other groups decided to move further away believing that the enemies would still pursue them arriving to the lands behind the First Dome.

For that reason some came to the shores of a new land that was to be "Lemuria" and settled there. The mystery arose when records of strange subway bases of unknown origin were found by means of hatches closed from the inside that prohibited the ancestral humans to go inside and investigate thoroughly. Then with the passage of time five more hatches were discovered along the coast of these new lands, and by means of a message to the leaders, the Anakim Giants approached Lemuria in order to unveil the mystery of the hatches.

It took a long time to penetrate them and then advanced and very strange machinery systems were found there, for this reason the Giants, Giant-Humans and experienced Ancestors joined together to carry out a deep investigation. Although the origin of these structures could never be revealed, it was conjectured that they could belong to a totally advanced hybrid race, since inside there were carried out studies of the manipulation of the temporal and genetic line, remote vision by advanced systems inside matter, and other studies that we cannot expose in these texts, but the study of these lands took another interest on the part of the leaders since the direct connection with Asgard and the beginning of the humanity refloated there.

Today they are inhabited by a strange race that has arrived from outside the Dome, which peacefully integrated into the nearby Ancestral and Anak lands.

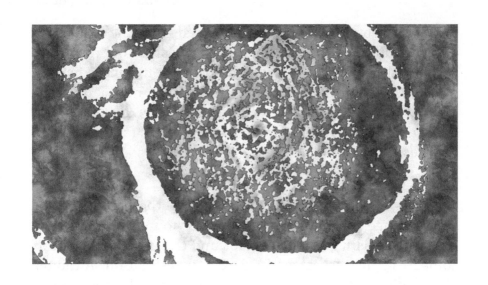

THE ARCANE ISLANDS

Ancestral Book - "The Conquering Crowns and Civilizations of Distant Lands" X95- CII / "Humanity Generation II - The

Battle of Mount Unai and The Ancient Titans" Book of the Great Ancestral Library in the Capital "The Ark"

In a remote place where few have dared to travel there are lands of great victors who have helped humanity Gen II (Second Generation), their bodies define and make the difference, but more their bravery and dedication to the fight against the conquering parasite. More than a hundred ships landed on the slopes that connect with the dividing Second Ice Wall, from there descended 53 creatures unknown to us at that time, our guard to see such a descent of creatures of more than four meters high that moved in a frantic and fast way, sent their signal Stop! So that they could appear according to engage in a peaceful communication.

The men stopped their descent abruptly and one of them with his hands in the air descended alone towards our position. He introduced himself as "Hulex" and commented that he came from the "Arcane Islands" and that the distance they had traveled was so great that the time-space shift between Domes was playing havoc with their genetics. They asked us for help, among other things, which we were able to exchange, it was a moment to take advantage of since we were just settling in to the new life in the Ancestral Lands, as good hosts we attended them and made their stay the best possible experience.

They thanked us for our hospitality and gave us several plans, technology and also helped with the creation of some of our structures and connecting highways between cities. They also told us the story of their ancestors and how they helped humanity of the past, also failing in their attempt against the oppressive custodian. That ancient humanity of the second generation, who also knew how to forge a great empire and who has left traces of that uprising, as well as the titanic giants "Arcane" that they themselves tell how they proudly helped in the Ancient Known Lands.

Some of their brethren were trapped in those lands in stone form, by the use of the Custodians against a group of humanity that had rebelled. Some of the arcane leaders with their more than four meters high were buried or mimetized in the environment that even today the new humans tread, they rest with their faces surprised by that unknown technology for those times, who stood up for the human liberation like so many other beings of the most recondite surroundings, who know very well that the human deserves full freedom and that the parasites must disappear once and for all from these great and mysterious worlds inside the Great Dome.

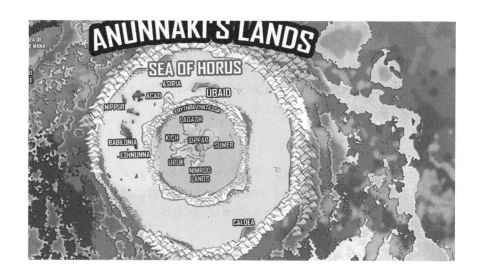

ARB013 - ANUNNAKI

Inhabitants: No Information

What we know about their civilization of origin: The originators developed early and sought to expand their knowledge and territory. They are Beings that seek to increase their power by colonizing other lands and other civilizations.

They are known for the creation of pyramidal structures that they use to reset/restart a Circle-Environment, as well as use it for other purposes in the same manipulation/control. They are also known as great creators and manipulators of Portals that transfer matter between distant places. Their development in weapons led them to be able to place themselves next to the Custodians in the dome of absolute power, they are hostile and devoid of any kind of emotion or feeling.

Their present: They are studying the edges of the Great Dome trying, as far as we know unsuccessfully, to be able to cross them. They have large colonies scattered throughout the plane.

There are a large number of Anunnaki leaders scattered throughout the colonized lands, believed to outnumber the Custodians and to be the most numerous beings within the Great Dome.

There is a great deal of information about their colonization of other lands, some of their technology, and structure of their lands, but penetration into "Erythra Thatassa", the great core of their lands, has never been possible by the Ancestors nor by the Giant-Humans.

The "Abduction Zone" near the "Atargatis Bridge" is a region that the giant leaders, ancestors and giant-humans try to avoid at all costs, it is a forbidden zone and marked in red on the great maps existing even today. The area besides being dangerous and completely hostile, there are also portals many of them in disuse that further complicate any matter that may be nearby, in addition to the existing radars and that some races live or patrol the area in search of other beings lost or transported by ancient portals across the width and length of the "Planets" within the Great Dome.

There is a danger that the Anunnaki may try in conjunction with other races to invade the "Atargatis Bridge" and try to colonize our lands in that position, for that reason, forces were deployed in time to install bases, some of them mobile to try not to be detected, the Anakim Giants deployed and developed technology to anticipate any attack that could come from "Argos" behind the Second Ice Walls.

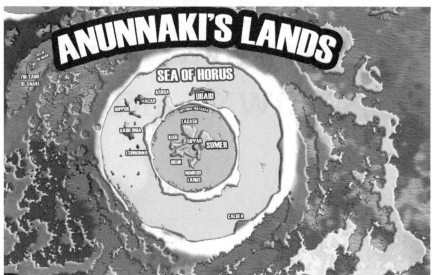

CONTINUATION OF MORRIS AND BUTLER'S JOURNEY TO THE KNOWN LANDS

THE INVISIBLE STRUGGLE, THE INNER STRUGGLE

Who would get up and argue today about the stars that are seen in the heavens every night? Or about the Moon or the Sun? Or about everything that is established?

Perhaps very few, it is that the conditioning of a lifetime or, rather, of past lives and lifetimes influences our thinking today, because the vast majority have simply accepted things as they were handed down from childhood.

We will be marginalized in the future if we simply comment this to someone else, we will be taken as insane people who have to be under observation of some professional, that professional who accepted all this, accepted the books he had to recite, accepted the "Earth" that he has walked and lived since he was born, accepted that he had to repeat certain words at the right time so that with a piece of paper and several signatures, he is granted permission to speak or study on certain issues. Who then will discuss about the educational systems? Or about what things should or should not teach us?

The world is empty for being justly full of confused and many times absurd ideas that we were simply adopting as time went by, and without even asking ourselves, we continue with the same plan, the same routine daily, when sometimes in that emptiness an inner voice resounds very loud saying "Hey, something is not right here" in that instant is when we seek to turn off our mind with another kind of thoughts, maybe and most probably some problem that is going around us.

The new generation is becoming and adapting every day more and more in simple robotic actions, it is far away from the previous one and it is already a mere spectrum of its first version, its competition with the other and its life based on mere biological functions is self-destructive, besides being easily manipulated, for this and many other reasons going into those lands where I was born become very difficult, because not only we fight against parasites but against many people who were contaminated by this manipulation under the same parasitic reign.

It is the price paid by humanity as a whole to fight for a freedom that never came, until now, and it remains to be discovered if we will be able to achieve it. It seems difficult being in these lands so polluted but even more being from outside, those lands are ours, they belong to us, as well as our absolute freedom and our infinite spiritual growth, human life was born with a purpose, "The Source" of the Celestial Lands took physical bodies to take care of this Great Dome, the races that inhabit it, and of course, to return the parasitic colonizers to their original form, the use of technology to dominate and crush into dictatorial control another entire race and not only prevent them from leaving but also manipulate their bodies, minds, their surroundings and their future is simply macabre and can only be carried out by utterly despicable beings.

I do not like to generate division even when it comes to these beings, but they have made of this Great Dome that offers the most beautiful beings, sights and places anyone has ever seen, a hellish place with constant fights, manipulation, control, psychological games and only for personal gain and search to increase their own power, but everything has an end and this is the gateway that will take us beyond, our growth and knowledge of our past and surrounding lands have to come to light, although as I said before, this places us in a place as dark as the distant seas crossing the Great Dome, the marginality is latent for those of us who dare to even ask that question that many hate due to the comfort they acquired, can we live otherwise?

Can we even call this freedom? Being in my homeland, there is a lot of noise and mental interference that originates especially in the big cities, the tumult, the rush and the absolute disorganization make the whole experience something difficult to digest.

People here run without really knowing why, are in a hurry to live, and focus or should I say "focus" one on the importance of physical appearance and the volatile achievements they carry in the mere environment What would happen then if one lives simply without having an image of oneself?

We should try to find out what would happen then with all that mental interference if our image disappears from one day to the next, I mean what you think of yourself, of the achievements and failures, of all the problems that your own mind has created for you, maybe the awakening is closer than we think simply with small changes. In the world around you right now you will never find the answer that we are immense because our spiritual growth is so, we are the purest creation that the parasites do not want to release, we are their greatest opposition that exists in this Great Dome for the dirtiest parasites of all, if only you could discover it for yourself in the silence, when your thoughts are silent and there is stillness, when you can see your surroundings in another way, without so much interference, without so much manipulation, you are not a coincidence or a mere point in the false universe, you are so important that they should have imprisoned you under Walls and manipulated your body, your environment, your history for seven long generations, the path to "awakening" is not to be better than another, it is not about that, it is about a path that sooner or later we will all walk, it is simply to realize how great it is to live this moment, despite being under the domination of these corrupt beings, a chain that we can break, not to let this state of unhappiness that in general seems to lead the new humanity be something accepted without questioning it at all.

Among so many thoughts Butler sat down again next to me, the great Captain, who had so many stories that made of himself a living encyclopedia, he had sailed so many seas that many of his stories could also be found in the Great Ancestral Library, not in vain I brought some of these books, to continue assembling this great puzzle, Butler knew very well how to enter and exit through the First Dome, he had done it several times until, at least, the discovery of the Custodians about the Portal we had opened and the military fortification with the installation of the thousands of bases that had been operating there for some time, and above all, because of the system of earthquake generating radars in the area.

Things had become complicated to sneak inside, but we were willing to do it once again even with the pain I felt throughout my body was nothing compared to the possibility of returning to the land where I was born and see my brothers again.

THE HIDDEN LAND NEAR ANTARCTICA

How would we do it this time? Well, by air, Butler would sentence, and it would be the first time for me to penetrate the First Dome with the famous "Iron Blue." This had to have surgical precision and was very risky, but considering the security moves that were taking place around the Ice Walls, it was better to be safe and do it by air.

That same afternoon we left for the Old Continents, I felt as much adrenaline as excitement inside me, I could not wait to take off, our great ship departed ascending at an incredible speed and reaching a height that I had never reached in my previous trips, you could clearly see the waters above over the Second Dome, everything was calm and according to plan, at least, until we approached the dividing edge.

It was planned to pass through the passage we were already well acquainted with Butler since my boat had long before sailed across, but this time, with a ship crossing the skies and going at great speed. Butler, knowing me, remarked several times to put my mind at ease, that everything would go as planned, there were only four of us inside, the pilot and one person who could indicate by sound alone what was the fault of those bluish beasts that were cruising the skies.

We descended several feet to reach an altitude that we

considered, a priori, "safe" since the radars should not detect us, suddenly we entered this passage and the experience by air is totally different, it is to enter a kind of tunnel where nothing is heard but silence, the speed although we had reduced it considerably before entering, there inside it seemed that we were being shaken frantically, everything lasted seconds and we appeared on the other side, flying upside down over the Antarctic sea.

The pilot quickly and with great astuteness controlled the ship and the situation brilliantly, everything returned to normal as the ship righted its course. The Ice Walls were perfectly visible, we were at about 2300 feet altitude.

We crossed part of the Walls without problems, but something was not right with our ship, several alarms went off inside and we began to lose altitude rapidly, we saw land in sight on the south coast, and the Lanner pilot made an emergency landing, everything was starting to go wrong in our return to the Known Lands, was this the unexpected end just minutes after returning to my beloved lands?

The Iron Blue broke into the quiet wooded areas between huge snowy mountains and with great care we managed to survive a forced but incredible landing between trees that hit our most precious bird that moved us and resisted the onslaught, one after another, we went from one side to the other, until suddenly peace invaded, we had passed the first test, but now what? I asked, Butler was beaten, but he was fine, and the other two ancestors had no major injuries either, my leg hurt quite a bit from the blows and my body too, although as you know, I had come with some problems since before entering these lands.

It remained to find out if this abrupt fall had been an error of our ship (something that was quite difficult to imagine) or if it had been caused by some technology that had been installed by the parasites or the forces that worked for them.

We were on some remote islands on the border with the Walls, which could not be seen in the distance due to the fog that covered the great forests but we knew exactly that they were there. The sun was peeking through the large trees and we left quickly to get away from the ship, in case there were forces in the area that could have spotted our fall.

We were mere mortals coming from the other side of the Walls, with a broken ship, strange clothing, although similar to the time that ran in my homeland, with ancient technology that fortunately still worked properly, but really if they wanted to attack us was our worst time and the worst way to have entered. We moved away about 900 meters from the area of the fall, although it had been resounding our ship had not generated any fire or something to consider that we could have been spotted from afar, the fog invaded completely and we could barely make out the road we were traveling in these cold forests.

Suddenly we began to hear strange noises coming from the north, someone was walking in the weeds, the fog prevented us from seeing if it was a man and we decided to stop our march completely. We crouched down in the thick grass and waited.

10,20,30 seconds passed and nothing, silence invaded, so one minute, two minutes, it was even five, when we overcame this we came out of the trees and ran head on into a human soldier walking towards us, I think we were both stunned, but the marine touched his gun with his left hand and raised his right to indicate that he would not shoot and immediately called us silently to come closer to his position.

Butler indicated that we should follow him and not say a word, he would speak, then the soldier asked us in perfect English what battalion we were from or where we came from, we let the Captain speak and he gave him concrete answers and exact locations to dispel any doubts from the soldier, we began to have equally great suspicions of this marine, what was he really doing patrolling alone in these latitudes? We were not even aware that humans had reached this remote southern part of the known continents.

Charlie, as the soldier introduced himself, received us in the best way believing Butler's version and handed us several fruits and food that he carried in his backpack, while he began to tell us about how he arrived to these lands and how confused he was in his way.

THE SOLDIER'S INFORMATION ON THE WAR BETWEEN HUMANS AND GIANTS IN HIDDEN LANDS IN THE SOUTH

Charlie patted my right shoulder and began to give me the "condolences" for being there too, "Human brothers, it is always good to see a brother walking beside me" Charlie commented strangely, we doubted his mental health at that moment, and not because there were not other beings around but we doubted that he was really aware, then we were going to understand the situation and what he meant in a perfect way.

I understand that you are new and surely you haven't seen the "killer beasts" commented Charlie, we all looked at each other without fully understanding, Charlie then continued: "Friends, it will be quite interesting to see your faces when you see those beasts coming against you in a hurry, I will understand since I have seen the same expression in everyone here".

Listen, what "beasts" are you telling us about? Butler asked, rather confused.

- "You'll see them," Charlie said, and then pointed his rifle towards the horizon to the east.

-There, look over there," he continued, "That one lying there, that's one of the beasts, you'll see it move in seconds, hold on."

We all stared at that sector and a Giant suddenly stood up, it would be about five meters tall, it was an incredible being and another race of Giants that I did not know in person.

"The blue beings, did you talk to the blue beings?" Charlie commented Again we made gestures of not understanding.

Charlie then commented:

- "You are the strangest new agents in this area," he then sentenced, "But time to time, you already saw and had the first experience with one of the beasts, and you will understand everything promptly."

Clearly being able to understand that situation could be beneficial to us, with a ship in shambles, the Custodians who seemed to walk all around us, in the most recondite land and at the mercy of Giants who knew little and nothing about us.

- "This war makes no sense at all," Charlie commented.

- "Rather none of it does, but this one much less so, we are at war against beings we didn't even know existed until now, that they don't understand our culture and only act out of repetition or defense, you know what I mean? It is a repetition, a loop that never stops, over and over again the same thing, every day like being in limbo itself.

- "I thank the Lord you guys showed up, I thought I was going crazy and ... I almost committed insanity, we must get out of here soon" commented Charlie already in a desperate way.

Butler tried to calm him down and sat him on a large rock and gave him water so that he could relax, Charlie's experiences clearly showed that they came from a Machiavellian and perverse game, from what other sector could this come more than the damned parasites? With Butler we understood it perfectly, although we did not yet know the details or in depth about these "beasts" as Charlie called them, we knew clearly that this game was about the Custodians and these lands were somehow hidden to perform this "kind of perverse game" although what was the function of all that?

THE CUSTODIAN GAME - THE WAR BETWEEN HUMANS AND GIANTS IN HIDDEN LANDS IN THE SOUTH

While Charlie recovered his breath and could calm down a little when he saw beings of his own race around him, we asked him questions to better understand the situation that surrounded us, and that we were going to have to face if we wanted to get out of there alive.

The answers would begin to give us a little light to navigate this new path that destiny had in store for us.

Charlie then began to detail his mysterious move to these hidden lands while an intense rain suddenly fell and meanwhile we were seeking shelter among rocks stained with mud.

"I can't understand how I got to these lands, because the final destination was to reach a base in Antarctica, or so we were told by a military man who claimed to be in charge, we had never seen him before, some of us were sent to a precarious base in southern Argentina, we were put on a warship, they explained the basics about the mission we were supposed to carry out in the Antarctic Peninsula, and it was only about logistics, guiding and taking care of the scientists who were going to transport elements for meteorological studies, that was basically what we were informed, among the military chiefs there were also other people with strange dark clothes, they seemed to come out of another time, they had dark glasses and did not seem to look directly at us, but avoided us or ignored us completely."

"Some companions asked some questions and gave us to drink something they said was obligatory, as I drank that rather disgusting and thick liquid my legs began to feel a strange tingling sensation, then my waist, then my chest seemed to burst, and I fainted. I woke up among the rocks and the swamp, while unknown people were running and screaming in pain around me, I had this gun you see and just as I was, I got up and started shooting at the beasts that were slowly approaching from afar, almost for the same survival, none seemed to understand the situation around, There was only one very quiet man who was sitting looking at the ground, but his calmness was really admirable, I approached him and shouted several times for him to follow us, those beasts were taking soldiers with their hands and were shaking them on the ground as if they were made of paper, the nightmare was beginning".

- Butler: Have you come across any of those strange beings with dark glasses around here? Or those blue beings? Who are those beings?

- Charlie: "The Blue Beings appeared before us when we spent the sixth night here, we moved away from the focus where those beasts seem to live, and secluded ourselves along the coast, we tried not to light fires, but the cold and hunger become a worse struggle than those beasts when they go whole days without tasting any food, then we had no choice but to make small and divided during the daylight so as not to raise so much suspicion, or so we imagined. But as I was telling you, after the sixth night, very early in the morning when the sun was just rising, a large boat appeared on the horizon and approached until it got as close to the coast where we were, three of those blue beings appeared overboard, they were very strange because the sun hit behind them and seemed to go through them. The sunlight turned blue when it "touched" their bodies, many of our companions who were camping there tried to swim towards the boat as an escape route, I do not blame them since I also thought so, but from the boat they started to shoot at them, confusion reigned among us again, we had huge beasts behind the vegetation waiting for us, and from the sea a boat arrived to shoot at us, how could we explain this whole experience?

This boat after killing several soldiers moved away throwing several huge boxes near the shore, we did not trust them at all after the most chilling scene we could live, but we thought that maybe it was information, something that would explain or give us a certain path to follow, or at least some food, so we had no choice but to bring them and open them as soon as possible. Inside them were more weapons of war, more advanced weapons than we had so far, grenades, and some night vision binoculars, in one of the three large boxes were sheets that in addition to detailing the inventory that had been sent to us, who knows what for or why, also had the list of all our names, and underneath it said something like:

"Freedom is obtained by killing the Seven Giants that live in these islands, once the last one is dead, the exit will be automatically enabled"

Some groups took weapons and left to the West side, others went to another sector, and some others stayed there trying to process everything, it was a very complex situation, and the division of the members was going to be even worse, at least I sensed it.

The following nights were even more terrible, we could hear gunshots, explosions and all kinds of screams of pain in the distance, one of those nights we saw how a soldier was shot through the air and the deafening scream of the beasts was chilling.

There were only eight of us left in our group, we decided to stay together no matter what, we approached one of the beasts without knowing it and it began to chase us emitting piercing sounds.

I am not sure how long we ran in the opposite direction to retreat, time in these lands is very strange to analyze, but this being reached us and when it was less than two meters from us it grabbed one of us with both hands, I shot him several times while running without thinking, one of the shots happened to enter through his right eye and the giant with a scream of excruciating pain fell down on top of the soldier who had between his hands. We seized the moment to run with all our might, lamenting another casualty and this time a very close one, I had known him for a long time, almost since I joined the army, he was like a brother to me.

Butler then interrupted saying that we were very sorry for his loss and that he had to go on with strength as we were clearly in danger, this absurd war against the Giants was a perverse game of the parasites, we don't quite know what the purpose would be, but many times it is impossible to come to a conclusion of the sick games they make the new humans play and especially with other races, especially the race they detest like the Giants.

Anyway, Butler knew that these Giants had no relation to the ones we knew, and they seemed to be genetically modified in an obvious way, they were possibly imprisoned here on these islands and might even have been moved from the Antarctic land itself to here to carry out this kind of manipulation.

Two of the giants suddenly appeared behind the rocks where we were waiting, one in front and one behind our position, they had us cornered, Charlie shouted something like "I am exhausted of this reality, damned giants" and ran towards one of them shooting with his rifle, the Giant was receiving bullet impacts but in the first seconds it seemed not to do him any damage, He had in his right hand a big piece of metal that he took to the top to take impulse and let fall from his fist with all the force to where Charlie was, who lost his life in the act, the Giant fell down defeated by the previous shots and we had no other option but to escape, we were terrified and confused.

The Giant that appeared on the opposite side did not follow us, we believe that when he saw his comrade killed he decided to retreat, we returned for Charlie's body to deposit it on the nearby coast.

Although it seemed a parallel reality, there was then hidden lands where a perverse war manipulated by the Custodians was taking place, where humans and a race of Giants were facing each other, the rules and weapons were given by the colonizing parasites to enjoy the bloody and brutal confrontations, how long had this been going on? I wondered.

Charlie had died like so many other soldiers, who were delivered as offerings to giant beings genetically modified and also used for this confrontation, we traveled another part of the coast and found no more survivors, this situation was another of the many that we had to stop, exterminate it at the root, clearly the parasites ruled, they felt they were the owners and were willing to take this manipulation to all levels.

Butler did not understand how this area was not known after so many previous trips and how we were not aware of it, but we could not focus on that at this time, although it should be clarified that Butler felt something different about the "reality" we were living there, anyway, we had to start planning our escape from those cursed islands near Antarctica. We couldn't leave our ship broken down in the middle of that forest either, for if they were found they would know perfectly well that the ancestors had returned to their homelands, if they weren't already aware of it by then.

Butler commented in passing that possibly the Custodians were using the race of Giants they called "Patagons" by moving them here, undergoing serious genetic modification and all that it entailed just to satisfy their pleasure of another cruel war. As he was saying that out loud as a form of catharsis and explaining in passing his idea about these lands, we were approaching a metallic gray structure and the beings standing at its gates were not going to be friendly to us at all but quite the opposite, Custodians, men in black and military men of the new humanity were there in some sort of meeting that seemed to be of the high command, as Butler would later confirm the presence of a Custodian Leader, according to our records he was known as "Agares" and there he was entering through a space inside this strange grayish colored structure right under our noses.

What do we do now? I asked aloud, confused by the whole situation and it was not for less, we were really in a critical moment, Butler nodded his head and knew then that we should return to our ship, I guessed then that he planned to send a rescue signal, but it was too high risk, in fact, I did not even think we would use that option ever. The truth is that we were really at a dead end since we didn't know this island, the ship couldn't stay there and we had a whole Custodian meeting going on in front of us.

We hurried as much as we could in our return to the forest, the signal would be sent immediately and it could cause us to be detected by the radars, not only in the air but also on the ground, and those would generate an earthquake of high levels around us, the Custodians would come out in search of us and the worst end would await us, what would happen then? Was it time to take a risk and look for a way out? Although I must also clarify that looking for a way out of that strange area was not very encouraging either.

THE RESCUE

Butler and our pilot Lanner had a heated talk where they could not agree, but inside the ship Lanner commented that we had a system to track and/or communicate with any other Ancestor that was piloting or even navigating in the vicinity, it served only with short distance frequencies, he called it the "OP.05" it was also risky to activate it but by then where there were discrepancies and also activating the other plan was even more dangerous, Lanner carried out the rescue plan of sending a signal to try to look for help in the surroundings.

We understood that we were close to the Antarctic Peninsula and there could be camouflaged ancestors in one of the bases operating there, the signal was sent and we waited a few minutes, Butler took the time we could not exceed 5 minutes 50 seconds, and so it was then that they were passing .... the first, nothing, the second, nothing, the third, nothing and the fourth was answered, in an incredible way and as a divine message we had located ancestors near the area (or so we thought) they headed towards us but during the wait the murmurs began again, we could not really know for sure that those who were coming for us were really ancestors or were sent by the parasites that had taken our technology, the next twenty minutes were in complete silence and we prepared ourselves as we could for a possible confrontation.

A small but modern boat arrived at the shores of that strange island, from there two people headed towards our meeting with an inflatable boat of those used for offshore rescue or simply to save themselves when the boat is in the last hours afloat.

Two agents introduced themselves as Josh and Riant, Butler greeted them cordially and Lanner fortunately knew them both, I think from both parties we breathed a deep sigh of relief as they later commented that they were also approaching thinking that perhaps it was a Custodian trap that had somehow picked up our signal using an OP.05.

Josh and Riant commented that they were very disturbed on the Peninsula and all bases alerted to earthquakes (hence many Ancestors were being detected). They also told in a very technical way to our pilot Lanner that the technology used there had changed dramatically in recent times and surely that was the reason that had made our ship in inoperable condition while in flight, so they believed that many brothers had fallen without much chance of survival, even if they could be ejected, the ocean at those latitudes was like falling into millions of needles sticking in the body at the same time, hypothermia would not take long to do its thing, in this way the Custodians knocked down any possibility of infiltration but the ships would not always be detected.

Josh and Riant were doing intelligence service being able to infiltrate human military bases with direct connection to some informant-mediator who spoke directly to high Custodian commanders, they generally used these islands, the most recent and what they were really upset about was possible infiltration in the Known Lands by Giants, that was even worse for them, since they clearly knew that in the not so distant past they could take away the custody of their most precious colony, the humanity of these walled lands.

Josh commented that She-Ki was possibly the one who had infiltrated these lands, Butler as I have rarely seen his eyes widened, he was blown away by that information, "She-Ki, you say? SHE-KI?" Lanner was also surprised asking almost the same question. Josh let a smile show nervously and Riant clarified that they were possibly looking for the connector portal number 609, that's when Butler and Lanner looked at each other even more confused than before, for what reason, what was the plan, what were the Giants looking for in that connection? I was once again, almost separated from them trying to remember the thousands of books I had read over and over again in the Ancestral database, I did not remember the numbers of the portals, in fact, there was not so much information on this subject, and the one there was did not reference those numbers, then I tried again to be part of this conversation and took advantage of the situation of complete confusion between Lanner and Butler, then I asked:

- What portal? What is Portal 609?

The one that leads to the gates of Asgard, said almost at the same time Josh and Riant. So now I joined the confusion and the same faces of Lanner and Butler, we really did not understand why She-Ki and the Giant-Humans sought to enter Asgard, also risking everything.

While Captain Josh's small boat took us all out of a very dangerous area as those southern islands between the Peninsula and the coasts of South America, we headed to areas a little safer, it should be noted that the ship had been completely destroyed with an ancestral system to carry out in situations like ours, we could not leave any trace that we had visited these lands and less a few steps away from a Custodian leader.

There were conversations about the plan that cannot be included here, but it was about the various human generations and the connection with the Anakim giants and other races as well. The gates of Asgard in the first generations were guarded by species of colossal sizes as it appears in several books of the ancient histories of the new humanity, for example, in Norse mythology and the serpent called "Jörmundgander". The Custodians had then brought several of these giant species from other worlds to guard the gates of Asgard and surroundings, why so much mystery there? Well, it was first necessary to understand that in these lands humanity was forged, the human bodies were taken by "The Source" from the "Celestial Lands", it is the place where it all began.

The direct connection that existed with Hyperborea, or "the core of the Known Lands" was destroyed, but Portal 609 was known by then to be still operational, without being able to give any great information about it either, it was between great mountains between what is known as Europe and Asia. Everything then began to close in my mind, first the great confusion of learning that the great and beautiful She-Ki who had given me her book and all the information that revealed in me and in all my group at that time a reality that I did not know completely, and thus gave me the necessary strength to return and try together with the ancestors to free my brothers that I had left behind and what I thought I would never see again.

Now then I could imagine that She-Ki knew of our journey and our plan to these lands, and his journey to the gates of Asgard was intrinsically related, Was She-Ki helping us to carry out this plan of human liberation? It was a possibility, a great possibility!

SHE-KI AND THE HUMAN-GIANTS SEEK THE DOORS TO ASGARD

In our excitement of interesting and deep conversations about everything that was happening there, we forgot for a moment that we were somehow escaping from the lands of the leader Agares. While it was true that they seemed unaware of our unplanned visit, the fact was that their technology had caused our ship to fall to earth like two magnets, a signal had been sent to the "Antarctic Peninsula" and two agents had arrived in a boat to their shores, it was highly unlikely that any of them had noticed our visit, but by then I think, we preferred to imagine that nothing could go wrong by then.

Josh had given us the information of where the infiltrated ancestors were located in several nearby points, most of them in military bases there, in this way we wrote down every corner to be able to visit them, we needed one of them to somehow provide us with a ship to return us to our lands, it was clear by then that the main mission we were about to carry out was not going to be possible due to the distance we were in, and with all the traces we could have left, it would be more than risky to carry it out with a secondary ship, we would not only put at risk our lives, but also the lives of every ancestral individual that would help us along the way, and also all the inhabitants of the lands behind the Ice Walls, the Ancestral Lands.

Clearly one of my desires now was to know what was happening with She-Ki and her plan towards Asgard, I regretted not being able to get there to see it, would the structures of the first humans still be there? The first great humans who settled and where it all began, to later fight in the first fateful clash against the parasites.

We sailed between small channels through the south of the continent, and we arrived to what Josh would tell us would be our final destination, since they had to return immediately and from there we should visit several points indicated by them that could rescue us, my body was really sore and dizzy, the ancestral medicine kept me still standing and with some strength, but I think more strength was provided by the fact that I would be able to make contact again with the society of the new humanity, my brothers that I had left so long ago.

THE CUSTODIAN'S TRAP IN THE SOUTH

Butler, as I always said, was the most experienced and possessed of an "innate nose" for all this sneaking around and not being found, I by then was between the pain in my body and my excitement to step on these lands again and see the faces of the families there walking around us, then the captain said to me:

"William, we must hurry to find these people, clearly something is not right here" It was not common for Butler to say these words unless there was real danger, no doubt he feared for our lives, my excitement was short lived and a deep crisis would echo inside me.

We visited several nearby points, but we did not find the agents and each visit was more and more risky, we were exposing ourselves enough that some military man would become suspicious and might report it to his superiors, and I think we already know what some superiors might do next.

When we had about four more points left, we visited an old hangar near a port, all gray and black numbers on the outside, Lanner spoke at each visit with his strange Spanish accent, one person called another, and another called another, and suddenly five people were surrounding us and asking us questions, I did not understand well what they meant but seeing Lanner's face and their posture was not pleasant.

I suppose they thought we were spies or envoys from another part of the continent or lands, indeed, we were in some way, but not as they surely imagined. One of the agents we were supposed to meet was present on the scene, and for some reason, which again I put down to divinity, the waters calmed down among the military, and with only this agent left with us, we gave him some information Josh had given us so he would know of our urgency and need.

The agent confirmed that he had a ship for us but not here, and we had to make a 318 kilometer trip to the north, he would come with us and so we could then enter the base where that jealously guarded and guarded by the ancestral infiltrated agents. We were not going to wait much longer, everything was getting quite strange around us, we felt people following us everywhere we went, Butler was quite tense, perhaps as he had never noticed before, and the next morning we left for the military base in the north.

The trip was short and we made it via land, when we arrived at this field where there was nothing but trees and overgrown grass that made it difficult for us to walk, another hangar appeared before us, but smaller than the previous one.

We crossed some military points where the agent spoke for us, and we passed one by one. I had little feeling in my legs, the pain was intense and it was hard to walk, in fact at the end

Lanner had to help me to get into a kind of very old "elevator", the structure was in a very bad condition due to the notorious disuse and passage of time.

This improvised elevator took us several meters underground, every meter we descended the nauseating smell mixed with humidity intensified. To our surprise, there were two ships there, one was similar to the one that had fallen and the other smaller, spotless, although full of dust, there was a majestic track to be able to go outside and get lost in the skies of the Known Lands, I breathed deeply again, although there was little oxygen down there, I looked at Butler who was still worried, and that was clearly a bad sign.

Butler commented to prepare the two ships and almost "forced" the agent to accompany us, he commented that he would help him in the flight since he was not so used to fly those, the agent commented that he could only help him with the small ship, and then Lanner agreed with Butler so that I would travel with our pilot, Butler would go in the small one next to the agent.

The agent informed us the path we were to follow and incorporated it into the destination of the ship, Lanner began pre-flight duties, checking every point in conjunction with the agent, then the four of us would do it in the small ship, the agent also informed us what we were to do when we arrived at the Ancestral Lands in case for some reason he did not arrive (this was commonplace in travel between worlds passages but nevertheless one prefers to avoid hearing it), who we were to talk to and that the ship be replenished immediately as it was needed for the times to come. I believed then that everyone was preparing for something big, very big, it was not my imagination that the plan was being carried out, and beyond the mistakes made, there was a great light of hope, all this was possible.

We got on the ships, the agent gave orders to two people there who opened some doors that led to a dark tunnel that we had to cross and then go outside, so was our departure from the beautiful lands of the south, lands of my brothers of the new humanity and those forgotten giants, it was certainly a "See you later" as I knew the area better and I had thought in my mind that the next ancestral visits could release much of humanity by air, at least I was excited about that.

FROM BUTLER'S EYES

The flight plan was correct, the speed and altitude were the right ones, everything was green light inside, but the alarms would soon turn on, and two ships began to follow us as we crossed the well known "Drake Passage".

The great concern now was clearly to be able to leave behind these ships that were chasing us, once confirmed that they were custodian maneuvers were initiated to move away from them, but everything was in vain, I was in permanent contact with Lanner from my ship, our great and experienced pilot assured that these ships could never cross the First Dome, I asked him several times to confirm, Lanner was even approaching the ships in a very risky way to reach a final determination, and the verdict was sentenced, never those custodian ships piloted surely by military of the new humanity could cross the First Dome, how the Custodians could deliver technology of this type to a confused humanity? It was a sign of total desperation not to lose their colony.

As Lanner stated, our ships were heading straight for the Ice Walls and over the plateau we increased speed to maximum. Again, precision would be essential, the Dome was meters away, I looked at Lanner's big ship and he gave me the order to get behind it so I could enter the passage following it. The two pursuing ships knowing the situation moved away from us, as our great pilot had stated, one turned to the right and another would turn to the left, the great concern was dissipating and it was time to cross the First Dome.

Lanner was ahead and I always had my point fixed on him, from one second to another as these tragedies happen in flight and at a similar speed, Lanner's ship crashed in front of us, I did not even have time to process it, my partner in the middle of absolute desperation and where only a second can annihilate you completely, took control, reduced the speed and put the front of the ship in the direction of the sky, I felt fire in my shoulder and right leg, but the deep pain was nothing of what was happening in my body, but that which I did not want to assimilate, that which I feared since we crossed this same passage when we entered, William Morris had died and took with him a great part of all of us.

Our ship had miraculously overcome that invisible wall imposed by the Custodians since we crossed the passage and they detected our route, the agent that I will call "Antony" so as not to reveal his identity, had been the hero who saved my life, The first thing I tried to do after crossing that passage was to return, but Antony kept repeating over and over again that there was nothing to do, and that they had undoubtedly led us into this ambush.

A NEW TARTARY

It is complex to interpret and digest a death, be it there within their lands or outside of them, be it in other worlds, wherever it happens, my father will always be present with me here in my heart, and not only in mine, in the hearts of so many ancestors who accept that William Morris was not only a visitor, but the one who led us all to better understand the atrocities that are carried out and suffered by the brothers of the new humanity.

And each one of the modifications that our bodies suffered from birth, whatever the generation, each one was entering a perverse and manipulated world, made our world a worse one every day, they not only contaminate their environment, but also their genetics so that each year is not a fruitful year but one less of life. Humanity is sick and slowly dies because of the famous aging that they call "natural process", they will fill their mouths talking about epigenetic alterations, telomeres, cellular senescence and many other factors to explain something that we believe that many leaders or people at the top know perfectly well, the alteration that human bodies suffer in the Circle-Environment, the environment vitiated by the custodian hands, and those pyramids that observe and define in the distance when to start the cycle.

We do not leave the plan to free humanity aside, it is our main goal, even when we know that we put at risk the lives of everyone behind the Ice Walls and the First Dome, all the lands that surround it and all the nearby civilizations that exist, as we already know She-Ki in her journey to the gates of Asgard could change history, a new path and strategy was opened forever and my father knew it perfectly since he learned of that movement, the Giants-Humans plunged back into the mud and that means that we will accompany them, we cannot let our ancestral brothers die in vain, giants and new humans who fought and fight for their lands, my dear father William Morris knew it and he came back here to tell us about his reunion with the brothers of the new humanity and also to say that She-Ki had returned to the Known Lands and was heading to Asgard, where it all began, and we then, have a mission to carry on just as my father wanted, today also begins here the path to human liberation, the Giants and the ancestral humanity unite for a new beginning, A New Tartary!

REFLECTION BY
HELEN MORRIS

HELEN MORRIS RESPONDS - MANIPULATION OF THE NEW HUMANITY

For the colonizing parasites to turn love into something cold and stereotyped, seems to be without a doubt their great primary mission, to turn it into a mere contract with guidelines to fulfill, it is a path full of pain that is only based on a contractual attachment, that is a purely physical choice and that is also based on pre-established images, added to the fear of the unknown, in the end and social alienation is unquestionable, here the individual is punished and pressured for so many things that it is almost so difficult to imagine that another life is possible.

It is similar to the work life and other aspects of life that you lead here, the system that they have created is so rooted in evil that it is repulsive, they make humans believe that they are this way by nature when the reality is that humanity would absolutely reject any type of war or conflict, only that in their minds is the same hostile system that they themselves implanted to carry it forward and make it develop every day without even being detected.

This system feeds back to you, and the answer is not to run away from it, but to take it from another perspective, from the same silence, the answer is intrinsically connected to be able to collapse in a single instant all the acquired conditioning, this is easier for children because they are not so contaminated, but the reality is that any human born after the last reset can do it, simply in the silence where you have no image of yourself, nor any image from outside, nor from the past, nor try to identify, it is the purest silence that anyone can find, then from there you can find a different answer than the one you would find with limited thinking, you would only hit against the walls that the same mind creates every day, with infinite negative possibilities that will lead you to pain, suffering and mere anxiety.

Love is pure nature, it is beyond the observer and the observed, beyond experience or desire, it is behind all that, you simply must get away from the chip you carry in your modern human mind, from the millions of messages you are bombarded with every day, from the tragedies you imagine in your mind that may never happen or will happen, you must spontaneously get away from the hatred of the colonizing parasites.

They were the ones who molded the new mind of the human because it would be more difficult for you to find the way, the true history of your own past. I understand that all this may be too much to process, and may be misinterpreted, therefore, we will leave it here for the time being.

YOUR REALITY IS
A SIMULATION

What can we do to free ourselves from the reigning custodian yoke?

There are many ways to achieve abstraction even at the very moment you are being punished, sometimes your life can become a torture, it is another part of the Custodian system, your life will have to be in constant danger and alert, you will seek security, and who do you think will offer you security? Bingo! the Custodians.

The indicated thing is that you can try to turn off those thoughts that at every moment your mind is transmitting to you about how or why you are going to perform some action, that does not mean that you should jump into the abyss, but in the figurative sense, then I could say that you should jump into the spiritual abyss, do you understand me? Crossing the dreaded gap between the reality you create through the custodian system and the hidden reality behind all limited thinking, the reality you are living is simply a lie, something properly simulated, you are in a system and even if you are immensely rich or incredibly lucky, you will feel the same emptiness as a person in a system, you will feel the same emptiness as a person who is in the opposite conditions, because that emptiness is your own memory that is latent but forgotten behind all the negative thoughts of your own mind, that memory is the Ancestral, it is the memory of your true past that is screaming to awaken, it is "The Source" that you know very well but you have been made to forget. Simply because by remembering who you are then you would also remember the true origin of humanity, then the parasitic race would have to force a new reset as it happened before.

What are they doing here?

The confusion is tremendous, they have you by the hands and feet, there is not much you can do (physically I mean), it is not possible a physical fight between you and them, there is no such technology nor any possibility, not even remote that they can be defeated today, nor is there any way to reach an understanding with them, they will never let go of their most precious colony on their own. You will always feel fear walking on a path that has no reference, there is no trail ahead to follow, you are alone on this path, you will feel fear and many other sensations, but like all costly achievements, you will enjoy double in the end, more important will be the reward of understanding who surrounds you at this moment, which lands are beyond, so far it is a mystery that we will solve today, clearly you can choose between this path and the other, the one you have been walking so far, but at least here you can get a forgotten knowledge and with it you will decide if you want to keep it and share it, or let it die forever.

THE HUMAN RESET OF THE FIFTH GENERATION

Ancestral Book - "Fifth Generation, Rescue during the end of the cycle - The Age of Giants 0503-X2".

THE TERROR COMING FROM THE SKY

02:58AM - I was in my room, somewhat restless and fearful for this new night, what would happen this time? I asked myself over and over again as the "watering time" as we had named this particular phenomenon approached. It would start at 3:00 AM as it had been happening lately, and many of us, excluding my father, were expectantly locked up looking out of the windows, waiting.

There was a generalized fear in the population, even though we had created new accesses to our homes where the water could not filter, as well as through the robust fortifications, and we had decided to leave the "home-scanners", even the old low frequency radars that some considered "conspiranoids" said they could detect the causes of this "Irrigation" out there in the dark in many specific points, and even inside our crops.

Darkness was said to be the best way to scare the "Waterers" away, but, the concern had become a worldwide thing, we were locked in from 1 AM until 5 AM, the waterings had started exactly 12 days ago and it was not only this strange rain and these "Waterers" walking around our crops and around our homes, but it was also a time of pure collective psychosis, things were happening that we had never seen before, suicides and criminality had increased even in the most peaceful regions and the rate had risen to levels never seen before.

Every day it was more difficult to distinguish between what was real and what was part of what the news reported, "hallucinations product of unfounded terror", but I refused to believe that everything that had been happening for 12 days was part of my mind, I was seeing it with my own eyes and feeling it with my body, something was clearly not right here, healthy people were suddenly starting to die, this "acid rain" was coming from these lights that were going back and forth, they were swinging in the dark sky, but they were also swinging along large surfaces close to the ground.

The one in the skies looked like "stars" that seemed to act in a planned way, but why weren't we doing anything about it? The news from the beginning and throughout the day spoke of emergency meetings by the important leaders of the great "Center-Regions" but nothing was being done. Our armed forces also did not seem to know or did not want to fight these lights with the false idea that it was a natural process, which mysteriously happened in every corner of the "Known Lands" exactly at 03:00 AM and ended at the same time.

The "spectacles" of these strange lights seemed to intensify every day, or at least that's what I believed together with some of my neighbors, but most of the people, although they were uneasy, did not seem to rebel against this phenomenon, some out of fear and others out of subordination. Also, as I was saying before, helped by the news by misinforming through supposedly renowned "scientists" who loudly commented publicly that this irrigation had already happened several times many years ago and that it was something normal, but the reality is that none of it was.

The clock struck 02:59AM, and while I was begging in my interior for prayers one after the other, I was screaming in my mind that please this time those lights would not appear, that the damned "Red Watering" would end once and for all. I felt in this deep terror that something was really being hidden and that they were killing us in silence, that it was all part of a macabre plan to assassinate us all in conjunction with the leaders of these "Center-Regions".

My father slept, I don't really know how he managed to fall asleep, I think that the media sooner or later end up making you docile and servile after so many years listening to them. I also think that maybe he preferred to immerse himself and believe in these big media that acted and were ready to put in your mind whatever came from the top, and today was no exception since they somehow brought the necessary tranquility both to his interior and to almost all the population in general, They kept us or tried to keep us in this state, repeating over and over again that these rains were natural due to a phenomenon they called "EDA" and that it could happen every so often, but how could something natural happen for so many days in a row, always at exactly the same time? Something clearly didn't add up, healthy people were suddenly getting sick all around.

At first we didn't believe this version so much, but after 6-7 days we all knew someone who was getting seriously ill. There were neighbors who were dying since those strange rains started watering us, and they always lasted exactly twenty minutes, all watering ended at 03:20 and those thick grey clouds also dissipated in the distance. My tremors came back, always since that fateful December 25th where it all started, it was 03:00 AM and at that moment nothing else mattered but to put my forehead against the small window on my right, and just watch, and pray... pray that this time nothing would happen.

My mind remembered again and again that "Pillar of Fire" that had taken place in another important Center-Region four days ago, or those strange gases that seemed to come out of the earth itself in distant earthquakes in the South, why did these events happen? And why did it seem that the great leaders who made decisions acted as if everything was natural? Many of these questions were going to take some time to arrive, but they would arrive.

FIRE ON THE WALLS AND POISONOUS IRRIGATION

The rain began to fall, drop after drop that accumulated along with my disappointment, again to go through this? I asked myself internally, I was really exhausted and with a lot of dread, it was not for less, a night that I would never forget was coming and everything would begin at this precise moment.

The drops of this supposed "poisonous irrigation" were falling again, but this time they were going to be accompanied. The immense columns that divided our regions and the walls that limited them began to catch fire completely and this irrigation instead of extinguishing it made the flames ignite with more and more intensity and expanded rapidly.

The dark night that was only illuminated by the holographic lunar sphere there in the heavens contemplated that furious fire that first illuminated the horizon and then seemed to slowly extinguish, all this was the harbinger of an announced end and that few had known how to interpret. I tried so many times to leave my home, from my window I saw the intense fire and then the sudden watering that fell with more intensity in some spotlights, but among the smoke I observed the shadows of the vile waterers that walked through the fields from one side to the other, they made noise like the legs of insects under the wood. I cringed so many times that I also hurt my hands pressing against that window without even noticing it.

I could not leave my father, who was sleeping in the next room without even knowing what was happening, I knew immediately, I feared it since the beginning of this hell, nothing of what was happening was natural and those sprinklers were present in great numbers in front of everyone's sight. In some strange way I felt inside me a great relief, everyone now knew the truth, although many would never be able to tell it.

The great column still had fire that went from almost its beginning to the middle of its path, it could be seen in the distance, it gave way and fell without mercy, seeing this the alarm of danger was lit throughout the City-Region, and as if it were an intruder, other bells began to ring in the distance. The fields were infested with these "Watering" beings that walked around with strange devices that emanated gases, they were not well distinguished but the amount of that night was superior even to the total of all the previous days. That day I felt what I had feared weeks ago, they were certainly killing us all.

When I saw that the situation was critical and that the usual twenty minutes had passed and none of this stopped, I ran to my father Gerald's room, I can't even explain today why it took me so long to come out of that shock, but I was terrified, so much so that my body seemed paralyzed for those minutes. I shouted to my father to wake up and that we had to leave urgently, the front door began to be hit hard, the alarm outside and the home-scanners sounded in unison, everything began to live in slow motion, between dazed and confused I could see that the "Regadores" entered our house.

PATAGONIAN GIANTS DEFEND HUMAN LANDS

Two beings entered and began to spray with those toxic gases, I put a mask on my father who just woke up sleepy without understanding the situation, while trying to do the same I was able to locate mine and then close the door of the room. I signaled my father that he should be quiet, and we both melted into an absolute sepulchral silence, the kind that lasts seconds, but your whole life flashes before you.

Deafening sirens and alarms could be heard outside, as the explosions began, but what would those explosions be? we wondered. At that moment it mattered little because the main danger was just behind the door, a creature was walking down the hallway outside while with my father in silence we waited for the worst, in that moment of desperation I looked out the window and the shadows of the Regadores were now accompanied by others, some giant shadows were present. I signaled again to my father so that he could observe it, could it be that our prayers had been heard? The "Patagones" or "Archons" were fighting, defending the human lands, those beings that, always far from humanity, lived in solitude in the cold south, and today they were here with us, trying the impossible, a battle that seemed lost from the very beginning.

The two beings we had in our home shot out, an unknown sound invaded the outside, I guess it was the call of one of their leaders or something warning them about the danger. They needed all the Regadores there since an unexpected visitor had appeared, these giants had no mercy whatsoever and while many fell by the gases that emanated and the blue rays of some kind of weaponry that these beings brought, many others were still knocking down Regadores with their overwhelming force, the difference in physical strength was abysmal in comparison.

I opened the door in panic and amazement but with some hope, I did not see any being crossing the door, I signaled again to my father and we tried to go out, although at that time we did not really know if we were better off outside or inside our home, but after that experience of confinement waiting for death before those creatures, we decided to go out and join somehow to those Giant Archons that gathered groups of humans around to help them.

ESCAPING WITH THE ARCHONS

We ran outside with all our energy towards a column with a tiled roof, there was no longer that rain, but we left our masks on because that deadly gas still existed in the atmosphere, and we did not even know the real symptoms that caused it. My father was already a bit older, he had turned 156 that year and although he was still physically well with the mask on, his vision was limited and he fell into the mud and the intense rain that had fallen minutes before.

I could see that he was trying to get up and place the mask that had almost come off his face, he was full of mud and I could not see anything at all, I tried to go back, but the figure of a giant stood next to me and extending one of his arms at a great distance, he stopped my intentions to move and kept me next to that column. Another Archon was on his way to save my father, but reddish-blue lightning bolts began to rain from a far distance over the dark sky, those penetrating the ground like raindrops.

One of them had penetrated the giant who was falling with signs of pain, and another had pierced the chest of my father who was lying on the cold ground. Regardless of the pressure the giant exerted on me, I made movements to escape from him and ran towards my father, taking off his mask I could see his face, and I understood that he was no longer among us, I took his hand and embraced his body knowing that I would never see him again. I could not understand the evil that was falling on me, this terror that stood in the way of human destiny that night and that we were all living, I removed my mask to embrace the body of my dead father, Gerald I shouted loudly looking at the dark sky without moon, why are we living this misfortune? Why the human has to live this end?

One of the Giants was lying next to my father, and his face was near my left foot, among all my confusion and absolute sadness I could see his face up close, he had stone features like a "Golem" from the stories my father told me, that with his outstretched arms he simulated that flight of his soul, that he was returning to the source of the Heavenly Lands and that sometime I will also return to meet him.

But not that night, it was not the time for me, because that Archon who also saved my life, took me with force of my torn clothes and took me to the group of several people that were formed simulating a large circle. Surrounded by a great wall of Giants that continued fighting against those tireless Regadores that returned again and again to try to penetrate to annihilate the few surviving humans that we were there.

Once inside the circle, many other neighbors that I knew along with other people from other Regions began to join our group, all of us with tears of pain on our muddy faces, without masks or any protection, we moved in unison with those Giants that acted as a wall and prevented any enemy attack. Reddish rays were falling from the skies and I cannot be sure even today about the Archon technology, but a great protective shield seemed to impede the passage and extinguished the forces of those deadly rays over our heads.

There were many children running with us in awe, I held the hand of one of them to make him feel some calm, all that was the strangest and most horrible thing that our humanity has ever gone through. The rescue of those giants in all the Regions was a heroic act of which I believe we will never be able to repay, a genuine and unconditional act of love for humanity, because it should be clarified that all the Archons/Patagons we knew lived far away in the south and could have escaped without us, we were only a few thousand, but we were able to start again, they gave us the possibility of a new beginning.

THE IMMENSE TREE MADE OF LIGHTS - THE BRIDGE TO ASGARD

After a while of hurrying we began to walk more slowly, many of us had taken the younger children in our arms since that walk seemed to have no end, I am not sure how long we had been on that road, but with the fear that instilled all the situation we were living around us I really lost count. I would only know that we had crossed large plots of land by looking at my injured feet, which were bleeding from the wounds along with the soaked mud.

The Giants were still walking alongside us, and were all around us in every direction as they covered our passage. We had stopped receiving those rays from the heavens, the rain had stopped and there was no strange gas in the atmosphere but there was fog that night and at dawn it began to become more and more noticeable. The Archons that were to our North put their arms up in the air as a sign that we should stop completely, so we did while they made their way generating a path for us to enter. A metallic fortification was born before our eyes, its doors wide open awaited our entrance. We did not know where we were going but no one wanted to be left out and alone in those lands that had become inhospitable to all mankind.

While I was entering I could observe everything around, on the outside that fortification that seemed to be made of crystalline limestone was shining, but inside the walls changed to a darker tone, with points of blue light at all angles that filled the upper part, like a holographic sky full of bright stars, for a moment I felt I was entering a small "land" within our own land.

When all the humans and Giants entered there, some of those bright blue lights of this artificial sky gathered in the center forming an immense tree, its roots penetrating the ground and forming its extension to heights that were even difficult to observe. A blue and immense glowing tree was born before our eyes that could not believe their eyes. A robotic and deep voice interrupted our contemplation, indicating that we had to enter there, some doors opened from the base of that tree made of lights, and we were all incredibly confused.

A war of human annihilation was going on outside, millions had died and among them my dear father, and now a group of thousands of survivors were in a fortification of the Archons in front of a tree created by artificial lights. My confused mind could not understand it. We all looked at each other without understanding anything at all, the children covered their muddy faces because of fear, the Giants indicated us with their hands that we should enter there, I remembered then the stories that my father told me as a child and that I believe we had all heard at some time during our lives. Were we perhaps entering the Great World Tree and Bridge to the first lands of Asgard? Were these giant fortifications part of the

Hyperborean Lands?

The first humans who entered there somehow "became" also thousands of points of light, somehow mimicked with that great tree and artificial stars. They were disappearing one by one, there was certainly an atrocious fear inside me, but also the hope of a new life, incredibly for my confused mind that knew that outside the human world was being destroyed in a thousand pieces and that the past of just a few hours no longer existed. It was my turn to enter, together with the boy I had helped to get there who was holding my hand tightly.

My whole body was completely illuminated, I could see while this was happening and I was now converted into thousands of points of light, my hand was melting with the hand of the child who was also, an abysmal darkness around us succumbed, I no longer felt fear, nor pain, nor cold nor hunger, nor the hardships and sadness of what had happened, two large doors opened and a bright sun came in almost blinding my sight, Then I could observe everything, it was exactly as my father had told me, I could deduce it then, we were at the gates of Asgard and as we walked along those roads made of stone, many other humans welcomed us with a smile and patted us on the back, somehow they knew of our pain, I understood then that another life was about to begin.

MESSAGE FROM HELEN MORRIS

The new humanity seems to have forgotten the true path and the path that their ancestors have left to walk it, rather it was not forgotten, but buried by the same conquering parasites, as in these writings and in many other ancestral writings we observe that the old humanity always fought against this reigning power, in our days outside the Ice Walls our humanity helps each other, moves away from objects, from the material, is interested in the welfare of the other, does not compete, has no desire for power and the fictitious growth that is supposed to grant that paper money they use, has no greed, It does not interpose or use any type of leadership to step on the dreams and destiny of any other being, that is far from the reality of the new humanity in its walled lands, and we must begin to realize that a life like ours is possible, we are human and brothers, and although our growth both in there by our ancestors and out here now by us has been different, the true human essence is the one that pursues the dream of freedom and that comes closer every day, although the environment seems so dark and desolate, we know that we can all together change this reality and return to understand the essence of the true being, the one that comes from and will always be connected to the Celestial Lands.

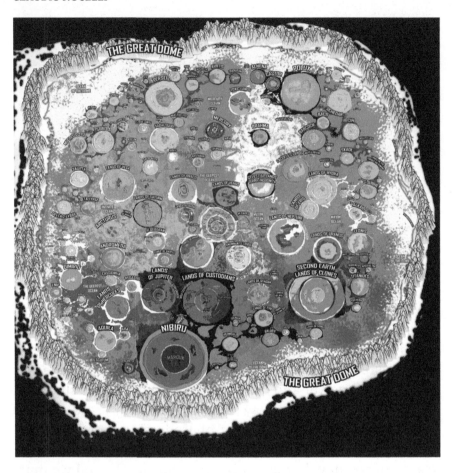

TERRA-INFINITA MAP - All Rights Reserved © Claudio Nocelli
© 2023

ABOUT THE AUTHOR

Claudio Nocelli

Born in Buenos Aires, Argentina,
Lover of occult stories since I was a child, I followed the skies closely after spending hours reading about UFOs and everything related to extraterrestrials. But something did not fit me in those interstellar travels until the story of the navigator would finally dispel so many doubts, in addition to the ideas of ancient books of mythology and travel that created a possible connection with lands and planets behind the Poles, everything began to have another perspective and sense, especially regarding the human past and the infinite spiritual potential.

As we all know the channels that talk about certain topics and do it with great respect, may not be so well received by the mainstream media, for this reason if any link of our social networks is not working we will always try to have the website active.

Creator of the YouTube Channel: "Nos Confunden" and "Nos Confundieron" with more than 6,300,000 views and the website: nosconfunden.com.ar that we invite everyone to join to continue growing.

BOOKS BY THIS AUTHOR

The Lands Of Mars: 178 Worlds Under The Great Dome

178 Worlds Under the Great Dome - Volume 1 - The Collection of the hidden Books about lands beyond the ICE WALLS
The lands of Mars hide much more than we imagine, here we can read the stories of the origin of the Martians in conjunction with the ancestral expeditions of the humans who live behind the Ice Walls.

Chapt. 1 - Where does the information from the Other Worlds come from?
Chapt. 2 - MARS, A Great Zoo
Chapt. 3 - The "Red Planet" Stained with Innocent Blood
Chapt. 4 - The Ancestral Expedition, The Writings of Captain Roald
Chapt. 5 - The Ship of Repentance Ones
Chapt. 6 - The Portal Hidden on Mars
Chapt. 7 - The Dark Membrane - Information Behind The Great Dome

Lands Of Custodians

In this book we will begin to learn more about our colonizing enemy.
Who are the Custodians? How did they come to colonize so many lands? Why have they gained so much power?
This parasitic race does not seem to want to leave our lands nor

let us know our true history and essence.

We will also take a journey into the past to learn about part of our origin and the importance of the "human soul."

The human being from the research and its subsequent results seems to have become the preferred race not to let it escape and set as its main mission to manipulate it to the point that it can not develop to its full potential, as this could be of great danger to the custodial race in their desire to continue to have the same power over these and all the lands surrounding this Great Dome.

Made in United States
Orlando, FL
05 August 2024

49955276R00212